THE BROTHERS ISAACSON

By
Jeff Lefkoff

Copyright © 2024 by Jeff Lefkoff. All rights reserved, including the right of reproduction in whole or in part in any form except in the case of brief quotations embodied in critical or review articles. This book or parts thereof may not be reproduced in any form, stored in any retrieval system, or transmitted in any form by any means – electronic, mechanical, photocopy, recording, or otherwise – without prior written permission of the author or publisher.

This is a work of fiction. Names, characters, places, and incidents either are the product of the author's imagination or are used fictitiously, and any resemblance to actual persons, living or dead, business establishments, events, or locales is entirely coincidental.

Cover design by Fiona Jayde Media

Published 2024 by Mount Nebo Press

www.jefflefkoff.com

ISBN 979-8-9899288-0-4 (paperback)
ISBN 979-8-9899288-1-1 (e-book)

Omnia vivunt, omnia inter se conexa.
--Cicero

Chapter 1
September 1980

JULES STRAIGHTENS HIS tie before knocking. Sydney Epstein opens his office door wearing a phone headset, gives Jules the finger-to-lips hush sign, and waves him towards a guest chair. As Sydney paces while talking – he's arguing with an IRS auditor – Jules surveys the room. The walnut-paneled walls are adorned with large photos of Sydney posing with confident men wearing golf attire or business suits. Jules recognizes the mayor of Atlanta, his arm around Sydney's shoulder. Jules' boss was treasurer of the mayor's re-election campaign.

Sydney completes his call, settles into his large leather chair, and hits Jules with his full attention. "I have a big opportunity for you, Jules. You saw the announcement that we've acquired an accounting firm in Miami and that Arnie will be running the office. What you don't know is the bigger picture – this is phase one of a regional expansion plan. We're already considering acquisitions in Charlotte and Nashville. And you, my boy, can be a major part of this. I want to prove to the other partners that I didn't hire you only because you're dating my daughter. If you help make this expansion a success, you could become the youngest junior partner in this firm since my father started it with Owen Taylor 35 years ago.

You've done well in your first year here and I see big things for you. It won't come easy, though. You'll need to work your ass off. What do you say?"

"What do I need to do?"

"Move to Miami, work as Arnie's right-hand man. Learn the ropes of merging a small existing firm into our business. After a year, move to another expansion city and apply those lessons. You understand what I'm offering you here?"

"Yes, it sounds great. But –"

"But what?" Jules startles at that fierce tone known by everyone in the office. He shifts in his chair.

"I'm not afraid of hard work. I think you know that. The thing is, I've never lived anywhere but Atlanta. I like it here, and I'd be away from Eileen."

Sydney's face softens at that. "I know you and Eileen are close. As her father I'm delighted. But as the managing partner here, I say you make sacrifices to get ahead. That's what every one of the senior partners has done. Our wives understand. Eileen will too. After all, this can be the start of a prosperous future for the two of you."

Jules forces a casual smile. How should he react to that?

Sydney moves on. "Anyway, what do you say?"

"I say yes, I'm in. Where do I sign?"

His boss grins. "No need for a signature. I know where to find you."

Two months later, Jules is driving down Miami's Dixie Highway. All he wants is to unpack and organize his new apartment, but his mom is dragging him and Eileen to visit her uncles. He's never met them but has heard about the four old bachelors who have lived together their entire lives. His family's timeworn excuse for his great uncles – "they took care of their mother" – has been accepted and repeated as if that were a meaningful explanation. Well, whatever. Hopefully, this will be quick. Then he can get back to alphabetizing record albums and folding T-shirts. There's a lot to do, and he needs to finish before starting work on Monday.

He turns into a quiet neighborhood in the city's old southwest quadrant. The houses are well-kept craftsman cottages with small porches and hurricane shutters, their yards trimmed and bright with flowers. Except for the uncles' house.

Pulling into the driveway, Jules sees peeling paint and sagging gutters. Bushes along the front of the house have grown taller than the windows, and the yard grass has gone to seed.

"Oh," Eileen utters from the back seat.

"Well, my uncles are old," Mom explains. "This house used to look nice. I guess they can't do the upkeep work anymore. Jules honey, now that you'll be living here, you could mow the grass and trim the bushes, at least keep the front yard from being an embarrassment."

"What? Mom, I'm here to work. I won't have time to be a gardener."

"You can do it on weekends; it won't take much time. They did so much for my mother, sending money while she raised four girls on her own, and I've never been able to repay them. It would mean a lot to me."

Jules sighs. "Okay, I'll try." Maybe he could spend a few hours here. He has enjoyed helping his widowed grandmothers with simple fix-it tasks in their Atlanta apartments. Such a *mensch*, they told everyone. But that work was for family he has known and loved all his life. These great uncles are strangers.

As they climb out of the car, Eileen says, "Tell me their names again."

Esther nods. "Izzy is the oldest and he's the boss. Then there's Jack, Max, and Davey. Davey's the baby. He's hard to understand because he had throat cancer years ago and they removed his voice box. He's the sweetest one, always has been."

Eileen holds hands with Jules. Under her breath she repeats, "Izzy, Jack, Max, Davey."

At the front door, Mom tries the doorbell. Nothing. Then she knocks with her fist, calling out, "Uncle Izzy? Uncle Jack? It's Esther!"

The door opens wide. Standing there is an old man in a white tank top undershirt and Bermuda shorts, with only wisps of white hair on his head. Thick dark tufts poke out from his ears. He smiles tentatively.

"Uncle Max! It's me, your niece Esther! How are you?"

"Esther? You're not Esther. You're too old."

"I grew up, Uncle Max. I'm 48 years old. And I have three children of my own, two of them grown. This is Jules, my first born."

Max ignores Jules. His eyes light upon Eileen. "Who is this beauty?"

"This is Eileen, Jules' girlfriend."

"I like girlfriends." Max grins, showing a mouthful of yellowed teeth.

Another man appears. "Max, what did we tell you about opening the door? ... Esther! Darling!"

"Hi Uncle Jack!"

"Come in, come in!" He enfolds his niece in a hug. Jack wears long white pants and a blue button-up shirt. A grease spot stains one of his pant legs. Jack's stoop brings him to eye level with Jules. His ears are tuft-free.

"Uncle Jack, this is my son Jules. You remember him?"

"Sure, I do. Jules, you were a pipsqueak last time I saw you. Now you're a grown man, how about that? I'm so glad you're here."

"This is my girlfriend," Max explains to Jack. "She's a beauty."

"No Max, she's not your girlfriend." Jack turns towards Eileen. "I'm sorry if my brother is bothering you. He doesn't mean any harm."

"That's okay. I mean, he's not... not at all. Um, I'm Eileen."

Max grins at her. "You see, Jack, I'm not bothering her. Her name is Eileen."

"Well, come on in the house. Izzy's in the bathroom I think, and Davey is still at *shul.*" Jack calls out, "Izzy! Esther's here!"

They follow Jack into the living room. Jules is struck with a musty smell that hints of mildew and stale urine. A sofa and

5

two matching chairs with tattered embroidery and faded fabric form a sitting area, surrounded by bulky, dark wood furniture. Every surface is dulled by a coating of dust. Jules turns to Eileen. Her eyes are scanning the room, her mouth agape.

A third old man walks in, wearing the same ear hair, sleeveless undershirt and Bermuda shorts as Max, except his undershirt is tucked in and the Bermuda shorts ride high on his waist. He's the shortest of the three, with hunched shoulders.

"Uncle Izzy!"

"Esther! I was wondering what day you would be here. We got your letter."

She kisses her uncle on the cheek. "How are you?"

"Me, I'm fine, fine." He lowers his voice and leans close to his niece. "But Max is not so good. He's always *farshluggineh*. He says he sees our mother, may she rest in peace, walking around the house. She tells him he's a good boy."

"You remember my son, Jules? And this is Eileen, his girlfriend."

"Sure, I remember Jules from before he grew up," says Izzy. "Okay, everybody have a seat. We'll talk." Jules sits on the stained mustard yellow sofa. Eileen sits carefully next to him, not leaning back on the seat cushion. "You want a glass of iced tea?"

"No, thank you," says Eileen. "I'm fine. That's a beautiful old television set. They don't make them like that anymore, inside a real wood cabinet."

"I bought that in 1954 for 280 dollars. The guy wanted 330, but I told him he was crazy. His store was overstocked, and he had to move merchandise. TV was great back then. Milton Berle and Sid Caesar. Groucho too. Then it all went to hell. We don't bother watching the crap they put on nowadays. Besides, the TV doesn't work anymore."

"Jules just moved to Miami," Esther announces. "He's an accountant."

All three uncles light up with this news. "Izzy has always been good with numbers," says Jack. "He's practically an accountant."

Izzy gives a vague wave of his hand. "I did a lot of bookkeeping. I know how to count money."

"You betcha," says Max. "Our brother Izzy is a whiz. He made lots of money for us. It's all in the banks."

Izzy frowns. "Shut up, Max. Jules, that's a good profession. People always need someone to keep the books, so you'll always have something to sell – yourself. You gotta sell in this dog-eat-dog world. I started selling when I was eleven. My pals and I sold ice cream at Coney Island. Hey, we got ice cream sandwiches. You want one?" He cackles. "I won't charge you."

"No thank you." Jules has never considered accounting as selling himself. That's demeaning. But he gets Izzy's point – a solid profession will serve him well.

Esther stands up. "Excuse me, Uncle Izzy, may I go use the bathroom?"

"Sure. Down the hall, you remember."

Jack turns to Jules. "Your mother has always been a darling girl. She had a tough time growing up without a father, but it never held her back. She was a great help to your grandmother, our sister Lilly raising four girls –"

Izzy interrupts. "What do you mean without a father? She had a father, that Ralph." He slaps the air with an outstretched hand, palm down. "Ack! What a no-good drunk. I told Lilly to stay away from that *shlemiel.* Instead, they ran off, got married and left Brooklyn. He dragged her all the way to Georgia. What kind of place is that for a Jewish girl? She had nobody except him, and he was always running around, trying to make it as a prizefighter. What a *putz.*"

"Let's not speak ill of the dead," says Jack, glowering at his brother. "You're talking about the boy's grandfather."

"Ack," Izzy gazes down at the floor and moves his jaw like he wants to spit. Jules is surprised by Izzy's anger, not by his judgements of Grandpa Ralph. Grandma Lilly told similar stories throughout his childhood, always with an edge of bitterness. Then there was the stink of stale alcohol during the occasional visits from Grandpa Ralph, who never had much to say.

Esther returns from the bathroom. "Uncle Izzy, why are there boxes of Saltine crackers piled up in the bathtub?"

"I got a good deal at K-Mart. Eighty-nine cents a box. They're a dollar thirty-nine at Publix, even with a coupon."

"But why are they in the bathtub? Doesn't it work?"

"It has a bad leak, so we shut off the water."

"Why don't you get a plumber to fix it?"

"Ack." Again his hand slaps the air. "Plumbers, they're all crooks."

"But how do you wash?"

"It's no problem. We do sponge baths at the sink. That's all we need, right Jack?"

Before Jack can answer, they hear the front door open. Izzy calls, "Davey, we're in here. Esther is visiting!"

Davey appears in synagogue attire: dull coat and pale tie, yarmulke, and yellowed *tallis* fringes hanging about his hips. His eyebrows are thick as caterpillars. Even from across the room, Jules can award Davey the brotherly prize for most ear hair.

"Uncle Davey! I'm so happy to see you." Esther leaps up to hug him.

Davey emits a gulping sound every few syllables. What comes out is so breathy it's barely audible. "Stay ... *ulp* here, I'll get you ... *ulp* some ice cream."

"They don't want any," cries Izzy, but Davey is already in the kitchen.

"I love ice cream," says Max. "It reminds me of girls." He gazes at Eileen, grinning broadly.

"Will you stop already, for crying out loud," says Izzy.

"What? You butt out. You don't understand women, and you know what I'm talking about, so don't tell me what to do."

Izzy looks at his hands, struck silent for an awkward moment while Max glares at his oldest brother. Finally, Izzy asks Esther about Jules' father Bernie.

Max whispers to Jules, "Hey, do you see that lady sitting in the chair by the cupboard? The lady with the chicken legs?"

"Uh... no."

"You sure?"

"I don't see anybody."

"Hmm. That's funny, I see her clear as day. She has chicken legs, sticking out of her dress. She has them crossed, ladylike. You sure you don't see her?"

"No Uncle Max, I see the chair and the cupboard, nothing else."

"I don't get it. Why is she here?"

Among the many elderly people Jules has known, no one compares to his great uncles. Max is demented, Izzy is volatile, and Davey can barely speak. A normal conversation is impossible, except with Jack, and their living situation is awful – pinching pennies on crackers and arguing over money. His parents fought about money when he was a child. Dad would rant at Mom for spending too much, then she yelled back over the cost of things the family needed. Jules hid under his bedcovers, terrified by their rage. Years later he understood his mom never confronted her husband on the real issue: his father didn't bring home enough money. Dad had given up the reliable drug store he inherited from his own father to embark on several business ventures, which cost him dearly and ultimately failed. Jules will never take on such a risk. He appreciates his steady paycheck.

Davey reappears carrying a plate stacked with ice cream sandwiches in their wrapper. Jules hears a soft sigh of relief from Eileen. She whispers to him, "Thank God, we're not having to eat with their bowls and spoons."

Everyone unwraps their sandwiches and starts in. Max begins humming then breaks into song:

"Whistle while you work,
Hitler is a jerk,
Mussolini bit his weenie
Now it doesn't squirt."

Izzy yells, "Max, what is wrong with you? There's ladies present, for God's sake."

Max is indignant. "Since when do you like Hitler? And that Mussolini, he ain't much better."

Izzy turns to Esther. "What am I going to do with him?"

Esther smiles. "Don't worry, Uncle Izzy. Everything will be okay." The worry lines Jules detects on her face don't match her reassuring words.

"Listen," Esther says brightly, "is there anything I can get for you? I'm flying back home to Atlanta tomorrow morning with Eileen, but I would be happy to pick up a few things, and Jules could bring them by later. Maybe groceries?"

"Nah, we don't need anything. We got plenty of TV dinners and ice cream and saltines."

"Well, now that Jules lives here in Miami, he can come over and drive you to the grocery store, right honey?" She raises her eyebrows.

Jules responds with what's expected of him. "Sure, I'll write down my phone number. Call me anytime." To his own surprise, he means what he says. He's curious about these bizarre old men.

"That's nice of you, Jules, but we don't have a phone," says Jack. "Just come over any time you want. We're always home."

"Not me," says Max. "I might be out with a girl."

"Why don't you get a phone, then you can call me when you need something?"

Izzy slaps the air. "You kidding? I'm not giving our money to those crooks at the phone company. Biggest bunch of shysters ever. They do whatever the hell they want. Roosevelt should have gone after them the way he did the oil companies."

"Izzy is smart when it comes to money," says Max. "That's why we have so much."

"Shut up, Max. Hey Jules before you go, let me give you something. Davey, go get those undershirts from the hall closet."

Davey comes back with two packs of K-Mart brand sleeveless undershirts, still in their original packaging. He hands them to Jules and smiles. "Take ... *ulp* them, we ... *ulp* won't use them."

Jules sees through the clear cellophane that the white cotton has yellowed. How long have these been sitting unopened? Have they absorbed the smells of these old men without ever being worn?

"That's very generous of you, Uncle Izzy," says Esther. "Thank you."

"Ah, it's nothing."

Jules is staring at the undershirts. "He's not kidding; it really is nothing," says Jack. "We're not exactly the height of fashion around here. It's been a long time since Coco Chanel visited."

In the car ride back to his apartment, the two women are talking away, something about somebody's wedding in Atlanta. Jules tries to focus on all the moving-in tasks to be done, but his head is filled with yellowed undershirts, ear hair, a lady with chicken legs, saltine crackers, and ice cream sandwiches. Come to think of it, that ice cream sandwich was tasty — a sweet bit of normalcy at the nuthouse.

Chapter 2
Brooklyn 1903

IZZY RUNS FROM his tenement apartment to the candy store on Pitkin Avenue. He is meeting his pal Joey and Joey's older brother Lewis, and they will leave without him if he doesn't arrive by seven o'clock. He races up the side streets, crammed with four-story walkup apartment buildings that house Eastern European immigrants and their American-born children.

He turns the corner onto Pitkin. On early Saturday mornings, the avenue is not crowded, so Izzy can run flat out on the sidewalk and easily dodge the few bearded men on their way to synagogue. The peddlers, shoppers and horse-drawn wagons will not be out for another hour. He smells horse manure scooped up by a street cleaner then gets a whiff of oven-fresh bread as he runs past Klein's bakery.

After the hot, still night in his family's cramped apartment, Izzy delights in the morning air. The cool breeze rushes past his ears as he runs. Though shorter than most eleven-year-old boys in Brownsville, he is quick, and his legs are strong. All week, Izzy has been looking forward to the chance to make some dough with Lewis and Joey. They're heading to Coney Island, his first time ever at the beach and, even more exciting, the first time Lewis has included Izzy in a money-making adventure. Today is gonna be a lollapalooza! As a bonus, he will be spending the day away from his father, who's been worse than usual all week, maybe because the stuffy heat is making sleep hard for everyone except his baby sister Lilly. Even his little brother Jack complained, but quietly to Izzy lest their father hear and answer with a slap. His father has been unhappy for a long time, always about money. Izzy hopes to bring some home today so his father will feel better and not drink so much.

Lewis and Joey Lefkowitz are waiting in front of the candy store. At fourteen years old, Lewis towers above the younger boys by a head. Izzy has heard how Lewis hustled for a dollar since he was nine, starting with shining shoes, running errands, and washing windows. Now Izzy has a chance to show Lewis that he can hustle too, so maybe Lewis will keep including him in money-making schemes that only an older boy could mastermind. Lewis smiles at Izzy. "Okay *boychik*, let's go make some moolah."

He leads the way down Pitkin, with Joey and Izzy one step behind. Joey is chomping on gum.

"Hey Joey, got a stick?" Izzy asks.

"Nah."

Lewis turns around and hands Izzy a stick of *Juicy Fruit*.

"Thanks Lewis, you're a pal."

"Yeah, well you guys will be working your asses off today, so I need you to keep up your strength."

"What are we going to do?"

"Ice cream, that's the ticket today. Stick with me, I'll show you."

Lewis' business venture is a multi-step affair. First stop is the Brooklyn Terminal Market that occupies a full city block. The boys rummage through trash bins until finding three abandoned vegetable crates, slightly damaged, along with several cardboard boxes. Watching Lewis demonstrate, Izzy tears and folds cardboard into liners for his crate. He then follows Lewis six blocks to the Steinman Ice Company on Blake Avenue. Lewis goes into the customer entrance by himself and comes out with nine blocks of ice, each the size of a brick and wrapped in mineral wool. He spreads three into each crate, after poking drainage holes in the cardboard lining. Next door is the Steinman Ice Cream Company. "Hey Lewis, can we go in with you?" asks Izzy.

"Okay but let me do all the talking. Keep your mouths shut."

Inside the front office, a fat lady with glasses sits behind a counter. "You boys want ice cream, we sell it in bulk, you understand?"

Lewis asks, "How much is a box of ice cream sandwiches?"

"Sandwiches, they're the newest thing. Everybody wants them, so they ain't cheap. Thirty-five cents for a box of twelve. You got money?"

"Yeah, I got money. How about a discount if I buy ten boxes?"

"Ha! A discount, he wants. Tell you what, mister wheeler-dealer, you buy fifteen boxes, I'll give them to you for thirty cents each."

Lewis takes a minute to respond. "That's four and a half dollars. All I got is four bucks, and a nickel. Deal?" Lewis spreads the money on the table, then pulls his pockets inside out to show them empty. Izzy's eyes widen at four one-dollar bills. He has only seen adults handling this much money.

"Oy, all he's got is four dollars, thank God for the nickel. You kids are going to bankrupt me. Okay, but only this once, and don't tell your friends I sold them this cheap."

Outside they load the boxes into the crates with the ice. Joey asks, "Hey, Lew, how we gonna get to Coney Island with no money?"

"Wise up, Joey. I got more stashed in my shoe. That's the way you get ahead in business. Buy low, sell high. When you're buying, let them think you're out of money. When you're selling, make them want what you got. Now we're going to sell those sandwiches at ten cents apiece and make a killing."

"Ten cents! Who's going to pay that?"

"All those saps at Coney Island. Nothing sells like ice cream on a hot day, especially if you get the kids going. They start whining to their folks and then we get a sale just so the kids will shut up."

Carrying their crates, Izzy and Joey follow Lewis back towards Pitkin to the closest trolley stop. As they wait, Izzy peers at their crates full of ice cream sandwiches and imagines each one as a dime. Fifteen boxes times twelve sandwiches each makes 180 sandwiches, so they're sitting on eighteen dollars! Yeah, that's the ticket. Lewis is one smart guy. Izzy can't wait to bring money home to his parents. They'll be proud he worked hard for the family.

After the trolley ride to Coney Island, Lewis leads the boys on a short walk to another ice company to replenish their jury-rigged iceboxes. After walking another two blocks, Izzy is fading in the summer sun. The crate is getting heavy, his arms are sore, and meltwater is dripping down his pants. He clenches from showing any weakness – he's resolved to work hard and do whatever Lewis says.

When they finally cross Surf Avenue and spot the beach, Izzy's spirits revive. There's a thousand people crammed onto that narrow ribbon of sand, all baking in the heat and ripe for a cold treat. He's never seen so much open space, without buildings to block the view. Peering beyond the beach towards the endless water takes his breath away. "Wow, is that the Atlantic Ocean?"

Lewis laughs. "What do you think? That's why the beach is here, with all these customers."

Lewis directs Joey and Izzy on dividing up the crowd and meeting back in an hour so he can check on how they're making out. He's already coached them during the trolley ride on sales techniques. "Look for guys with a gal. They always want to show off by buying things for them. And families – go for the kids first. Talk up the ice cream and get them to bug their parents. Then go to the dad or grandpa and say 'sir' a lot. Don't let anybody talk you down from ten cents apiece. If they try, say that there's plenty of customers here and act like you're walking away."

Izzy scans the crowd and goes right to a small group of three guys and three gals, exactly as Lewis said. They're old enough to have money, but too young to be married. Speaking loud enough for them all to hear, he addresses the skinniest guy. "Want to buy an ice cream sandwich for one of these lovely ladies? They're the newest thing, everybody wants them."

The guy glances at one of the girls, who replies by smiling at him sweetly. At that moment, Izzy knows he has him. That knowing brings an exhilaration unlike anything he has experienced, a delicious certainty that this helpless sap will be putting money into Izzy's hand. The guy buys two, then his sap pals follow. Izzy moves on, filling the rest of the hour with more sales.

One person tries to talk him down in price. The man is smoking a cigar and sporting a thick mustache. With him is a wife and a bunch of kids. He speaks with an accent Izzy does not recognize. When the man offers to buy eight ice creams for five cents each, Izzy responds as Lewis taught him. "I got lots of full-paying customers." He starts walking away.

The man laughs. "Okay Rockefeller, you cornered the market, I'll pay your price. What's your name?"

"Izzy. Izzy Isaacson."

"Is that so? Did you get a good wholesale price for that ice cream, Izzy Isaacson?"

"Wholesale?"

"Wholesale, wholesale. You're a retail man, you got to buy wholesale."

"We paid less than thirty cents a box."

"What are they, twelve to the box? So you're selling for a dollar twenty. Good, very good. Keep that up and you *will* be a Rockefeller. Let me tell you something, Izzy Isaacson. My name is Galermo, Giussepe Galermo. I came from Italy with almost nothing in my pocket, nothing! Now I own a pasta factory. I buy flour and eggs, I hire people to work in my factory, and I sell the pasta to Italian grocery stores all over Brooklyn. Manhattan too. America is a great country." Galermo quickly makes the Catholic sign of the cross.

"Uh, we're Jewish."

"Is that so? With a name like Izzy Isaacson, what a surprise. Your name reminds me of a bible story. Tell me, Izzy, you go to Bible Studies?"

"Bible Studies?"

"What they teach in Sunday School. Or maybe it's Saturday School for the Jews, what do I know? So, you heard about Jacob and Esau from the Bible?"

Izzy has no interest in Judaism. His parents tried to push it on him, but religion is old country, only for the immigrants, like speaking Yiddish. Izzy and his friends are Americans – they speak English, they hustle for money, and they don't need immigrant religion. Anyway, he remembers Jacob and Esau from bedtimes stories his mother told when he was younger. Esau is the older son of Isaac, so he should get all the sheep after Isaac dies. Isaac is very old and cannot see well, and the younger son Jacob pretends to be Esau, so Isaac gives him all the sheep.

"Yeah, I know that story." Izzy has no time for a lecture – Lewis will be waiting and expecting more sales. "I got to go. This ice cream is not selling itself."

Galermo laughs again, loud this time. "Izzy, you're a boy after my own heart. Let me tell you one thing first. That rascal Jacob, with his mother's help, tricked his father and cheated his own brother, to get ahead. That was not nice, but it was clever. Jacob was the clever one, same as you and me. Right?"

Izzy does think of himself as clever, but it's a quality that usually goes unmentioned. His parents don't recognize it, but Galermo does. "Right!"

"That's right, and Jacob became successful. He became famous even, and nobody thought much about Esau after that. So, what's the Bible teaching us? If you want to come in second, be nice. But if you want to get ahead in this world, be smart, smarter than the other guy. That's how the real Rockefeller did it. And that's how I'm doing it. You can do it too."

"That's what I'm doing! Thanks, Mister Galermo." Izzy pulls out eight ice cream sandwiches. "That will be eighty cents." Galermo places a dollar bill in Izzy's palm. Izzy's hands tremble as he counts out twenty cents in change.

Galermo grins. "A pleasure doing business with you, Mr. Isaacson."

When Izzy returns to the rendezvous point, Lewis and Joey are waiting for him. "I sold it all," Izzy announces. He shows Lewis his empty crate, and hands over the cash he collected.

Lewis turns to Joey. "Joe, I want you to team up with Izzy. Watch what he does, how he talks to the saps. Then you copy him." He grabs three boxes from Joey's crate and moves them to Izzy's, flashing Izzy a big grin. Izzy understands that he's done well, he's good at selling, and Lewis will want him on his team again.

By eleven o'clock they are sold out. As they wait for the trolley back home, Lewis explains the finances. "We made eighteen dollars. After the cost of the ice cream and the ice and the trolley fares, that's twelve dollars profit, boys. I get half then you each split the other half. Here's three dollars each."

Izzy objects. "Wait a minute, why do you get half? And why does Joey get the same as me when I sold more?"

"Why? I'll tell you why. I get half because I'm in charge of this outfit and I say so. It was my idea and my money that got us started. Without me you'd have nothing in your pocket. You're lucky that I'm only keeping half – most bosses are sons-a-bitches. If you don't like it, you don't have to come next time."

"Okay, okay. Don't get sore, Lewis. I was just asking." Izzy decides Lewis is right; he's the boss, after all. Izzy is lucky to be along with Lewis and he best not complain.

On the trolley ride Joey falls asleep. Lewis reaches into his own pocket, counts out fifty cents and hands it to Izzy. He whispers, "That's for being such a good salesman. You earned it, *boychik*."

Izzy is dog tired but triumphant when he finally gets home and climbs the two flights of stairs to the cramped Isaacson apartment. The family is at the lunch table, slurping chicken soup, though it's mostly potatoes, carrots, and onion with a few bones from yesterday's leftovers. His father looks up. "Vere you been all day? Your mama's vorried sick."

Izzy grins with pride, pulls the three dollar bills and two quarters from his pocket, and lays the money on the table in front of his mother. "I been out making dough, with Joey and his brother Lewis."

"What, you got a job?"

"Yes, Papa. I got a job selling ice cream sandwiches."

"Who pays you three and a half dollars for that?"

"Nobody pays us. We buy low and sell high."

"What? Whaddaya talkin'? You steal that money?"

Izzy is stunned. He thought his father would be proud of him.

Izzy's mother protests. "No he didn't steal anything! Vhat's the matter with you, Mo? Right Isidore?"

"That's right, Ma. I made it fair and square. Lewis and Joey and me, we're in the retail business. We buy wholesale for cheap. Then we sell the ice cream one at a time for a good price."

"You buy wholesale? What's a wholesale? You make ice cream out of it?"

"No, papa. Wholesale is the *way* we buy the ice cream. We buy a lot at one time and pay two and a half cents each, then sell them for ten cents each."

"Then who pays you three and a half dollars?"

"Like I said, nobody pays us. We *made* the money."

"Whaddaya talkin'? Nobody pays you because you didn't do no work." Mo raises his voice. "Now you tell me where you got that money! Tell me or I'll smack you." Izzy takes an instinctive step back, knowing too well his father's volatile rage. How did Izzy doing something good for the family become a reason to be slapped?

Jennie raises her voice to match her husband's volume. "He told you, Mo! He bought the ice cream, he sold the ice cream, then keeps the difference. What's so hard to understand?"

Mo is flustered. "But he didn't do no work! He must be stealing!"

Now Jennie is full throated. "He did not steal. Can't you understand anything? This is how you get money in America. You been here fourteen years and you still don't understand. No wonder we're so poor!"

"I'm poor because my boss is a cheapskate miser," Mo yells. "I wash dishes all day, and he don't pay me three and a half dollars. How can a boy get more money than a grown man?" He slams his fist hard on the table. Little Max and Lilly both start crying. Bessie and Jack are terrified.

Jennie bolts up and gathers Max in her arms. "Izzy, take care of your little sister. Mo, what's the matter with you? You're scaring your own children."

Izzy watches the anger drain from his father – his shoulders slump and his voice becomes morose. "This country America, I don't know. They pay you plenty to do nothing, but when you work hard they pay you a pittance, barely enough for a bottle of schnapps." He grabs the three bills on the table, leaves the two quarters. "I'm going out."

"Where?"

"Out!"

"Don't you spend that money on booze!"

"Shuddup, woman. I'm the man in this house." He storms out.

Izzy is sick to his stomach. He turns to his mother. "I made that money to help the family, Ma. Not to help him buy booze."

"I know, darling. You're a good boy." She hugs Izzy around the neck. "I'll tell you what. Next time, be quiet about money you bring home. He doesn't have to know."

Lying in bed that night, Izzy hears footfalls and muffled chatter from the apartment above. It's another hot night so all the windows are open, letting in snippets of conversation from the sidewalk below. Jacob and Esau's father must have been an idiot – how could he not know one son from another? Even Izzy's father would never make that mistake. Or he could if he was drunk enough. Anyway, Izzy would never cheat his brothers, never! He's going to keep taking money from the saps and give it to his mother and not let his father know. He's going to be rich.

He drifts off to sleep, picturing the dollar bill that Mr. Galermo placed in his hand.

Chapter 3
January 1981

JULES DIVES INTO the waves as the sun breaks over the horizon. He has fallen in love with Miami ocean swimming, so elemental and expansive after his years in cement pools. Pools gave him athletic confidence without the humiliation of teenage team sports – he was terrified of missing the easy basket or bumbling the simple fly ball, then would inevitably commit the error and disappoint his teammates – though swimming laps lacked the euphoria of coursing through seawater. Now immersed in the untamed ocean, power surges through his arms, legs and lungs. His strokes accelerate.

A seagull glides low overhead. He was fascinated with gulls as a boy while visiting Grandpa Harry and Grandma Ann in their high-rise condo on the Hallandale beach, not far from here. After lunching on corned beef sandwiches, Grandpa showed him how to throw bits of rye bread to expectant gulls from the breezy twelfth floor balcony. The birds hovered in wait, then swooped to catch a tossed scrap in midair. Watching these masters of flight from eye level gave Jules his first sense of wonder at wild animal life.

That was fifteen years ago. What will he be doing fifteen years from now, when he's pushing forty? He'll be a senior partner at the firm, living in a nice house in Atlanta with Eileen. When he's sixty? He'll be the managing partner; Eileen's father will be long gone. Jules will be so successful his name will be added to the firm: Taylor, Epstein, Boyce, and Rothman. He'll be old then, but nothing like his great uncles, strange and lonely. He'll be normal, married to Eileen with lots of friends.

He misses Eileen. The last time they had sex, the full weight of her body was on his, pressing him into the mattress. They kissed deeply. She tasted of bubble gum toothpaste and smelled of floral shampoo.

Her memory lingers as he returns to his apartment and gets ready for a day at the office. When he steps out of the shower and grabs the periwinkle towel, he returns to their argument months ago at Burdines. He was bored and sullen – department stores do that to him – while Eileen fawned over bath towels. "Which color do you like, Jules, powder blue, royal blue, or periwinkle?"

Jules perked up. "Periwinkle? Is that related to Bullwinkle? I like Rocky and Bullwinkle."

"Be serious. We might have these towels one day when we're living together."

"Let's worry about that then."

"Jules, just tell me which color you prefer."

"Periwinkle, definitely."

"You're not even looking. I'm trying to help you and you don't care."

"I do care, now that I know there's a color called periwinkle. It will remind me of Bullwinkle in wintry Frostbite Falls during the sweltering heat of Miami." Jules grinned at his own wit.

Eileen shot him a hard glare. "Stop being sarcastic. You know I hate that."

"Then stop requiring me to have an opinion on things I have no interest in."

"Jules, we need to make decisions together. That's what couples do."

"On big things, sure, but not on bath towels. This is a stupid waste of time."

"Don't call me stupid."

"I didn't. It's this conversation that's stupid."

"Fine, be that way."

After that, Eileen gave him the silent treatment until dinner.

Two months later, the memory still burns as he dries himself with that same towel. He throws the damn thing on the floor, stares at it, then picks it up and hangs it neatly. Why is he indignant over a silly old argument? Anger is no way to start the workday – he needs to dispel its energy. He enters the bedroom and crawls to the floor for pushups. With each downstroke, the earth-tone carpet rises to meet him, like the time in kindergarten when he fell face down from a playground slide and the ground whooshed up into his face. After landing hard and recovering his breath, he realized he was not physically hurt but cried because no one saw him fall or cared to keep him safe.

Jules is poring over the tax files for Paul Perlman Pest Control, the accounting firm's largest client in Miami. His relocation from the Atlanta office is going as planned. Everyone here accepts him, and he enjoys the work. The order and precision of the accounting world is the best part. As a young boy, he loved to organize and recount his collection of pennies, nickels, dimes, and quarters. He would try different stacking systems — ten pennies next to the dimes or five nickels next to the quarters — to create order out of chaos, clarity out of confusion.

After hours of checking and double-checking, he concludes the Perlman depreciation tables are incorrect. He gathers the files and walks next door to Arnie Zender's office. The door is open, and Arnie is at his desk. "Hey, Arnie, got a minute? I think I found a problem."

"Another problem?" Arnie sighs. "Okay, Jules, come on in."

Arnie is a senior accountant who has worked at the firm in Atlanta for 25 years. Knowing that Arnie would oversee the Miami venture made it easier to accept Sydney's proposal that Jules relocate. Arnie had always been patient and generous with Jules when they worked together on several accounts, with Arnie tutoring him on finer points of accounting. Now that they are in Miami, Arnie is uncharacteristically tense. "What's up?"

"I've been reviewing the Perlman account. The firm has been using accelerated depreciation for capital equipment that doesn't qualify." Jules hands Arnie the tables and supporting equipment lists.

"I see." Arnie sighs again. "Go check with Marty, maybe he can shed light on this."

Marty Spiegelman is one of Schlesinger and Associates' long-time accountants who stayed on after the acquisition. Jules has yet to work on a project with Marty, though he's pleasant when they small talk in the break room. Three inches shorter than Jules and balding, Marty speaks with a New York accent and always leans forward as if he's in a hurry to get somewhere.

Jules heads down the corridor towards Marty's office. How should he approach Marty on this? Will Marty feel criticized by Jules and resent him? Jules is young and was given a relatively senior position in the office. He's proud of that, though it's awkward at his age. So far, everyone has been respectful, but that could change for the worse if he comes across as a finger-pointing brat. It's good that no one here except Arnie knows Jules is dating Sydney Epstein's daughter.

Jules knocks on Marty's door.

"Come in."

"Hi Marty. I'm sorry to bother you, but I'd like your advice on these depreciation tables."

"Sure Jules. Have a seat."

"Thanks." Marty's office is filled with baseball paraphernalia. Jules eyes signed photographs, a baseball under glass, and a 1955 Brooklyn Dodgers pennant. "Wow, you're really big on baseball."

Marty smiles broadly. "It started in Brooklyn when I was a kid. My friends and I loved the Dodgers. We *loved* those guys.

Jackie Robinson, Pee Wee Reese, Gil Hodges, Duke Snyder. I knew their batting averages, home runs, the whole *megillah*. The Dodgers were everything great about Brooklyn. Smart and scrappy, like the whole town. You know where the team's name came from, Jules? In the old days – I mean going back to the 1910's when my dad was a kid – they were called the Brooklyn Trolley Dodgers. If you lived in Brooklyn, you had to be quick and alert all the time when you walked the streets. You even had to dodge the trolleys."

"Wow, I never knew that." Jules relaxes into his chair.

"The 1955 season, that was a dream come true. We dominated the league all summer, then beat the Yankees in a seven-game World Series. I was fifteen years old, and I'll never forget that seventh game. I was overjoyed. It was the best day of my life."

"Better than the day you became a CPA? Better than your wedding day?"

Marty hesitates, then lets out a partially suppressed laugh. "How old are you, Jules?"

"Twenty-three."

"Have you taken the CPA exam?"

Jules sits up straighter. "Not yet. I plan to in the fall."

"Are you married?"

"No, but I have a steady girlfriend."

"Well, big days in life are not always what we expect them to be. Anyway, what did you want to talk about?" Marty sounds upbeat.

Jules describes what he found in the depreciation tables. "Yeah, it's a gray area, open to interpretation," Marty responds. "But one thing is certain: we don't want to piss off

Paul Perlman. He's our biggest client, and his business keeps growing. He's used us for years but is already nervous the acquisition will change us."

"Right, that makes sense," Jules says, though it's not a gray area. This could put the firm's reputation at risk. "Thanks for the advice, Marty."

Jules gathers the papers, bids Marty goodbye, and reports back to Arnie. "Marty's right," says Arnie. "We can't afford to lose Perlman."

"But Arnie, this is over the line. We could become liable for big IRS fines."

Arnie lets out a groan. "I hate making these decisions."

"Should we call Sydney? Or one of the other partners?"

"No, they put me in charge. It's my job to figure this out." Arnie purses his brow, pushes his glasses up the bridge of his nose. "Let's do this. We'll submit corrected depreciation tables in the quarterly filings, without bringing it to Perlman's attention. Hopefully he's too busy to notice."

"What if he does?"

Arnie winces. "Then we'll blame it on the transition, say it won't happen again, and give him a credit on our fees. Whatever it takes to keep him happy. For now, we keep quiet."

On Saturday, Jules is driving to his great uncles' house. Like most weekends since his arrival in Miami, he is checking on them in case they need help with anything. Despite their protests, he has convinced them to let him mow the lawn and trim the bushes – small wins but victories nonetheless. It's gratifying to convert the riotous mess of a yard to neatness and order. Plus, as he promised, he's repaying their past generosity towards Mom and Grandma Lilly.

Other than time spent with his great uncles, life in Miami is what he expected, though he misses Eileen even more than he foresaw. They talk on the phone, but that's no substitute for holding her and being held by her. Good thing he has Richard to temper his loneliness. While planning the move to Miami, Jules had called Richard, an Emory friend who had grown up in Miami, to ask for help in finding an apartment. Luckily Richard found one in the same complex where he lives with his wife Deborah. Richard's a fun guy. He and Jules get together regularly, often for a walk to the University of Miami campus, less than a mile from their apartment complex.

He pulls into his great uncles' driveway and studies their house. Now that the yard is in decent order, a paint job will spiff up the place nicely. How will he convince them to let him take on such a project, especially Uncle Izzy?

Izzy answers the front door, wearing the signature sleeveless undershirt and Bermuda shorts. "How are you, *bubbellah*? Life treating you okay?"

"Yeah, everything's fine."

Jack approaches from the living room. He walks gingerly and holds onto furniture or a wall. "Hey there, Jules!"

"Hi Uncle Jack. I'd like to put a new coat of paint on your house, to brighten up the roof eaves and window trim. How would that be?"

"Nah, don't bother," says Izzy. "That's a lot of work, but we got a favor to ask you. Can you take Jack to the doctor on

Friday? He needs to see a urologist. A few days ago, I saw blood in the toilet after he went."

"Oh, it's nothing," says Jack. "I feel fine, except for the usual aches and pains. A little blood never hurt anything."

"You need to go to the doctor."

"Doctors, shmocters, what do they know?"

"I'll tell you what I know. When you go *pish,* only *pish* should come out. Blood is not good."

"I'm fine, I'm telling you."

"You see what I have to put up with, Jules? The only way I could convince him to go is if you take him."

"Sure, I can take time off work on Friday, then put in a few hours on Saturday. I'm happy to do it."

"Good. Come on in, I'll get you an ice cream sandwich." Izzy pulls Jules into the kitchen, out of earshot from Jack. "It's nice you are taking Jack. Be sure to listen and let me know what the doctor says. Jack keeps to himself about these things."

"Okay." The sudden intimacy with Izzy gives Jules an idea. "Uncle Izzy, can I ask your advice? We have a client who expects us to lower his taxes by filing documents that are not right. We can't afford to lose the client, and my boss says it's a gray area, but I know that he knows it's wrong."

"You want my opinion? In business, you do what you have to do. The main thing is you take care of your own. Simple."

Jules nods, trying to hide his disappointment. He was hoping for sager advice.

They walk back into the cramped hallway. Max appears, wearing standard-issue uncle's attire. He stares blankly at

Jules. Izzy says, "Max, it's Jules, our great nephew, Esther's son. Remember he was here before with Esther and his girlfriend?"

Max lights up. "Oh, the one with the nice *tokhes,* I remember. Two cheeks you could really grab ahold of. Know what I mean, Jules?" Max looks at Jules hopefully.

Jules smiles at him. He's beginning to appreciate the irony of Max's consistency, the focus amidst the muddle.

Izzy interrupts. "Shut up, Max. That's his girl you're talking about!"

Max ignores his brother. "And beautiful knockers. Yeah, beautiful." His smile is serene as his eyes focus on something faraway.

"Jules, don't pay him any attention. Listen, whatever you do, be careful about getting married. Most girls run around and spend your money and you got nothing in the end."

Jack staggers in from the hallway. "Izzy, don't you tell him what to do." He glances at Max quickly, then continues. "Haven't you meddled enough? What do you know about love and marriage?"

Izzy is suddenly downcast. "I'm trying to help the boy," he says meekly. Jules is startled to see Izzy cowed. What's going on?

Jack glares at Izzy, starts to speak, but Max interrupts. "I saw Marcia this morning. She came to visit, didn't say a thing, just smiled at me. She forgives me. Such a beautiful child." He wipes tears from his eyes. "But when I asked her about you, Izzy, she frowned and shook her head. I don't think she likes you."

Izzy stares at Max, dumbstruck. Jules wonders who Marcia is but dares not step into a troublesome subject between the brothers. Jack is watching Izzy, then Max. He breaks the tension. "Jules, come into the living room and visit with us."

Jules follows the three brothers. Davey is sitting on the sofa, leafing through *The Kosher Kitchen Kookbook,* open on his lap. His head is bent low so that his face is near the pages, an awkward position for reading. Why doesn't Davey instead hold the book up to his face? Davey smiles at Jules, breathes heavily as he gasps out a few words. "Hello ... *ulp* Jules. Nice to ... *ulp* see you."

"Hi Uncle Dave. Are you planning to cook something?" Jules moves closer so he can hear Davey's underwater voice.

"Oh no, I ... *ulp* just like to ... *ulp* think about it. These days all I make is ... *ulp* strawberry Jell-O, sometimes lime. The ... *ulp* ladies at the *shul* make breakfast for us, after ... *ulp* morning services. So nice of them ... *ulp*."

Max pipes up. "Davey goes to *shul* every morning. He's *frum*."

Jules asks, "*Frum*? What does that mean?"

Izzy responds, "*Frum* is, you know, *frum*... religious. Davey's a good Jew."

Davey smiles. "We are all ... *ulp* good Jews. So ... *ulp* maybe *shul* is not for everyone."

"Waste of time, if you ask me," says Izzy.

"No girls," laments Max.

Jules is at his desk the following week when Marty bursts into his office. "Paul Perlman's on the phone, and he's mad as hell. Did you modify those depreciation tables?"

"Arnie told me to."

"Well Arnie's out of the office with a client, so you need to talk with Perlman."

Jules swallows. "Me?"

"Yes, you. You made the mess, you clean it up."

A knot grips Jules in his stomach. What should he do? He'll follow Arnie's guidance – make Perlman happy. "Okay, I'll take the blame. Will you be on the phone with me?"

"Let's take it in my office." They hurry to Marty's desk. He pushes the blinking light on the phone, then puts the call on speaker.

"Paul, I asked Jules Rothman to join us. He worked on those tables we filed."

Perlman doesn't bother with introductions. "Listen, do you want me to find another accounting firm? When Jerry Schlesinger sold the firm to you guys, he told me everything would stay the same. Now fix this or I'll find somebody else I can trust!"

Jules' hands are shaking. He tries to keep his voice steady. "Mister Perlman, I'm sorry we made a mistake. It was my fault. Marty has explained it all to me, how we should have used accelerated depreciation. We'll reimburse you for the increased taxes you're incurring, out of our pocket. And we'll waive our fees for the time spent on this."

"Okay, that's good." Perlman's voice is smoother. "But no more mistakes, you guys. I'm running a business here, and I need to know you got my back."

Marty speaks up. "It won't happen again, Paul. We'll review our quality control procedures, especially for your account, to double check everything. You're growing your company so damn fast that we need to put more horsepower into the financial accounting."

"Ha. Don't bullshit a bullshitter, Marty. Jules, you listen to Marty from now on, and send me the calculations on the increased taxes you'll be paying for."

Crisis averted. "Sure thing, Mister Perlman."

After Perlman hangs up, Jules looks at Marty. "Thanks for your help. He likes you."

"No problem. You did well, Jules, offering him a credit and not arguing accounting rules. And don't worry about future filings. The IRS isn't going to bother us about fudging accelerated depreciation. Everybody does it."

Riding with Jules to the Friday urology appointment, Jack fidgets in his car seat. "Are you uncomfortable, Uncle Jack? We can adjust the seat."

"As comfortable as I can get. My lower back hurts all the time, it's not the seat. But never mind that. Let me ask you something, Jules."

"Okay."

"That girlfriend of yours. You two have plans?"

"Sort of. We talk about getting married someday, but not before she finishes law school. Her father is the managing partner in the accounting firm where I work. Hopefully one day I'll be a partner."

"Sort of? That sounds like a real plan. You love this girl, right?"

"Oh yeah. I miss her when we're apart. We've been dating since high school."

"And you want to raise a family with her?"

"Sure." Jules glances towards Jack. "I guess."

"You guess?"

"I mean, that's so far away." He has considered fatherhood only as an abstract idea. The thought of actual children with Eileen now seems so ... permanent. There's no going back from that move. Is that how it was for his great uncles? Did the permanency of children turn them off to parenting? "Uncle Jack, it's interesting that you and your brothers never raised families of your own."

"We took care of our mother; may she rest in peace."

"Yes, I heard that, but Max mentioned a Marcia. Who is she?"

Jack draws a sharp breath, holds it, then releases a sigh. "We try not to discuss her, for Max's sake. But you're related, and I'm old and I get sick and tired of secrets. Especially now when Max is so confused, he doesn't know what's what. Marcia is .... she was Max's daughter. She died of cancer over twenty years ago. Breast cancer."

"Max had a daughter? How?"

"In the usual way, that's how. He was engaged, but they never got married."

"What? My mother didn't tell me."

"Out of respect for us, I'm sure. Turn right at the next stoplight. Don't let my brothers know I spilled the beans. I don't need the aggravation, and Max doesn't need to get riled up, with him already seeing people that aren't there. He's getting worse. Izzy is very worried."

At the red light several pedestrians cross in front of the car, including a young couple. The woman is waving her hands and yelling at the man, who walks silently beside her, scowling. "Uncle Izzy doesn't seem worried. He seems .... angry."

"That's his way. Ever since he was a boy, he scraped and clawed for every dollar. In those days, in Brooklyn, you had to be tough. It became a habit, I guess. He's always watched out for us, our entire lives. Our father was a drunk, so Izzy took care of the family. He brought money home to my mother then got us jobs when we were old enough. If not for him, we'd all be in the poorhouse."

They *do* live in a poor house. "So when was Max engaged? What happened?"

"It was a long time ago. He was young, barely into his twenties. She broke it off, and we all thought she had betrayed him. Years later we found out that ... well, it was more complicated than that."

"How old was Marcia when they split up?"

"She wasn't born yet. The mother got married right away to another guy, so for a long time Max didn't know the baby was his."

"So why the big secret?"

Jack looks hard at Jules. "It was a shameful thing. Not like today, when everybody sleeps with whoever and people have babies as if it's nothing, like they're getting a haircut or a new suit. Max was in love, then it all went bad. He was left with a broken heart. Completely broken. When we found out about Marcia years later, we ... we ... never mind, that's a long story."

Jack's voice carries a bitter edge. Despite his curiosity, Jules decides against any more questions. A few minutes later, he pulls into a parking stall outside the medical office building.

Jules runs around the car to the passenger door. He helps Jack swivel his legs out to get footing on the ground, then heaves Jack up by his arms to standing. Jack winces in pain. Jules winces as well, in involuntary sympathy. He offers his left arm. "Hold on to me, Uncle Jack. We'll walk together." Jules closes his right hand over Jack's forearm for extra security. They move gingerly towards the front door.

"Ah, this getting old, it's *farcockteh,* all messed up."

"It's better than the alternative. That's what my grandmother says."

"That's not necessarily true. I'm 84 years old, Jules. That's a long time. None of us lives forever."

Inside the urology office, Jack asks Jules to accompany him into the examining room. It's brightly lit and smells of rubbing alcohol. He helps Jack into a chair, then stands aside, jiggling the coins in his pocket.

The doctor waltzes in, smiling and confident. "Hello Mr. Isaacson, I'm Doctor Meltzer." He shakes hands with Jack. "I bet you speak *mamma loshen.*"

Jack smiles. "What do you think? I grew up in Brooklyn, when all the immigrants spoke Yiddish. Now I'm rusty, so I only use the choice words."

"My parents grew up there, too." Meltzer turns to Jules. "And who is this young fellow?"

"This is Jules, my great nephew. He drove me here, took off time from his work. Such a good kid. He's an accountant."

Meltzer and Jules shake hands. "That's a good profession. What kind of work did you do in Brooklyn, Mister Isaacson?"

"I worked with my brothers, in family businesses." He glances at Jules. "In those days, Jews couldn't be doctors or accountants. Even in New York there was anti-Semitism. Besides, we were children of poor immigrants, and as teenagers we took full-time jobs instead of finishing high school. I'm glad that's changed. I'm proud, looking at the two of you."

Meltzer nods at Jack. "Thank you, that's kind of you to say. So, what's the problem? How are you feeling?"

"Fine, I feel fine for a person my age. It was my brother's idea I should come."

"Alright, you're lucky to have a brother who cares about you, and a great nephew to drive you around. So why did your brother want you to see a doctor?"

"There's blood when I go to the bathroom."

"In your urine?"

"Yes, yes, in my urine."

"How long has this been happening?"

"How long? At my age, who can remember?"

"How's the flow?"

Jack clears his voice. "What do you mean?"

"The stream of urine. When you use the toilet."

"It's not the Hudson River."

Meltzer chuckles. "Okay, but is it a faucet or a leaky pipe?"

"Dribs and drabs. It takes a long time."

The doctor puts on a latex glove. "Jules, why don't you step to the other side of that curtain while I examine your great uncle. Mister Isaacson, please pull down your trousers. I'm going to check your prostate. You understand?"

"Yes, yes, I know what you need to do. Don't worry about it."

As he hides behind the screen, Jules flinches at the thought of a doctor's finger in his own rectum. Poor Uncle Jack.

When Meltzer is done, he says, "I'm going to have the nurse come in to draw blood from your arm."

"Okay, fine."

Hearing Jack zip up his pants, Jules returns to stand by his great uncle. Jack asks the doctor, "So, what did you find in there?"

"Your prostate is enlarged, and that can be a problem, but it's also common in men your age and does not create any issues other than loss of pressure and frequent trips to the bathroom. The blood test will tell us more."

"Tell us more about what? Whether I have cancer?"

"Let's not jump ahead of ourselves."

Jack looks Meltzer in the eye. "Listen to me, doctor. I'm 84 years old, there's blood in my urine, and I have an enlarged prostate. Does that say cancer to you? I want you to be straight with me. No sugar coating."

Meltzer frowns. "Okay, Mister Isaacson. Tell me, do you have pain elsewhere in your body? Maybe your hip joints or lower back or shoulders?"

"Yeah, pain in the low back for a few months. Now my hip hurts."

"Your prostate is rigid as well as enlarged, so yes, putting all this together suggests prostate cancer, but I can't be sure until I have results of the blood test and an X-ray."

"Thank you for telling me."

"You can treat it, right doctor?" Jules asks.

Jack turns to Jules. "I'm not interested in treatment. I know what's involved, and I'm not going through that."

"But – "

"No buts. Listen Jules, I wanted you to bring me here rather than Izzy because I don't want anybody telling me what to do. That goes for you too."

The doctor shakes his head. "There's no need for this conversation now. Let's wait until the test results."

Jack continues, "Another thing, Jules, this is between you and me, at least for now. You understand?"

"Yes. I understand. But …"

"But what?"

Jules already agreed to Izzy's request for a report back on Jack. Now he's caught between the two brothers. Does he lie to Izzy or betray Jack? "Um … never mind. You can count on me, Uncle Jack."

That evening in his apartment, Jules grabs a beer from the fridge and plops onto the sofa. After driving Jack home, he managed to avoid Izzy by leaving Jack at the front door and scurrying away. Finding himself enmeshed among family members keeping secrets from one another is familiar from his Atlanta family. The best policy is to keep quiet, then feign ignorance if directly confronted. Besides, his growing loyalty to Jack outweighs his fear of Izzy.

He picks up the television remote and surfs the channels until he comes across *The Graduate*, a movie he watched years ago. Again he pities the aimless young man vulnerable to other people's opinions and confused about love and work. Good thing Jules has a reliable girlfriend and a secure career.

During the night, Jules dreams he's standing at an altar with Eileen, clothed in a traditional wedding dress. She stares at him disapprovingly, shaking her head. He's wearing a periwinkle tuxedo that clashes with the bridesmaids' powder blue. The wedding cannot continue. He hears someone shouting his name, looks up towards the balcony and spots Uncle Jack calling out, "Jules! ... Jules! ... Jules!" Everyone is laughing at him now – he's in Bermuda shorts and a dingy sleeveless undershirt. With a finger he probes his ear canal and finds a thick tuft of hair.

Chapter 4
Brooklyn 1911

"JACK, WE GOT a big delivery from Gordon's," Mr. Katzenbaum calls from the upstairs office. "Go around back and bring in those boxes."

Jack gathers the cleaning supplies he used to wash the display windows facing Bushwick Avenue and hustles through the store towards the alley door. A fifteen-year-old Brownsville boy with a job, Jack has finally joined Izzy as a breadwinner for the family, proud to be contributing. His favorite assignment is opening delivery boxes from Gordon's, the textile mill located upstate.

Hands busy with anticipation, Jack stacks the boxes on the stock room floor, pulls one onto the table and cuts it open. As a young boy he opened the occasional box of Cracker Jack – a gift from Izzy – that always held a treasure to discover. His favorite was a plastic pinky ring that he pretended held a diamond. Now the treasure is new fabric, each Gordon's box filled with the textures and colors that the Katzenbaum seamstresses will transform into beautiful dresses.

Jack pushes aside the wrapping paper to find a roll of baby blue satin, top of the line at Katzenbaum's. The rolls underneath are satin as well: spring green, sunflower yellow, ruby red. He unrolls a bolt of the red and holds it to his cheek, eyes closed. What a delight!

After a moment, Jack opens his eyes to find the younger Katzenbaum brother watching him. Flushed with embarrassment, he stammers, "Uh...I was unloading this shipment like Mister K told me to."

Howard smiles. "I doubt my brother told you to unload quite that way, but I understand. I love the satin too. I love all these fabrics, how they each feel different on the skin. Of course, I also love the way they look after I've made them into dresses, with waists and busts and shoulders to fit a woman's curves."

Relief washes over Jack. Howard is kind, so different than the older brother always barking orders. "Uh, I thought the girls downstairs made the dresses."

"They cut and sew the fabrics, but they start with the patterns that I make."

"Patterns?"

"A pattern is a template that shows the seamstress exactly how to cut the fabric. I'll show you. Come with me."

Howard leads Jack through a door he has never entered. Inside is a workroom with a large table and several dress form mannequins on floor pedestals. Howard pulls sheets of thick brown paper from a wide drawer under the table. They have been cut with wavy edges into shapes unfamiliar to Jack.

"These sheets fit together to form a pattern. The dressmakers follow the pattern when they cut fabric into pieces, then sew the pieces together to make a dress. I develop the pattern, so I give the instructions for how each dress should be made."

Jack had not understood there was an important step before the dressmakers did their cutting and sewing. He is enthralled. "You create dresses! Gosh, you're an artist."

"That's nice of you, Jack, but the real art is in the original design. That's done in Paris. My brother gives me pictures of dresses in fashion magazines, then I make the patterns that will reproduce the dresses. We pay the captain of a trans-Atlantic ship to buy the magazines in France, then Herman pays a runner to meet the ship at the port in Manhattan, so I get those dress pictures as soon as possible. I have my own ideas about dress design, but Herman only lets me use the Paris originals."

"Why?"

"Because if we're going to succeed in business, we have to give our customers what they want, and what they want is the latest styles from Paris. Fashion is what sells. My brother is the businessman here."

"So's my brother. That's how we survive."

"We all need to survive, and I'm grateful that Herman's so good at running the business, keeping our family housed and clothed and fed, but we also need other things in life, such as beauty and art, don't you think? Not everyone appreciates that, Jack. I can tell you do, by the way you enjoy the fabrics." Howard smiles, gazing right into Jack's eyes. Jack looks away, towards the floor.

"What the hell is going on in here?" Herman Katzenbaum suddenly appears at the door. "Jack, I told you to unpack that shipment. Pronto, boy! Time is money, and I don't have money for you to waste time. You want I should dock your pay?"

Jack freezes. Bringing home less money would be a disaster. How would he explain that to Ma and Izzy? He starts to answer Mr. Katzenbaum but he's fighting back tears. He manages a strangled, "I'm sorry."

"What? What did you say? Speak up!"

"Ease up, Herman. It's my fault. Jack was doing what you said, but then I asked him to come help me move these mannequins into better positions so I could work faster on the next set. We just finished. Thanks for helping me out, Jack."

"Sure," Jack mutters as he slides past the older Katzenbaum. He regains his composure. "I'll have that shipment unloaded right away, Mister K."

Jack goes straight to the stock room then quickly unloads the shipment and sorts the rolls for the show room. Adrenalin courses through him. In that moment Howard understood him, saw him as he has never been seen before. One day he could be like Howard, creating patterns that transform bolts of cloth into beautiful dresses. Jack could be an artist.

That night at home, Jack sits with Izzy in their usual spot on the roof, stomachs full of the baked chicken and potatoes with onions their mother cooked for dinner. The evening air is warm for late March, carrying the promise of spring. Pigeons flutter and coo on the railing. It was a peaceful evening in the apartment – once again his father did not show up for dinner. The family has come to rely on Izzy for material support, with Mo increasingly scarce, staying away for days at a time after Izzy gives him a dollar or two. When he does appear, he is sullen and volatile, usually stinking of alcohol. Everyone walks on eggshells when he is home.

All afternoon Jack has been imagining himself doing what Howard does, designing and creating women's clothes. How can he learn dressmaking? Could he work with Howard as his helper? Would Mister K allow that? Should Jack ask Howard to persuade Herman?

Izzy leans back in his chair. "So how's the job going?"

"I like working there. Today Howard – he's the younger brother – showed me how he makes dress patterns for the seamstresses to follow. The older brother gets fashion magazines from Paris, then Howard copies the pictures."

"The older brother's the boss, right?"

"Yeah, he runs the place."

"Then be sure you do whatever he says."

"But Howard is the one who designs the dresses. Without him, they wouldn't have dresses to sell. He's an artist."

"Artist? He paints?"

"No, he doesn't paint. But he makes beautiful clothes."

"Beautiful shmootiful, he's a tailor. That's for losers."

Jack raises his voice. "Howard's not a loser. He's an important part of the business, and Katzenbaum's Clothing and Fabric is a good business. They have lots of customers, so I guess they make good money."

"That's because of the older brother, not the tailor. The older one knows his customers – that's the first rule in business. Katzenbaum's customers are ladies who want to look pretty, and he gives them what they want."

"He couldn't do that without Howard. He would have nothing to sell."

"So?"

"So, I want to do what Howard does, but Mister K wants me to stay busy with stocking and cleaning and all that. How can I learn to design clothes?"

"You don't. Like I said, you do what the boss tells you to do. Period."

The next afternoon Jack carries loads of fabric down to the Katzenbaum basement for the sewing girls to convert Howard's latest pattern into merchandise for the sales floor. Mister K gave Jack a long list of tasks for today, and Jack is anxious to please the boss after getting yelled at yesterday.

The basement contains a large room filled with ten Singer machines, each operated by a young woman with her head down, focused on her work. The sporadic whir of each foot-powered sewing machine blends into a single continuous hum. Jack hauls bundles stacked to his chin towards the supply table squeezed between the sewing machines and the bathroom. Before he can deposit the load, one of the seamstresses emerges from the bathroom. The door opens outwards but is caught mid-swing by the load of fabrics in Jack's arms. With the door edge blocking his way, he cannot reach the table, and the young woman is stuck behind a partially opened door. "I'm sorry," she mumbles, receding back into the tiny room.

"My fault," Jack replies. He steps back, the bundles still in his arms. After an awkward moment, he calls to her, "You can come out now, there's room."

She cracks the door, checks that the coast is clear, slips out and closes the door behind her. "I'll help you with that." She slides her arms under the stack of bundles opposite Jack, relieving some of the weight. Her hands touch his bare arms.

They step sideways and lay the stack onto the table.

"Thanks," says Jack.

Now he has a clear view of her. She's a bit older than him, though a good three inches shorter. Her hair is pinned up into a smart bun, similar to the other seamstresses.

She smiles brightly at Jack. "I'm Millie Weintraub."

"I'm Jack. Jack Isaacson."

"You're so strong, carrying those heavy bundles in these tight spaces. Lucky for me, or I might have been stuck in that water closet all day." She giggles, briefly touches Jack's shoulder.

"Oh, I'm just doing my job." Despite the risk that Mister K could catch him idle, he wants to hear details from a seamstress on how they follow Howard's patterns during the sewing process. "I've noticed you working here."

"You noticed me?" Millie pats her hair, tucks a stray strand behind her ear.

"Do you enjoy sewing dresses?"

"It's okay." She lowers her voice. "I wish the pay was better. My big sister Shirley also has a job sewing, and she works at a big factory in Manhattan. She has to work nine hours a day plus seven on Saturdays, but she gets paid twelve dollars a week. That's almost double what I make. She might get me a job there."

"You would have to trolley every day to Manhattan. Doesn't that cost a lot?"

"Yes, but the extra pay is worth it. Twelve dollars a week!"

Jack considers this. It doesn't make sense, crossing the Brooklyn Bridge every day even if it is more money. He has been to Manhattan twice, both times with Izzy who had an errand to run for Lewis. The tall, uncaring buildings reduced Jack to an insignificant nobody. "But here you get to make such beautiful dresses. If you stay, maybe you'll learn more about design."

She beams at him. "Maybe I will."

Jack smiles back. Millie is nice. He's not been interested in a girl before – he hasn't met the right one – but with Millie they would have dressmaking and fashion in common. "Do you know Mister K's brother Howard? He makes the patterns for the seamstresses to follow."

"Sure, I know him. He's nice, not like his older brother." She juts out her chest, wags her finger, and deepens her voice. "You there, get back to work. No loafing around here or I'll dock your pay."

Jack laughs. "That's pretty good." He looks around to check that no one is watching, then does his own imitation of Mister K, frowning and adopting the finger wag. "Time is money, and I don't have money for you to waste time."

Millie giggles.

"Howard sure is nice. I'm hoping to learn from him how to make dress patterns."

"Really? Then I can sew what you design." She smiles generously, gazing at Jack. "We could be a team."

"That would be great. You can show me how you cut the fabric to match the pattern, and then set up the sewing lines. I have lots of questions."

Millie keeps her smile, but the brightness fades. Did Jack say something wrong?

"We could meet after work today, and you can walk me to the trolley," she says.

"Okay. I'll meet you out front." Jack glances towards the stairs that lead to the showroom. "I better get back to work before Mister K shows up. I need to sort these bundles."

"See you later, Jack." Millie turns away and walks towards her sewing station.

Jack starts in on the piles of fabric, sorting by type and color. The materials are smooth and clean on his hands. He looks forward to learning from Millie exactly how she follows Howard's patterns when cutting the fabrics. Does she first draw cut lines on the material? Or does she use a knife while holding the pattern against the fabric? He can't chance an involved conversation while on Mister K's clock, so he'll ask her out to the movies, then they can talk shop afterwards. It will be his first date with a girl.

He finishes the sorting, rushes through the basement to collect a large stack of freshly pressed dresses, and carries them to the showroom, bounding up two stairs with each stride.

Izzy hurries down the Pitkin Avenue sidewalk on his way to meet Lewis. In addition to their usual transaction today, Izzy intends to propose an idea to Lewis: if he hustles to sell more tickets than his average, he gets a larger share of the higher revenues from the numbers racket, say 33 percent. Higher revenues will mean more for Lewis too, so it's a win-win, as long as Lewis doesn't think Izzy is being disloyal or ungrateful. Izzy rehearses his pitch, this time starting with an avowal of his fidelity.

At the corner of Herzl Street, he turns into Gurewitz's Kosher Deli, where Benjamin Gurewitz stands behind the counter with his oldest son, Pauly.

"Hey Izzy," Pauly says with a grin, "how's it going?"

Lately Pauly has become interested in Izzy's sister Bessie, which is okay with Izzy. Pauly usually shows up to the Isaacson apartment with a gift from the deli, such as a brisket or a whole chicken, and always makes a point of talking with Izzy's mother for a while before he and Bessie go out for a walk. He would be a good provider for Bessie.

"Hey Pauly. I can't complain. How's business, Mister Gurewitz?"

"Fine, business is fine." The elder Gurewitz grins. "Don't get me wrong, I got my share of troubles, but who doesn't? Here, have a *shtickel*. It's on me." Gurewitz points to a plate of sliced salami ends displayed on the deli counter, with a taped handwritten sign that reads, *Have a shtickel, they're only a nickel.*

"Thanks. Here's some news. I had a $400 winner last week. He bought ten lots, so he even got a discount."

"Is that so? Who is this lucky fellow?"

"Manny Finklestein. He works at Frankle's Furniture store, way down Rockaway Avenue near Hegeman. You should have seen his face when I counted out twenty 20-dollar-bills."

"Don't know him, but I know that store. Since when do you give a discount?"

"If you buy ten tickets, you get an eleventh one for free. Same as any ticket, you can double down or choose a different number."

"Too rich for my blood." Gurewitz glances around for his wife Golda, spots her at a table chatting with a customer. He opens the cash register, pulls out two dollars. "But I'm feeling lucky, so I'll take two this week."

"Number 44?"

"Sure, same as always."

"You got it." Izzy pockets the two bills, pulls out a notebook and pencil. After a quick scribble, he takes a seat at the corner table farthest from the door. Izzy always arrives first for the weekly exchange with Lewis. He delivers this week's sales, with the list of names and chosen numbers, 00 to 99. The winning number is determined by the two hundredths digits of the Dow Jones on Monday, as reported in the *Brooklyn Daily Eagle* on Tuesday morning. The timing is good for sales on Friday, when people get paid and are feeling flush. In return, Lewis gives Izzy two envelopes, one with his cut – 20 percent of total sales from the previous week – the other with cash for last week's winners. The winner's cash is clipped together in small packets, each with the lucky person's name attached. The payout is 40 to 1 and each ticket sells for a dollar, so five dollars can win two hundred, an appealing prospect for Izzy's customers. That leaves 60 percent in profit: 20 for Izzy and 40 to Lewis and his boss Arnold "The Brain" Rothstein.

Izzy fidgets in his chair, eying the front door for his mentor's arrival. While practicing his pitch one more time, he rearranges the table items: salt and pepper shakers, mustard dish, and napkin holder.

After a few minutes, Lewis walks in, spies Izzy and takes a seat at the table. "Hey, *boychik*! How's my best salesman?"

"Doing great." Izzy pulls the wad from his jacket pocket, passes it to Lewis under the table. "That's $622, best week ever. You were right about that big payoff. I sold ninety-six tickets on the spot at that furniture store – ninety-six dollars without moving my feet – not just to Frankel's staff but there was a bunch of customers, too. I had them egging each other on. Three of them bought ten-packs."

"Yeah, that's the way. Let the saps convince each other what a good deal they're getting. Nobody wants to miss out when they see a big winner. Here's your share from last week." The exchange again occurs under the table. Unlike every other transaction in their lives, neither needs to count the money. Mutual trust runs deep.

It's a good time for Izzy to present his proposal. Lewis is hesitant at first, but then appreciates the potential in it. "Okay, we'll both come out ahead if you sell more. But the higher percentage will have to come out of my share, not The Brain's, so let's make it 30 percent. Deal?"

Izzy extends his hand, and they shake. "Deal!"

Lewis nods his head approvingly. "I've always known you're a smart guy, Izzy. Stick with me, you'll go far."

Delighted, Izzy throws out another idea. "Hey Lewis, I been thinking. You got the numbers business covered in Brownsville. You got me and the three other guys to do the retail work. Why not go out on your own? You don't need to pay a cut to Rothstein. Then there's even more for you and me."

Lewis glances around in case anyone is within earshot. "Shush! Are you crazy? No way. We don't cross The Brain, not unless we want our faces rearranged. He's got an organization, you understand? The organization takes care of any problems that come up. If somebody tries to cut in on our turf, they'll get a not-so-polite visit. If the fuzz bothers you or the other sales guys, Rothstein's boys will grease the right palms. There's lots of money to be made Izzy, but you need an organization to keep it going."

Might violence be needed? Izzy shivers, but he sees the way it is – all he needs is the threat of Lewis calling in muscle to keep competitors away. "Okay Lewis. I'm with you, so if you're with Rothstein I am too. You can count on me."

"Right back at you. Don't worry Izzy, we got plenty of opportunity ahead of us."

The next Sunday morning, Jack wanders down Pitkin Avenue, pondering the events of last night. Pauly came over to ask Jennie and Izzy for permission to marry Bessie, which was easily granted. Then Bessie and Pauly sat on the sofa close to each other, holding hands and sharing their plans with the family. They're drawn to each other, like magnets. Will Jack ever know romantic love like that? There was no inkling on his recent date with Millie, though he did enjoy the time with her.

What worries him more deeply is the conversation he and Izzy overhead later in the evening. Jennie and Bessie were talking softly in the bathroom with the door ajar. Jennie was counseling her daughter on marriage. "Now listen, *bubbeleh*. On your wedding night, Pauly is going to do what husbands do. It will hurt down there, but you got to let Pauly do it so he can get you pregnant. Your father hurts me, but God says a wife should obey her husband and the man should go to the wife, especially on the Sabbath."

The taste of vomit rises up in Jack's throat. Is he supposed to do that one day? Hurt a woman with his sex? He knows the basics of intercourse, but female body parts are a mystery. Why would a woman experience pain? And how could his own father do such a thing?

Izzy was furious. He told Jack it's not supposed to cause pain in the woman, at least not after the first time. Before Jack could ask why the first time is different, Izzy proclaimed he will not let their father hurt their poor mother anymore. Jack said he would help, though he has no idea how he might protect his mother.

A paper boy rounds the corner, carrying a bundle of the Sunday *Brooklyn Daily Eagle* and hawking the headline: "Big fire in Manhattan! Hundreds dead! Two girls from Brownsville! Read all about it!"

Jack joins the small crowd gathering around the paper boy. People exchange nickels for newspapers, scan the front page, then read aloud for the crowd: "It was a shirt factory....Terrible fire....They were young girls.....some jumped from the ninth floor, some burned alive....*Oy gutinue*...140 dead....140 dead girls!"

A woman cries out, "Two from Brownsville? Who? Who are they?..... List of names on the back page!" Another voice shouts, "It's Deborah Plotnick and Shirley Weintraub.....Oy oy oy, those poor mothers, what *tsooris*, what heartache....Do you know them? Who knows them?"

From the group's perimeter, Jack starts to speak up, but his throat constricts, choking on the name Shirley Weintraub, obviously Millie's sister. To speak Shirley's name to these strangers would be a betrayal to Millie. He stumbles away from the crowd, heading towards home.

On the next street corner, another small crowd has gathered. As Jack approaches, he hears bits of conversation: "Didn't they have fire escapes?....... Ah, you know the bosses, they don't care about the poor workers.....There ought to be a law....." Jack passes a similar gathering on nearly every street corner. Pitkin Avenue is awash in sorrow, a community grieving for two if its own.

Two blocks from his family's apartment, someone grabs his arm. It's Izzy. He scans Jack's face. "You okay, pal?"

In the safety of his brother's orbit, Jack starts to cry. "Izzy, one of the girls who died, I know her younger sister from Katzenbaum's. Millie was talking about getting a job with her sister Shirley – she would have burned up with the rest of them. Burned up, Izzy." Jack sniffles, wipes his nose. "All those girls burned up."

Izzy pulls Jack through the crowd into their building and up the stairs to their spot on the roof. His voice rises with each flight they climb. "Those sons o' bitches, locking those girls inside to keep an eye on them, blocking the exits. They ran a goddamn fire trap, those bosses. It's not right, Jack. Those girls had nobody to stand up for them, but you got to stand up when people aren't treating you right. Well, no one's going to take advantage of me or you or the rest of the family. No one! Take that *shyster* landlord Moskowitz who tried to raise our rent when he heard that I'm making a little money running numbers with Lewis. I told him 'You don't want any trouble with me and my friends, so if you know what's good for you, you better change your tune.' He backed down when he saw I meant business, that son of a bitch."

The intensity of Izzy's rage calms Jack. He's back to himself, no longer crying. "Izzy, that fire was an accident. Bad things happen."

"Bad things happen when bad people let them happen. That Katzenbaum you work for is no different. You think he cares about those girls in his basement? Or about you?"

"He doesn't want us to burn up in a fire."

"Maybe not, but he won't spend a dime to stop it from happening. You know what? It's time for you to quit. Tell Katzenbaum to shove it up his ass."

"No, I like working there. I want to learn from his brother how to make clothes out of fabrics."

"You want to be a *tailor*? Eh, no money in that. No brother of mine is going to be a poor tailor, then get trapped in a fire. I'll talk to Lewis about getting you a better job."

Jack pleads. "Izzy, I…. I love the fabrics!"

"What? That's nonsense. Now listen to me, my mind is made up, and that's that."

"Don't tell me to quit. I won't do it!"

"Oh, yeah?" Izzy frowns, pokes Jack in the chest. "You have to do what's best for the family. You know that. Besides, I'm trying to protect you. This is for your own good, even if you're too young or stupid to get it."

"I'm not stupid. And you can't make me quit."

"We'll see about that." Izzy sneers. "You'll come around, I know, and you'll do the right thing."

Jack says nothing. Izzy may be his big brother, but not his boss.

When Jack returns to the apartment with Izzy, he's hit with the sour, alcohol-infused body odor announcing his father's return. His little sister Lilly is playing on the floor with Davey – they are making the most of the two wooden toy trucks that Izzy bought Davey for his third birthday last week. Jennie and Bessie emerge from the kitchen, wiping their hands on their aprons. Jennie reports that Mo is asleep in their bedroom.

"Did he ask you for money?" asks Izzy.

"No, but he gave me a dirty look and called me a word that I don't care to repeat."

"Ma, I'm so sick of him treating you wrong. You who does so much for our family."

Jennie smiles weakly. "You're a good boy, Izzy, a real *mensch*. You're the one taking care of the family." Bessie clears her throat, hands on her hips. "And you too, Bessie, I don't know how I would look after everybody without you. My little girl is practically a woman, soon to be married."

Jack figures that Shirley Weintraub was a year older than Bessie. Shirley might have been standing in her mother's kitchen two nights ago, eating dinner with Millie and their family. Now Shirley is gone, gone forever.

Little Davey breaks out crying. During his play with Lilly, he tripped over a toy and fell flat on his face. Bessie rushes over, picks up Davey from the floor, and tries to comfort him. The commotion draws Max from the boys' bedroom. "What happened?"

Davey is now howling full throttle, calling for his mama. As Jennie rises, Mo emerges from the other bedroom, eyes bloodshot and balance unsteady. "I'm trying to sleep in here!" he yells. "Get that kid to be quiet, or I'll do it myself."

"You leave him alone," Jennie yells back. "It's not his fault that his good-for-nothing father decides to sleep off a drunk in the middle of the day."

Mo reaches her in two strides, followed by a hard slap on her face. "Shaddup, woman!" The force of the blow knocks her onto her hands and knees. Jack gasps.

Izzy erupts. "Don't you touch her!" He pushes Mo away from his mother, both hands square onto Mo's chest. Jack has never seen Izzy confront their father physically. Izzy glares at Mo. "Leave her alone! Leave us all alone! Just get out!"

Mo stares back, stunned at his son's explosion. "You don't push me." He lunges, gets both hands around Izzy's neck. Unable to get free, Izzy starts punching his father in the abdomen. Jack considers separating them, or joining in on Izzy's side, but he's afraid of their rage, their unrestrained brutality. Instead, he puts his arms around Lilly and Davey, who are cowering in the corner.

"Stop it, Mo!" screams Jennie, "you're hurting him." Jack wants to help his brother but moves neither his feet nor his mouth. It is ten-year-old Max who tries to pull Mo off Izzy. He is too small to make a difference, but his efforts distract Mo enough that Izzy can free himself from the neck hold. Izzy regains his composure, bends low, throws his shoulder forward, and plunges into Mo's midsection with all his might. Mo is thrown against the wall with a crunching thud. He collapses on the floor, gasping for breath. Between gasps, peering up at his eldest son, Mo manages to say, "I'm your father, the man of the house."

"You're not a man, you're a drunk and a dumb immigrant. You're not providing for this family – I am! You're leeching off us so you can buy booze." Izzy reaches into his pocket, throws a few wadded dollar bills at Mo. "Take this and get out!"

Mo turns away. He looks to Jennie for support, but she is frowning at him in grim defiance. He slumps on the floor, utterly deflated. Jack witnesses his father's degradation, his weakness, his shirking of responsibilities. Mo gathers the money, slowly picks himself up, and stumbles out the door.

Izzy yells after him. "And don't come back! Don't ever come back!" Breathing heavily, he turns to face the family. His eyes fix on Jack. "And you, you're going to quit that job. I'll get you a better one, better for you and better for the family. No more tailor work for my brother. You hear me?"

Jack's head droops. He looks at feet. "Okay, Izzy. I'll do what you say."

Over the next few weeks, the *Brooklyn Daily Eagle* carries front-page stories on the Triangle Shirtwaist Factory fire. There are photographs and heart-rending accounts of the young women who died while working 60 hours a week to provide for their families. Editorials call for criminal charges against the owners and for new building codes and more government oversight of safety conditions in New York factories. Reports tell of labor unions finally succeeding in their attempts to organize the garment industry, buoyed by public sympathy in the wake of the tragedy.

One day the paper contains a brief piece on page 14. An unidentified man was struck dead by a trolley in Flatbush. It's the third fatal accident this year involving a pedestrian and a Brooklyn trolley car. The driver said the man tried to dodge the trolley but misjudged its speed and crossed the tracks too slowly. Police reported that there was no identification on the body, only an empty bottle of schnapps and a wadded-up dollar bill.

Chapter 5
February 1981

DRIVING HOME FROM work, Jules clenches his teeth while muttering to himself. Paul Perlman is a snake. On the phone today with Marty and Jules, Perlman explained his plans to expand his pest company into Palm Beach County, which means obtaining a hefty bank loan. The bank will want a list of the company's assets, and Perlman expects the accountants to inflate their value. These assets include the previously depreciated equipment, so the firm will be undervaluing and overvaluing the same items at the same time.

Jules cannot afford to challenge Perlman on this. He would fire the firm, the Miami venture would fail, and Sydney would blame his young accountant and future son-in-law. On top of that, Perlman is robbing Jules of accounting's best part – its systematic order – and replacing it with … chaos. He's also demanding the accounting team completes the valuation by Monday, so Jules will be working all weekend and canceling his plans to go snorkeling with Richard.

He needs to clear his head. At home he changes into swimming trunks and heads for the beach. He splashes into the water at a run, then dives into the first wave. The shock of cold immersion gives way to a visceral aliveness, punctuated by the bite of saltwater trickling into his mouth. The ocean buoys his body, no longer weighted by anxiety and anger. He adjusts his goggles, then swims parallel to shore at a vigorous pace, the water rocking him in gentle swells. After a while he spies a nurse shark, lying motionless on the sandy bottom, and stops to admire the big fish. It's at least eight feet long. Jules marvels at its double dorsal fins, elongated tail, and the distinctive barbels hanging from its broad flat head, exactly as he recalls from marine wildlife photography books.

When he turns to continue the swim, someone in the water ahead is waving. It's a blonde girl, maybe his age. Is she waving at him? There's no one else around. He waves back, and she motions him to join her. He rushes to reach her.

"Are you okay?" She's treading water, no sign of distress.

"Oh thanks, I'm fine. I wanted to say hi. I'm Cathy." She speaks with a Southern accent, beaming him a million-dollar smile.

"My name's Jules. Did you see the nurse shark?"

"Shark? Where? Let's get out of here."

"Oh no, nurse sharks are harmless. They don't act like other sharks at all. They usually lay on the bottom, scrounging for small crabs and snails."

"Are you sure?" Her eyes are wide. And bright blue.

"I'm sure. They never hurt anybody."

"Just the same, I'm getting out. Will you swim back with me? I'm scared."

"Sure."

As they emerge from the surf, Jules tries not to stare. She's wearing a bikini and could pass for a fashion model.

"Want to sit with me a while on my towel?"

"Yeah! Uh, I mean ... that would be nice. Thanks." Does he sound like an idiot?

"So how do you know so much about nurse sharks?"

"I've always been interested in marine animals. It started when I was a boy, and my father gave me a conch shell. He showed me how to hold it to my ear to hear the ocean sound stored inside. That was magical. After that, I started collecting coral, sand dollars, starfish, clam shells, marine fossils, anything that came from the ocean. I became fascinated with illustrated books by Jacques Cousteau and stories of the sea by Jules Verne and Jack London. I read *Moby Dick* when I was twelve."

"You sound smart. I bet you're good at school. Are you in college?" She pulls out a ponytail band to let her hair fall over her shoulders. Jules' heart jumps into his throat.

"I finished last year. What about you?"

"I'm in college now. I go to the Florida Bible College. It was easy to get into. You probably went to a big place."

"Pretty big, I guess. I went to Emory, in Atlanta."

"Wow, I knew you were smart. And nice, too." There's that smile again. Is she flirting with him? He blurts out, "I have a girlfriend. She lives in Atlanta."

"I have a boyfriend too, back home in Ocala. Well, he's sort of a boyfriend. Anyway, it's nice that you're honest, Jules. A lot of boys aren't. That girlfriend of yours is lucky to have you."

"I guess. But I'm not much to look at.

"Oh Jules, don't hide your light under a bushel. That's what Jesus teaches us."

"Um ... I'm Jewish."

"You are? That's wonderful! Like Jesus was. I mean, used to be. Pastor Mark says we love Jewish people. We're lucky there are so many here in Miami." She rifles through a beach bag, pulls out a brochure that she hands to Jules. The title is *Why Jews Are Turning to Jesus*, lettered in a font that mimics Hebrew.

So that's it – she wants to convert Jules. That's why she's interested in him. "Uh, you keep it, Cathy, else it will get ruined when I swim back. Well, I better go. Time for me to get home."

She makes a pouty face. "Did I say the wrong thing? I say whatever comes into my head, that's one of my faults. Does it bother you if I talk about Jesus?"

"No ... well, kind of. I'm just not used to it. It's okay, now you're the one being honest, I mean honest about yourself, and that's good. I hate it when people pretend to be somebody they're not." Where did that come from? Why did Jules say that?

"Oh Jules, you are so sweet. Before you go, let me give you my phone number." She pulls a pen from her bag. "And this way you can't lose it in the ocean." She grabs his hand, places his forearm on her outstretched legs, and holds him in place while inking his arm. The touch of her skin, on her upper leg no less, triggers a semi-erection. Horrified, Jules tries to cover up by rearranging his legs, a difficult maneuver with Cathy holding one arm in place. As soon as she releases him, he rolls the other way, quickly adjusts his swimsuit, stands up and checks his arm. She drew a heart next to her number.

    She stands as well. "Thank you for saving me from that mean old shark, Jules. You're a knight in shining armor." She gives him a quick hug, the moment passing before he can hug back. "I hope you call me."

    "Okay. Um, it was great to meet you."

    "You're very nice, Jules. Not like other boys."

Back home, he turns on the television to watch *Jeopardy*. A commercial is playing. It's a cheaply made animation, depicting a cluster of skulking termites. One turns to the viewer, speaks in an exaggerated Hispanic accent. "Hola, boys and girls. We come from Columbia to eat your family's house foundation. Don't worry, we be quiet. Tell your parents NOT to call Paul Perlman Pest Control, hee hee." Then a giant fist smashes down from above, flattening the insects. The screen switches to Paul Perlman himself, wearing a white coverall uniform, pointing and shouting at the camera. "You got termites, ants, roaches, nasty crawly things? Call Paul Perlman Pest Control – we kill 'em good!" He pounds a fist in the palm of his other hand emphatically on 'good.' "Right boys?"

    The camera pulls back to show a group of similarly dressed employees behind Perlman, who respond in unison, "We kill 'em good!" using the same fist-in-hand motion.

    Jules shakes his head. Perlman is a pig as well as a snake, exploiting fear of Columbian cocaine smugglers to portray termites as dangerous to children. He tries to ignore the guy as *Jeopardy* begins.

The categories whet his appetite: Interstate Highways, Notable Team Names, Woody Allen Moments, Fish in the Sea, Fashion Statements, and Pun Fun. He aces several questions, which feeds a hunger for more. He stands up from the sofa and paces around the room, eyes fixed on the television.

The phone rings. He considers unplugging it from the wall, but he won't take his eyes off that TV set. The phone continues its clamor until the answering machine kicks in. He hears Eileen's voice. "Hi Jules, it's me. I'm surprised you're not home right now, but anyway it's important that I talk to you right away."

Jules grabs the phone. "Hello."

"Hi Jules."

"Hi Eileen. Hold on a minute." With his hand over the mouthpiece, he reaches over to mute the television. He can watch *Jeopardy* without her knowing. "Okay, sorry. Is everything okay?" he asks.

The game continues with Fish in the Sea for $100. The answer displays on the screen: 'Because they lack scales and noticeable fins, these fish are often mistaken for snakes.' He says to himself, *What are eels?* The returning champion got it – a giveaway. Jules starts to sweat.

"Oh Jules, I miss you so much. It's been three whole days since we talked!"

"Yeah." Fish in the Sea for $150: 'An underwater ecosystem held together by calcium carbonate.' *What is a coral reef?* "I miss you too."

"We'll be together soon. I booked my flight to Miami during spring semester break in April, as we planned."

"Great, I can't wait." Fish in the Sea for $200: 'The most common members of Subclass Elasmobrachii, these fish have skeletons made of cartilage, not bone.' *What are sharks?* Right again.

"I already called Deborah, and we're planning to take you and Richard shopping. Deborah says there's a new mall called Dolphin Mall, isn't that cute? I need a blouse and I know you could use another suit, maybe a navy one…" The *Jeopardy* game shifts to Woody Allen Moments. Jules flashes to that scene where the girl is chattering, while the guy is wondering what she looks like naked.

Three weeks later, Jules opens his front door to greet Richard. Jules finally has a Saturday off from work for their snorkeling adventure. Richard gives him a grin and a big hug, enveloping Jules in his stocky upper body. His brown curly hair is cut fashionably, short on the sides and back. "You ready to go, *boychik?*"

"First come inside for a minute. I want to show you what I just bought." He leads Richard to his new aquarium and turns on the viewing light. The fish have been keeping him company the past few days. "That bright blue one is a cichlid, the orange fish with the big tail is a flamingo guppy, the striped one is a tiger barb, and the multi-colored one is a gourami. In the wild, these species live in coral reef habitats. We might see one today."

"Wow, that's cool. Is this your first aquarium?"

"I had one when I was growing up, but this one's much nicer."

"I didn't know you're into tropical fish and ocean stuff."

Jules' childhood passion for the ocean had waned in high school, as his attentions turned to the practicalities of teen life. Residing in a tropical coastal city these past months has reignited his old interest, and he's eager to experience snorkeling for the first time.

The guys head out in Richard's car for breakfast at *Lots of Lox* on Highway One, listening to Crosby Stills and Nash on the cassette deck. It's a beautiful mid-winter day in south Florida. The sky is a deep blue with brilliant cumulus clouds catching the sunlight. Where the highway leaves the mainland at Manatee Bay, Jules catches his breath at first sighting the water. "Wow, it's so beautiful, Richard. It makes me wonder why I spend so much time working in an office, when all this beauty is nearby."

"Gotta pay your dues, man. You and me both. That's why we have money to go snorkeling. Not to mention that excellent pumpernickel bagel stuffed with lox."

"I know, but I wish I had a better balance. This is my first Saturday off in three weeks. I want more time outdoors, in nature."

"Jules, be patient. Put in your time at the accounting firm, and one day you'll be a partner. You'll be wealthy enough to go on trips to the beach or the mountains or wherever you want to go."

"So, in the meantime, it's nose to the grindstone?"

Richard wags an index finger, keeping his other hand on the steering wheel. "No, in the meantime you make the job fun."

"You have fun being a stockbroker?"

"Absolutely. I adore my clients and I spend most of my working time with them."

"The old Jewish ladies who call you up worried every time the market clicks downward? Or their husbands with their exaggerations of how smart they were running their businesses back in the day?"

"Hey, I love schmoozing. It's a win-win. My clients get to spend time with a Jewish boy who reminds them of their grandson that lives in another city and doesn't call enough and doesn't want to listen to their stories anyway. I enjoy their life stories, how things were when they were growing up in New York or wherever. They like me, and I like them. They trust me with their money to invest and I make more for them than they would putting it in a bank. I earn more commissions, then they introduce me to their friends, and I become someone else's surrogate grandson and keep expanding my client base. It's a virtuous cycle."

"Virtuous? Really?"

"I'm having fun and everybody's happy with nobody being hurt. The point is that you need to have more fun."

"Okay, here's something fun. I met a girl at the beach. Her name is Cathy, and she's a total knockout. Long blonde hair, beautiful smile, incredible body. She was flirting with me."

"You're shitting me."

"I shit you not."

"Have you seen her again?

"No. She gave me her phone number, but I haven't called her."

"Why not?"

"I don't know. She's out of my league. And it would be unfaithful to Eileen."

"Does this Cathy know you have a girlfriend?"

"Yeah, I told her. She said she has a sort-of boyfriend, whatever that means, also out of town."

"Then you're okay. You can at least call her. Listen, you've never been with any girl besides Eileen. You need to get more exposure, and I'm not talking sex, or even romance. Getting to know more women is good for you, and for Eileen actually."

"What? How can that be?"

"If you haven't been around enough to know you're in the right relationship, you harbor doubts, and little issues become major ones because you lack perspective. There are always issues, in any relationship."

It's true that small things about Eileen bother Jules. "But if I tell Eileen about this girl, she'll blow her top."

"You don't have to tell her, not unless something happens. This girl Cathy gave you her phone number, she's not proposing marriage. Just call her to talk, don't even ask her out. Or you could invite her for a daytime walk on the beach, so it won't be a date."

"There's more to this situation. She goes to bible college. She got all excited when I told her I'm Jewish, gave me a Jews for Jesus brochure."

Richard bursts out laughing. "My friend Jules, the Jesus Jew."

"I'm glad you think this is so funny."

"It is funny. I'm picturing you wearing a *tallis* and a big crucifix, holding hands with an adoring blonde girl who came out of a Norman Rockwell painting."

"She wants to convert me."

"That's good. If she's in it to convert you, she's not interested in dating you, so you can relax about Eileen. Just get to know Cathy as a new friend, a person with a different world view. You might learn something."

"Like how to put mayonnaise on a corned beef sandwich?"

"See, it is funny. And fun is what you need, like I said."

Captain Pete's Diving and Snorkeling Adventures is housed in a small wooden building decorated with nautical-themed tchotchkes. Inside is a fortyish woman with long sun-bleached hair standing behind a counter. She's wearing a T-shirt that highlights her ample breasts and reads, *At Captain Pete's, We Do It Deeper.* She smiles at them. "Hi, can I help you swabs?"

Richard lights up. "Yes, we have reservations to go snorkeling. My name is Barnacle Bill. This is my mate Smee."

She glances at a clipboard, "Ah yes, well Smee is on the list, but there's no Bill. Oh, I have you down as William."

Richard grins. "Oh, I hate that name. That's what my mother calls me."

"Yes, you look more like a Bill, and William is no name for a pirate." From beneath the counter, she pulls out a pirate hat, puts it on, closes one eye and does an "Arrrr."

"I didn't know they had lady pirates in these parts."

"Hey, careful who you're calling a lady. She rechecks the clipboard. "Bill, I'm guessing you and Smee might be using the aliases Richard Steinberg and Jules Rothman?"

"That's right! And I'm guessing that you are Missus Pete?"

"That's Miz, not Missus. I'm Miz Captain Pete."

She has them sign forms, takes their payment, and helps fit them with snorkeling masks, tubes, and fins. As other customers arrive, Jules lathers up with sunscreen and insists on spreading it on Richard's back and shoulders.

Then Captain Pete appears, failing to fulfill Jules's image of a sea captain. He wears a baseball cap and a ponytail, flip top sunglasses with the shades up, and is clean-shaven. He gives a safety lecture to the group and reviews the planned excursion. Everyone follows him to the dock and loads onto the boat.

As Captain Pete pulls away from the dock, Jimmy Buffett blasts on the boat's tinny stereo system. How predictable. Jimmy Buffett is too pop for Jules, though Buffet's lyrics occasionally stick with him – those dreamy songs about searching or reflecting, such as *Changes in Latitudes*.

After twenty minutes, Jules cannot spy land anymore. The ocean is so vast, stretching to the horizon and thousands of miles beyond. Beneath the surface is another world, where fish breathe water and dolphins talk to one another and coral polyps build intricate reefs. A lull of serenity arises within him so quickly that his eyes water. He wants to check in with Richard, but his pal is busy flirting with the captain's mate, Katrina. She giggles as he gestures at the snorkeling gear while telling her some story. How does Richard do it? He's always able to entertain an audience, whether it's old Jewish couples or Ms. Captain Pete or even Jules himself.

Pete brings the boat to a slow idle, then a stop, one hundred feet from a ring of buoys with signs that read, "Divers Present" and "Motorboats Stay Back 50 Feet." He jumps down from the bridge and has everyone gather around. Pete says they are in John Pennecamp Underwater State Park, one of the best locations on the East Coast for exploring coral reefs, then reviews the rules everyone must follow to protect the coral. In addition to the natural wonders of the reef, the snorkelers will see an underwater statue of Jesus, nine feet tall and weighing 4,000 pounds.

They move to the stern and don their flippers and masks. Katrina is standing on the rear platform, helping each snorkeler into the water. Richard clumsily climbs onto the platform holding Katrina's arm. In his best New York accent, he says to her, "*Oy vay*, I haven't felt this shaky since they told me *Manischevitz* is cheaper by the case. Good thing you're here, hon. Such a strong, healthy girl. Nice teeth too."

She giggles again. Richard plops into the water. Jules follows but all he manages with Katrina is a weak "thank you."

Jules takes to the water immediately, floating face down and breathing easily through the snorkel tube. The water is warm and clear and quiet – the only sound is the internal wind of his own breath, solid and rhythmic. Now that his face is below the surface, the coral formations and myriad creatures are visible: angelfish, parrotfish, zebrafish, damselfish, sea cucumbers and urchins, all flashing iridescent colors as their movements reflect filtered sunlight. Sunbeams penetrate the wavy ocean surface from fluctuating angles, turning the water itself into multiple shades of blue and green. Swimming with arms extended, Jules watches the refracted sunlight dance on his arms and hands, a bright yellow net shimmering in a silent breeze.

    The statue appears. Jesus is deeper than Jules expected, with the top of his head a good eight feet down. Jesus stares up towards the surface, his arms raised high, palms outstretched.

    Richard swims over and they explore the reef together, silently pointing out fish or coral shapes to each other until they drift apart. Jules takes in the quiet underwater beauty. This is a precious place, an aquamarine temple. Jules spreads his arms wide and lets himself drift, nudged by the waves. He relaxes into it, letting the random movement of the water push him this way and that. When the waves move him towards the pleading Jesus, a tightness clips his breath. He turns away, continues drifting, then the statue comes back into view. He moves more forcefully to avoid that face. Jesus is watching him, pitying him, warning him.

    Two hours later, they are back on the boat heading to shore. Jules sits at the bow, contemplating the horizon while Richard naps, head slumped on his life preserver. Something silvery in the water catches Jules' eye. Is that a fish? No, it's a dolphin! Two of them! They are keeping pace in front of the boat on the starboard side, two dorsal fins knifing the water.

Jules stares agape at their sleek, strong bodies. Then the one on the left breaks the surface with a small leap. A moment later the partner follows. Now they are doing synchronized jumps, their entire bodies in the air every fifteen seconds or so.

Without taking his eyes off these magnificent creatures, Jules nudges Richard. "Hey, wake up. Look at this."

Richard sits up and follows Jules' gaze. He puts his arm around Jules, who responds by leaning in towards his pal. The two friends watch the dolphins in silence.

As Richard steers the car out of Pete's parking lot, he pulls a joint from the ashtray. "Let's find a quiet place to smoke this before we get on the highway." They spot a driveway going to the beach with plenty of parking. Richard hands Jules the joint with a lighter. "Will you do the honors, mi amigo?"

Back on Highway One driving north, Richard gets up to cruising speed and cranks up the stereo. Jules rolls down his window, puts his head out, and lets the wind roar in his ears. He screams a howl as loud as he can, right back to the wind. Richard laughs. "Hey wild man, come back in here, we have music! Woo, I'm pumped up! Now we're ready for Talking Heads!"

Richard pops in a new cassette. Jules has not heard this before. In the middle of *Once in a Lifetime*, David Byrne switches from singing to sermonizing, warning Jules that one day he may regret the path he chose: the house, the wife, the whole package.

At the doctor's office as a child, he dreaded the imminent hypodermic shot, his panic rising with the knowledge that something bad is coming and he can't do anything to stop it. But now circumstances are different, now it's *his* choices and what *he* does. Jules is making it happen, bringing it on without grasping how or why. He wants to ask Richard for help, but he's unable to formulate a question.

That night lying in bed, Jules leafs through his new book, *Tropical Ocean Fauna*. He had gone straight to a bookstore after Richard dropped him at home late in the afternoon. The book contains rich color photos of marine mammals, fish, and birds. He starts on the text but is too tired to concentrate. He drifts back to floating in the water amidst the blues and greens and the Jimmy Buffet song about mother ocean.

Jules snorkels above the coral reef, watching the Jesus statue. Through the hushed water, Jesus speaks to him, though the statue's mouth is unmoving. Jesus pleads for help, staring right at Jules. "Why does everyone swim around me without helping? Don't they know I am drowning?" Now Jules is standing on the bottom, looking up at the snorkelers, arms raised. How did he get here? He can't breathe. He struggles to swim up to the surface, but he weighs 4,000 pounds. He's going to drown. "What have I done?"

He wakes up panic-stricken, heart racing and panting for breath.

Chapter 6
Brooklyn 1920

MAX CHECKS HIS appearance in the men's room mirror mounted in a gilded frame above the line of washbasins. He adores his usher's uniform with its deep red color, crisp folds, and dandy brass buttons. It bestows him with authority, at least for teenage patrons barely junior to him. He keeps order in the Olympic Theater by enforcing the unwritten rules Izzy has established: no talking during the movie, no feet on the seatback in front of you, no necking in the back rows. At nineteen years old, Max is a reluctant policeman of the necking rule, often lingering behind a side curtain where he can surreptitiously watch the couples who come to the dark theater to escape the eyes of Brownsville adulthood. He thrills at the girls who give themselves over to their boyfriends with closed eyes and parted lips. He eventually makes his presence known by shining his flashlight at them, startling the newcomers and annoying the regulars.

They are showing *The Mark of Zorro*, now in its fifth week at the theater. Max has still not tired of it. Douglas Fairbanks uses wit, charm, and master swordsmanship to rescue the townspeople and save Lolita's honor. It's no wonder she falls for him. In the final scene Zorro discretely conceals their long kiss behind a handkerchief, but their passion is undeniable – Lolita's hands, visible below the kerchief, are aflutter. The hero's kiss so overwhelms her she cannot control herself, her helplessness divulged by her trembling fingers. Until five weeks ago, Max had no idea that a woman's hands could be so exciting. Now he daydreams of those feminine fingers and the hidden desire they reveal.

Live music accompanies every movie. Since Hannah joined the Olympic's staff of rotating organ players four months ago, Max has been stealing glances at several parts of her anatomy: the nape of her neck, the curve of her hips, the swell of her breasts. Now his eyes roam towards her hands, even when she's away from the organ. As her hands move to grasp ordinary objects – a paper cup, a thick pencil, a ream of sheet music – he imagines her tapered fingers expressing the passion of Zorro's Lolita, but now the passion is for Max, the victorious hero, and his irresistible kiss.

Not that such a thing could ever happen. Hannah is a married woman, five years older than Max. During their chats between shows, she teases Max about being nineteen, an "adorable boy yet to learn the ways of the world." He should act indignant and protest, but her attention – those warm eyes and soft giggles – fills him with such pleasure he doesn't mind that she thinks of him as a boy rather than a man.

Hannah alternates on the organ throughout the day with her uncle Zachary, who was brought to the Olympic six years ago by Mordechai Boshnik, the old Ukrainian immigrant who was playing organ when Lewis Lefkowitz' boss bought the place. According to the story Zachary told Max last week, Mordechai was a respected musician in Kiev until the 1881 pogroms forced him to flee for his life. In America he could get work only as a piano teacher – Zachary had been one of his students – until the rise of the silent movie theaters and their steady need for organ players. The theaters had been a godsend for old Mordechai. Since 1910, the number of Brooklyn movie theaters had grown faster than the supply of qualified organists, pushing up wages and offering steady work.

After thirty years in Brooklyn, Mordechai could finally earn a decent wage, but his luck was short lived. Arthritis developed in his once reliable hands, bringing pain that had to be endured for him to continue his livelihood. Then in 1915, after playing for the opening day of *The Birth of a Nation*, he collapsed backstage. Zachary rushed to his side and partially revived him with smelling salts. Mordechai was inconsolable, denouncing the widely hailed movie as vicious propaganda, reminiscent of the anti-Semitic leaflets that had triggered the pogroms. He was crushed that such wickedness was not confined to Ukraine or Russia, but was here in America, his refuge. He died minutes later from heart failure.

Max was baffled by this story. How could a movie kill a person? What did the American Civil War have to do with Ukrainian pogroms? Max decided these events were long ago and had nothing to do with him, other than proving life is unfair. It's not fair that Hannah is so alluring yet far beyond his reach. He will never know her touch, never experience her passion. He can only dream.

This miserable fact weighs on Max as he trudges towards the front lobby to prepare for customers coming to the next show. Lewis strides in through the front door, wearing a tailored suit and silk tie. "Hey Maxie, you seem down in the dumps. Why so blue?"

"Oh nothing. I'm just tired."

"Izzy working you pretty hard, is he?"

Max nods. "We all know who the boss is around here."

"Yeah, that brother of yours is one tough son-of-a-bitch. That's why I can always count on him. So you heard any good jokes lately?"

"Nah." Max's despair deepens. He normally knows lots of jokes but right now can't think of a single one.

Lewis studies Max's face. "Something else is bothering you. What gives?"

"Girls." Max sighs. "I mean ... I've never had a girlfriend. And I'm nineteen years old!"

Lewis snickers. "So, you're alone at night and all you can do is buff the baloney, right?"

Max is speechless. His face turns red.

Lewis puts his arm on Max's shoulder. "Don't worry about it. I've been there, we all have. Getting a girl is not a hard problem. Lots of girls would go for a good looking, good talking guy like you. You ever been to the Jewish Social Club dance?"

"Never heard of it."

"It's in Flatbush, on Bedford Avenue. I used to go there when I was your age. Lots of cute girls who want to dance, though most of them are out for a husband. It used to be every other Saturday, after sundown. Check it out. I'll see you later, Maxie. Say hello to your mother for me."

Max doubts he's good looking, but he is confident in his ability to make conversation. A social dance with lots of girls? That's a good idea – maybe he'll meet someone. He'll get Jack to go with him.

In the theater office, Izzy peruses a catalogue of movie theater supplies while he waits for Lewis. A new display case for the candy concession might boost sales. It's his decision – Lewis trusts him to maintain the theater and pay wages with box office cash. The real value of the theater to Lewis and his boss, Arnold Rothstein, is in the books that Izzy creates. The Rothstein organization launders more money through the Olympic Theater than any other single business in all of Brooklyn. In Izzy's books, shows are sold out and expenses are minimal. With 1,500 seats "selling" at 25 cents apiece, Lewis can launder over $15,000 a month in Rothstein money taken in from casinos and numbers games spread throughout New York. That gives Lewis the means to pay Izzy a nice salary.

Lewis comes by to talk business once a month or so. He used to come twice a week to pick up the cash stored in the office safe, but now he's assigned that job to his brother Joey. It's a good job for Joey – being a mule takes more brawn than brain, and Joey has grown into a six-foot, broad-shouldered fellow. To Izzy he's still a sweet kid, despite the hard-edged stare he's adopted for guys he doesn't know.

Izzy sits up when Lewis walks into the office, smiling. "Hey *boychik*, how's business?"

Izzy shrugs and puts down the catalogue. "I can't complain. With Jack in the box office and Max making the rounds as usher, I got a good grip on the place. I just have to make sure those candy girls don't get sticky fingers when their hands go in the till."

"Plus, you keep filling the house, even on matinees." Lewis grins. "That's superior selling skills I taught you." He takes a seat in the easy chair and lights a cigarette.

"Oh yeah, we sell more tickets than the sky is blue. My only problem is with one of the organ players, the girl."

"She's not good?"

"She's good alright, good at making eyes with Max. He falls for it, a sucker for a skirt. Lewis, I see trouble for that boy." Izzy had his own trouble with a woman, five years ago when he was still running numbers. Her name was Fannie Frankel, the daughter of Eli Frankel who owned the furniture store on Rockaway where several of his steady customers worked. She flirted with Izzy, made goo-goo eyes at him, the whole bit. They went out a few times, got to smooching wherever they could find a private place. He bought her things: chocolates, shoes, a fancy dress, even jewelry. Then he caught her with another guy at a restaurant, making the same goo-goo eyes and letting him fondle her hands. To top it off, she was wearing the earrings Izzy had given her. His humiliation still burns – he had trusted her, and she betrayed him. Worse was the powerlessness. He had let the situation get out of his control, all because he had feelings for a gal.

Since then, he's taken women out without getting emotionally snagged, staying in control.

"Relax, Izzy," says Lewis. "It's normal for a nineteen-year-old guy."

"Normal? What's normal is for the guy to call the shots, then the gal to follow. Max would follow that girl anywhere."

"Give him time, he'll grow up. It took a while for you to learn about women, right?" Izzy flinches at the reference to his shame, which Lewis witnessed at the time. Lewis moves on, "That reminds me, I've been going with this new girl, Mary, and she's a real doll. It's true what they say about Catholic girls – they're looser than Jewish girls, way more fun. They confess their sins to the priest, get forgiveness, then they're ready to do it again. Mary has a younger sister, Catherine, same age as you and even better looking than Mary. Want me to set you up?"

Izzy shrugs. "Sure, why not?" He's getting tired of the girl he's been going with anyway. She talks too much, and her laugh is annoying. He fidgets in the chair. "So back to business. Anything new with you?"

"Plenty. That's why I came to talk. Mister Rothstein had a meeting yesterday with me and the other boys. Ever since the politicians been talking Prohibition, he's been making plans, buying a brewery upstate and a distillery in Jersey. I tell you, that guy is smart. We don't call him The Brain for nothing. Anyhow, now that Prohibition is official, he's telling us it's going to be a big business opportunity for the organization. Those clowns in the government can make drinking illegal, but that won't stop people from buying booze. All we need to do is make it easy for them."

"That means a lot more cash to wash, but the Olympic is already maxed out. We need another theater."

"You're halfway right. We do need more capacity in the money management side of the organization. The Brain is putting me in charge of that, and we got to go bigger than movie theaters limited by the number of seats. We need higher inflow, more merchandise."

Izzy sits up straight. "Merchandise has to be bought, and that means more outflow. Plus, you got to store it. The theater's perfect – all we store is three reels of movie film during each run, then use it over and over."

"But what if you're a middleman? The only storage you need is enough for show, in case the fuzz comes snooping around. What you do need is cooperative suppliers and lots of fake customers who can't be tracked. You ever been around lumber yards?"

"A couple of times. What are you thinking?"

Lewis launches into the most sophisticated scheme he has yet devised, involving phantom logging operations in the Catskills and Adirondacks, small town sawmills upstate with creative bookkeepers, and the General Construction Trucking Company that will move enough lumber into New York to hide its real cargo, booze. Izzy will run a lumber yard in Brooklyn, "selling" to the mushrooming construction industry that's building apartments and houses all over the city. Izzy listens intently to everything his mentor says, including the sham corporations and bogus sales transactions that will be mutually validating in case some *shlemiel* auditor from the government ever shows up.

When Lewis pauses for a breath, Izzy brings it back to what matters most for him. "So I'll be the boss of a lumber yard. Okay if my brothers work there?"

"Sure, bring them both. Jack can work the register, he's solid that way. Max can be the salesman telling jokes to any actual customers. Same as here, your brothers don't need to know the ins and outs beyond it being a regular business. I'll get another crew to work the Olympic. Might as well keep a good thing going, even if it will be small potatoes compared to our new venture. One more thing, *boychik*, you're moving up in the world, and it's time you earn a commission."

"You mean a percentage?"

Lewis beams. "Three percent of flow. On top of your salary."

Three percent of the theater's monthly booked revenue is $450, and Lewis expects the lumberyard to be much bigger. Izzy will be able to buy new furniture for his mother, better clothes for his sisters, better food for everyone. His family can finally shake off the poor immigrant legacy. He did the right thing years ago when he kicked out his father, that good-for-nothing loser. "That's great! Thanks Lewis. You can count on me."

"I'm proud of you, Izzy. You're like a little brother to me." He stands and prepares to leave. "Hey, weren't you going to move the family to a new place?"

"We moved last week after all these years. New place is on the second floor, so Ma doesn't have to walk up as many stairs. It's way bigger than the old place – three bedrooms plus its own bathroom. No more walking down the hall to pee then having to wait for old man Metzenbaum to get out of the crapper."

"Sounds nice. Where is it?"

"Four blocks from the old place, on Amboy Street between Pitkin and Sutter. My brothers and I carried the furniture over, so the move cost me nothing."

"Nothing? That's a good price." Lewis smiles broadly, extends his hand to shake Izzy's. "Keep up the good work!"

That night the last feature of *The Mark of Zorro* ends at 10:30. It takes another 30 minutes to empty the theater and lock up before the three brothers start the walk home, in silence. Jack replays his surprise encounter today with Howard Katzenbaum, who he had not seen for eight years. They recognized each other right away when Howard walked up to the ticket window, wearing a royal blue blazer with a herringbone weave, along with a winsome smile. "How have you been, Jack?"

"Hey Howard! It's so good to see you." A warm tingling vibrated under Jack's ribs. "I'm fine. How are you?"

"I'm good, thanks. I heard that the Isaacson brothers had gotten into the movie theater business, but I didn't know you worked at the Olympic. It must be nice to watch so many good movies and bring them to people in Brooklyn."

"Yes, and we're earning a good living with my older brother in charge. Of course, you know all about that."

Howard laughed. "Herman and I are still at it."

"You're still making art."

"Well, I'm still making clothes." Howard took a step back from the window, turning towards his companions, two teenage girls. "Jack, these are my cousins Arlene and Maureen. Girls, this is Jack. He worked in the store with me back when he was a teenager."

The girls peered through the window and waved, obviously sisters. The older one smiled and spoke. "Nice to meet you Jack."

"Nice to meet you, Arlene. You're lucky to have Howard as a cousin, taking you to the movies."

"You were always such a nice young fellow," Howard said to Jack. "You must have been Arlene's age when you worked at the store. Now you've grown up into a handsome man." He beamed at Jack.

Jack blushed. "You were always kind to me. No need to pay, the tickets are on the house."

"Thank you, Jack. Why don't you come by the store? I'll show you our latest silks and cashmeres."

"I would like that."

"Tell you what. Can you come over this Saturday?"

Now, walking home with his brothers after their shift, Jack returns to his days at Katzenbaum's, his admiration of Howard and the warmth Howard always showed him. What if Jack had kept working there? Would he be alongside Howard, helping with dress patterns and developing his own ideas? He would love that sort of work instead of selling tickets at a movie theater. Why has he always done what his brother says? He peers sidelong at Izzy, clenching his jaw. He could stop right now, tell Izzy that he's going to quit the theater. He could .... no. No, he can't. He works with Izzy not only because his brother demands it, but also out of loyalty to his mother and younger siblings. He would make less money as a tailor, and Izzy would have to pay someone else to cashier, leaving less for the family. Jack is a good son, and the movie theater is a good business, thanks to Izzy. He shouldn't blame Izzy – this is the way it has to be.

Jack notices three people walking towards them, arm-in-arm. In the center is a middle-aged man, a snappy dresser, with a woman on either side. Max whispers, "Geez, look at that. Some guys have it made."

As the threesome pass by, Jack catches a smirk on the guy's face that reminds him of Lewis. "So Izzy, Lewis stayed extra long today. Everything okay?"

"More than okay. He has ideas for making more money than we can at the theater. The three of us might be getting into the lumber business."

"Lumber? We don't know anything about lumber."

Izzy shrugs. "So, we'll learn. It's a business, same as any business. You got customers you sell to, you keep them happy, and the more you sell the better off you are."

"What about the theater?" asks Max. "I like being an usher."

"You'll like being a salesman more. You can tell your jokes to the customers, be their friend. You'll see." Izzy puts his hand on Jack's shoulder. "And you can run the front desk and cash register." He rubs his right ear lobe. "I think tomorrow I'll visit lumber yards, nose around and see what there is to see."

"I'm up for something different," says Max, "but I'll miss ushering. Tonight, I watched a girl necking with her beau in the balcony. She unpinned her hair, and it was flowing down her shoulders. Her guy had his hands all over her! I won't get any shows like that at a lumber yard."

"Just as well," says Izzy. "We need to get you away from all those girls. Hannah too. I see how she flirts with you."

"What's wrong with that?"

"Max, you can't let a girl twirl you around her finger. That's what they do, so you got to show them who's boss. In the meantime, it will do you good to be working where it's mostly men."

"You're no fun, Izzy, you know that? Isn't that right, Jack?"

"Uh ... I don't know." Jack is not listening to his brothers. He's picturing the tender smile Howard flashed him today.

Twenty minutes later Max follows his brothers up the stairs to their apartment. How can he get a girl like the one he watched at the theater tonight? One who will let him kiss her and caress her and maybe more. A girl who will be crazy for him, like Lolita, her hands atremble when they kiss.

When they enter the front door, Max's mother wakes from her nap in the easy chair. Same as every night when Max and his brothers get home from work, she pulls dinner from the oven and sits with her boys as they eat. Twelve-year-old Davey emerges from the bedroom, carrying a book. Izzy smiles at their little brother and cups his hand around the back of Davey's neck. "How you doin, *boychik*?"

"Good. I like this book. It's called *The Wonderful Wizard of Oz*, and it's about going to a magical land, where everything is beautiful."

"That's magic alright."

After dinner, Max and Jack go up to the roof. Moonglow bathes the neighborhood rooftops and building walls. The air is warm and heavy, carrying the whir of electric fans propped in bedroom windows as Brownsville tries to sleep. Though nearly midnight, people are still out, loafing on front stoops sharing stories and cigarettes. Snippets of conversation and laughter sporadically drift up to the brothers' rooftop.

A light flips on in an open window across the street. Max spies a young woman wearing a bathrobe, her back to the window as she fills a claw-foot tub. She moves to the sink, studying herself in the mirror. Max cannot make out her facial features, just her black bob-length hair. His gaze wanders to the plunging neckline of her robe. Is she wearing anything underneath? She moves out of sight, then the light switches off. The thrill that surged through Max is abruptly squelched. His heart sinks.

He keeps his eye on the dark window, imagining her in the bath, luxuriating with her head back and throat exposed. Someone opens a window in his building and the repositioned glass reflects the moonlight at the precise angle needed to illuminate the woman's bathroom. Max has full sight of her again, now in moonglow. She is in the tub, sponging her shoulder and neck and bare breasts. She lifts her right arm, rubs the sponge across her armpit, around her ribs, back over her breasts.

Mesmerized, Max stands utterly still, his breath slow and shallow. Her sight fills the back of his skull with electricity that crackles down his spine. He is frozen in place, a dog fixated on an exposed rabbit. A slight moan emerges from his throat. Jack follows his gaze. "Oh my."

Max whispers, "Yeah. My oh my."

"Max, we shouldn't be peeping on her."

"She can't see us. There's no harm."

She stands, brushes the water off her body before stepping out of the tub. After dabbing herself with a towel, she turns back towards the tub, places her right foot up on the edge to dry her leg. Max takes in the roundness of her breasts, the pinkish brown of her nipples, the curve of her hips. "This is the best moment of my life."

"Max, there's more to life than this."

"Then I'm ready for more."

The young woman puts on her bathrobe, opens the door, and exits the bathroom. The show is over.

Canarsie is immediately south of Brownsville, but it's another world from Izzy's home neighborhood. Riding the Rockaway trolley, he notices the change as soon as he crosses Ditmas Avenue. Crowded tenements and storefronts give way to sparse industrial buildings and bare lots. Rockaway Avenue widens, easily accommodating the flatbed and cargo trucks bustling in both directions. He steps off the trolley at Flatlands Avenue, stretches his arms towards the open vistas. The air smells fresh with possibility.

He walks two blocks to Morgan's Lumber Supply at the corner of 95th Street. A large flatbed is parked along the side of the building, where men are unloading lumber and plywood, singing a ballad in baritones. The fragrance of fresh cut wood reaches Izzy as he steps through Morgan's front door. This is a place of men's work, of physicality, of progress. Izzy stands taller in his five-foot-seven frame.

A salesman approaches. He's a bit older than Izzy, maybe 30, and wears a thick black mustache that compliments his olive features. He must be Italian. The size of his belly says he eats well. "What can I help you with?"

"My name is Izzy Isaacson. Could I talk to Mr. Morgan, the owner?"

"You could if he was here and if his name was Morgan, but it's a no on both counts. The owner's name is Nicola Moriani. I'm his son-in-law, Joe Galermo. Why do you want to talk with him?"

The name Galermo ignites a spark of recognition, though Izzy cannot form the memory. "Do you think Mister Moriani might want to sell the business?"

Joe's face lights up before he regains a neutral expression. "Excuse me," Joe begins, "but you're too young to have enough money to buy such a successful business."

"It's not only me. I have ... partners who will put up the money. They got plenty."

"Okay, so bring them here. We'll talk."

"They'll have questions for me to answer before they decide whether it's worth a visit. How about you show me around?"

"Listen, I don't have time to mess with a … junior partner. If you're serious, I need to talk with the guys who have the money."

Izzy's hackles go up. "You listen. If I walk, I'm not coming back. Now unless you have a line of buyers, I'm all you're getting. If I like what I see and hear today, my guys will put up the money. And we'll pay cash up front, no payment plan spread over time, so you could get a clean deal and wipe your hands of this place." He crosses his arms. "What do you say?"

Galermo glances at the floor, then returns Izzy's stare. "You're not bullshitting me?"

"Scout's honor."

"Ha, you're no boy scout, but okay, I got a few minutes. Let's start out back and I'll give you a tour of the yard."

After the walk-through, Izzy stays for another hour, questioning Joe on the customer base, monthly sales, cost of goods, supplier relations, labor costs, and taxes. He takes it all in with no need to write notes. He's hearing plenty of exaggeration and half-truths but there will be time to get to the bottom of it when he goes through the books. Regardless, he's satisfied he could make this business profitable, even if Joe is stretching the truth. Besides, Lewis' boss has bigger plans that don't depend on Joe's veracity.

When he reaches the street after their meeting, Izzy turns around to gaze at the building. In his mind's eye, the "Morgan's Lumber Supply" lettering above the door is gone. In its place a much larger sign spans the building façade: Isaacson Brothers Lumber and Building Supplies.

On Saturday Jack hops off the trolley before it comes to a full stop. Lighter than air, he floats down the sidewalk towards Katzenbaum's Clothing and Fabric Emporium. What luck that Howard ran into him at the Olympic, then invited him to come visit. Jack never considered initiating such a reunion on his own, being too shy after all these years. Now he and Howard will become friends and he can visit the clothing store more often. He already smells the fabrics and visualizes the finished dresses.

Howard is waiting for him inside the front door. They shake hands. "Jack, I'm so glad you could make it!"

"Thanks again for the invitation. I'm so excited to be here again! I love this place." Jack scans the showroom, a home away from home. "I see the store hasn't changed much. The dress styles are updated, of course. I can tell from the mannequins."

"You always had an eye. Have you ever thought…" Howard peruses Jack's face. "Never mind, let's go to lunch. I know a good deli two blocks from here."

The Bushwick Kosher Deli is a step up from the Gurewitz delicatessen where Jack usually goes. The seating area is more spacious, and the counters less cluttered. The aroma of sour pickles and cured meat, however, are the same. The place is filled with people.

They find a table and order Rueben sandwiches. Howard asks about Jack's family.

"Everyone is doing well. Business at the theater is good. My younger brother Max works as an usher. As you know, I run the ticket window, and my older brother Izzy manages the place. Izzy says we might leave the theater and get into a new business, a lumber yard. Our brother Davey is still too young to be working – he's almost twelve – but I expect Izzy will get him a job with us eventually, whether it's the theater or a lumber yard. My sister Bessie got married to a nice guy named Pauly and my younger sister Lilly helps our mother with the chores."

"Same as my family working together, except I have three sisters and of course the one brother. Herman and I have been at the clothing store for over ten years now."

"I remember he had you following the Paris magazines. What about now? Do you create your own designs?"

"I do. I finally persuaded Herman we should try it, as a supplement to the main business. I started slowly and cautiously, not doing anything too bold. Sometimes my designs sell, sometimes they don't, but either way I love doing it."

"That's wonderful. I'm proud of you, Howard."

Howard smiles. "I've been thinking, Jack. The business keeps growing and we could use your talents. Would you like to join me? I could teach you. I know you would be good at it."

"You ... you mean come to work at Katzenbaum's again?"

"Yes, but it would be completely different than nine years ago, when you were doing a teenager's work. You would be right alongside me, choosing fabrics to buy, creating dress patterns, checking on the seamstresses, and more. Of course, the pay would be much higher."

Jack averts his eyes downward. The table's wood grain is visible on the edges but obscured in the center, where countless water glasses have left their marks. He wants to say yes. Why not say yes? Because it's a fantasy, that's why not. "That's very generous of you. I'm honored." He looks up at Howard. "But I can't leave Izzy and the theater. Or whatever business we're in."

"Why not? Family loyalty?"

"Exactly. I would be turning my back on them. Plus, I would catch hell from my brother. He doesn't approve of clothing as a career for me."

"I understand, Jack. Believe me."

"It's hard for me to say no. I would love working with you, Howard."

"Well … here's an idea. You just come to the store whenever you can, say on a day off from the theater. I'll show you what I'm doing, and you can help if it suits you."

Should Jack dare do such a thing? He can, he can do this. No one needs to know how he spends his time off. "That would be great, but I don't want to be in the way."

"You won't be. I like being with you, Jack. And I know you'll love the fabrics and the dress design process. You might create your own design."

Jack's eyes are suddenly moist. Howard is a true friend – he understands Jack. "I'm so happy you're willing to do this, Howard. How can I thank you?"

"It's me who should be thanking you, for the help I know you'll provide. And I'll enjoy our companionship, so whatever time we share will be a gift to me."

A yearning arises in Jack's chest, an unfamiliar ache. He peers at Howard's soft brown eyes. He wants to speak but can't find any words.

Howard studies his face. He smiles gently. "Come on. Let's go back to the shop for that tour I promised."

———

That evening Jack rides the Flatbush Avenue trolley with Max, heading to the Jewish Social Club. The chilly evening air, heralding autumn, adds a shiver to his anxiety. He has never danced in public, and he might look foolish. Jack was ambivalent about coming tonight, but Max had pleaded so desperately that Jack reluctantly agreed. Now he wishes that he hadn't.

Stepping off the trolley at Avenue D, they walk two blocks to their destination: the Flatbush Community Hall. Above the front door a handwritten banner reads "Hadassah Social Dance," adorned with musical symbols and Stars of David.

Inside, the foyer is filled with young people and energetic chitchat. Girls are wearing the new drop-waist dresses with straight lines and loose fits. A waiting line circles the foyer and leads to a table where three middle-aged ladies sit, talking with the would-be dancers and writing notes. The table stands outside the doors to the dance hall. Above the hubbub of voices Jack hears the musicians warming up inside.

When the brothers reach the front, the lady in the middle calls them over. She's wearing a traditional navy-blue dress, styled with a puffy chest and thick waistband. Her glasses are perched on her nose, and she peers at Jack over the top of their rim. "Admission is ten cents, please."

Jack hands her the coins. She scans the two boys up and down. "You must be brothers. Am I right?"

Jack speaks up. "Yes, we're brothers."

"Your names?"

"I'm Jack, he's Max." Her nametag reads Mrs. Ruth Shapiro. From her salt-and-pepper hair and smooth complexion, Jack guesses she's a similar age as his mother.

"You got a last name, Jack and Max?"

"Isaacson."

She writes this in her ledger. "And your parents' names?"

"Our mother is Jennie Isaacson. Our father was Mo, but he, uh, disappeared years ago. We think he died."

"May he rest in peace. So, you take care of your mother. What good boys."

"Not only the two of us. We have an older brother, Izzy, who lives with us too. He's twenty-eight."

"Is he married?"

"No, not married."

"Then bring him here next month. We'll find him a nice girl." Jack bristles at this stranger interfering in his family. Why did he even mention Izzy?

Mrs. Shapiro's welcoming demeanor turns sharp. Wagging a finger at Jack and Max, she warns, "Now you boys listen to me. We *yentas* have a nice dance here so nice boys and girls can get to know each other. We got rules, you hear me?

No touching except hands, shoulders, and upper back. You understand? And no shimmy dancing! Charleston and Fox Trot are okay. We'll be watching. You understand?"

Jack doesn't respond. He understands the touching rules but has no clue how to Charleston or Fox Trot. What if he dances a shimmy without meaning to? A tightness grips his stomach.

Max smiles and speaks up. "Yes ma'am, we understand the rules, but we've never been to a social before, so we don't know those dances. What should we do?"

Her voice softens. "Watch what everybody else is doing. You'll pick it up. And don't be shy. Ask girls to dance – that's what they're here for. They'll be happy to dance with you, even if you are a beginner. Besides, you boys are handsome. Now go on in and have a good time."

Jack follows Max towards the dance hall doors. His brother wears a big grin, rubbing his hands together as if he's about to join a feast. "Okay, let's go!" He leads the way in.

The room is brightly lit, and the music is upbeat. People are everywhere, though most of the crowd huddles into groups of guys or gals spread around the perimeter. Clusters of boys backslap and banter; their boisterous energy unsettles Jack – he could never fit in with them.

Jack shadows Max to the punch bowls, where he's surprised to come across Joey Lefkowitz, Lewis' kid brother. They see him regularly on his cash pickup runs at the Olympic. He's a bit old for this crowd. Jack extends his hand. "Hey, Joey, how you doing?"

Joey scowls. "Don't call me that here, with girls around. You call me Joe."

"Sure, okay. Sorry. How's it going?"

"I can't complain."

Max asks, "You seen any pretty girls here?"

Joe's frown morphs into a smirk. "Love 'em and leave 'em, that's what I say."

Jack is not sure what he means. "This is our first time here. I don't even know how to dance."

"Aw, it's easy. Watch me, then do what I do." Joe pulls a small flask from his jacket pocket, hidden in his palm. "Hey, you want a snort?" He extends it towards Jack, then Max. They both shake their heads – like Izzy, they are devout teetotalers, given what booze did to their father.

Joe shrugs. "Suit yourself." He pours the flask into his cup of fruit punch, downs the drink, and strides towards the nearest gaggle of girls. He offers his hand to one of them, who glances back towards her friends before allowing herself to be pulled onto the dance floor. She's wearing a peach-colored, dress with short sleeves. It's an attractive style, simple and tasteful. The band starts a new number, and more couples join in. The brothers position themselves a few steps away from the refreshment table and watch the dancers.

Joe is half a step behind the music. His partner tries to follow his lead, though her attention keeps returning towards her giggling friends on the sidelines. The brothers study other couples who move smoothly with the rhythm. After two songs, Max turns to Jack. "I think I'm ready. You?"

"No, I need more time. I don't want people to watch me until I practice."

"But the only way to practice is to do it."

"Well, I'm going to wait."

"Who should I ask to dance?"

"Find a girl that's shorter than you, but not by much. One who isn't surrounded by other girls."

Max searches the perimeter and cuts across the dance floor. The girl he's headed for is the right height and is turned away from her friends, watching couples dance. She smiles softly when she sees him coming.

Max is a natural on the dance floor. Sometimes his steps are too big, and he loses the timing, but he quickly recovers. By the end of the song, his movements are smooth. Max bows a goodbye, then drifts back to Jack.

"Max, you looked great out there. Who knew one of the Isaacson brothers has dance in his blood?"

"It's not hard. I just followed the music."

"Well, you have a fan. That girl to the left of the bandstand, wearing the red shawl? She was watching you."

As if on cue, the girl turns towards them. "She reminds me of Lolita, in *Zorro*," whispers Max.

Jack nudges him. "Go ask her to dance."

"I will, but only if you ask a girl too."

Watching Max has given Jack courage. "Okay. Which one?"

"There's one, on the other side, in the green frilly dress. She looks nice."

Jack spies her. "I'm going."

"Atta boy."

To reach the girl, Jack walks around the dance floor perimeter. He notices Max stride towards the red-shawl girl, their eyes on each other. She takes two steps in his direction, extends her hand without waiting to be asked. Max pulls her onto the dance floor.

I can do this, I can do this. Jack approaches the girl from the side. Her dress is forest green with a stylish shoulder cut and light brown trim around the neck and sleeves. "Excuse me, would you care to dance, please?"

"Oh! You're so polite. What's your name?"

"I'm Jack. I guess my manners are better than my dancing. This is my first time."

"I'm Leah. I've done lots of dancing so don't worry." She smiles kindly at Jack. "The main thing is to listen to the beat of the music. I'll show you."

On the dance floor, Leah counts out the beat for Jack. "One, two, three, four, one, two, three, four." He counts aloud with her, watching her foot movements, and matching with his own feet. She offers her right hand and puts her left on Jack's shoulder. He mirrors her hand positions, and they start moving together, taking small steps. "Now keep counting to yourself, then let your feet follow," she says.

Jack's body begins to move with the music, his awkwardness melting. He releases her shoulder, turns away while holding hands, then turns back to her, emulating other couples. "That's it!" says Leah.

They move in synch, letting go of each other and coming back to touch in time with the music. He recalls playing tag during fifth grade recess, the thrill of being "It" and catching a squealing girl – or a boy – simply by touching their arm.

As soon as the song ends, Jack gushes, "Wow, that was fun. Will you dance with me again?"

"I'd love to. You picked that up so quickly. No one would know you're a beginner."

Jack swells. "Thanks, you're a good teacher."

They stay on the dance floor for another Lindy and then a Fox Trot. As the couples applaud the band, Jack spies Max and the red-shawl girl at the refreshment table. He turns to Leah. "Would you like a glass of punch? I want to introduce you to my brother."

"Sure. Lead the way."

Jack holds her hand as they weave through the crowd and approach the punch bowl. Max is chattering away with the girl, obviously enjoying himself. She clutches his arm and laughs open-mouthed, her teeth a fierce white against deep red lipstick. Max calls out, "Hey Jack, this is Ida. Ida, meet my brother Jack."

She grins at Jack. "Your brother is so funny! Such a doll."

"Yeah, he knows how to tell a joke."

"Humor and charm, it's enough to sweep a girl off her feet." Ida giggles, gazing into Max's eyes.

As Jack introduces Leah to Max and Ida, they hear a woman's voice come over the loudspeakers. It's Mrs. Shapiro, at the microphone on stage. The room quiets. "First, I want you to know we ladies organize this dance so you boys and girls can get together and have fun. Let's hear a round of applause for Hadassah of Brownsville." After a moment of tepid clapping, she continues. "Now for a special treat. A real singer is going to serenade us with that beautiful song 'Let Me Call You Sweetheart.' He has performed at classy clubs all over Brooklyn, a nice young man, Mister Gabe Gellman."

As Gabe steps onto the stage, Jack hears Max whisper to Ida, "Oh, here's a pretty boy, ready to sing *shmaltz*. The *yentas* love him, I'm sure."

Ida giggles. Gabe is out of place, older than the crowd but younger than the Hadassah ladies. He sports a white suit and thin mustache, with his hair parted in the middle and slicked down. The band starts up and Gabe croons:

"Let me call you sweetheart,
I'm in love with you
Let me hear you whisper that you love me too
Keep the love-light glowing in your eyes so true
Let me call you sweetheart, I'm in love with you."

Max looks Ida in the eyes, raises his eyebrows up and down, and sings with a high-pitched Yiddish accent. "Let me call you shveetheart, I got such a pain you voodn't believe."

Ida giggles again. "I think you're jealous."

"You're right, I'm so jealous. I could never impress the old *yentas* the way he does."

"I see. You impress only young women."

"Sure. With my irresistible charm and sense of humor. Like Zorro."

"Yes, you do remind me of Zorro!" Ida's laughter is full throated. She grasps Max's upper arm. "But Zorro has a sword."

"I can get a sword," Max grins. "If any bad guys bother you, I'll cut them to pieces."

"Ooh, my hero." Ida wraps both hands around his arm, beaming at him through her eyelashes.

Jack turns to Leah, embarrassed by all this flirting. He smiles apologetically, unsure what to say. "Do you like the punch?"

Walking home that evening, Max asks Jack, "Did you ask Leah for a date?"

"No, but when we said goodbye, I thanked her for dancing with me and said maybe we could dance again next time." He hopes that's enough to get Max off his back.

"Maybe? That's not asking her out, Jack, but you should. She's your type."

Jack snickers. "My type? I have a type?"

"Well, she speaks only when she has something thoughtful to say, like you. Not me, I chatter on about anything to make conversation or kid around. Ida's that way too. Anyhow, Leah's nice and nice looking and I bet she would love you to ask her out."

Jack did enjoy dancing with Leah. She was kind and patient. Asking her out would certainly make his mother happy – she's been after him to find a girl and get married, claiming he's such a catch, so considerate and tall and handsome, the girls will fall for him. He's tried going out a bit, but he hasn't yet met the right girl. Could Leah be the one? His mother would approve of Leah's soft-spoken manner. "Okay, Max. I'll do it. Let's go again to the dance social, and if Leah's there I'll ask her out. If she's not, I'll ask Mrs. Shapiro how I can get in touch with her."

"Great. In the meantime, I did ask Ida out. We're going to meet next Saturday night at Gurewitz's Deli, then take in a movie. She gave me her address too, in case I need to contact her." Max pulls a piece of scrap paper from his pocket, studies it. "Can this be? Jack, this is the address for the building where we saw that girl bathing from our roof. That could have been Ida. Her hair fits, so does her height. Holy moly! This means I've seen her naked before we've had a first date. She's even more of the cat's meow than I thought. Boy, I can't wait until next Saturday."

How can Max be so excited over a girl he just met, even if she was the one in the bathtub? Is that normal? Some guys are crazed that way, but not Jack. He has a calmer demeanor, like Leah. Yes, she could be the one.

Chapter 7
March 1981

JULES STARES AT Cathy's phone number in his address book. Her inked version on his arm persisted several days, forcing him to keep his shirt sleeves rolled down at the office. Faint vestiges remain, no longer discernable. He can't put off calling her any longer.

There was another time he could have phoned a girl. He met Lizzie at a party during his senior year at Emory. Squeezing through the crowd searching for Richard, he found himself crammed in a kitchen next to a skinny girl with a pointy chin and nervous fingers. *Blood on the Tracks* was playing on a stereo, and Jules declared that Bob Dylan was a great poet. The girl laughed. "He writes good songs, but that's not poetry. 'Joy and woe are woven fine, A clothing for the soul divine, Under every grief and pine, Runs a joy with silken twine.' That's poetry!" The defiance in her eyes frightened Jules, until she smiled. He hung in there.

"Wow, did you write that?"

She laughed again. "I wish. That's William Blake."

"Who?"

"He wrote poetry in the early 19th century." She pushed her black-rimmed glasses up on the bridge of her nose.

"Oh. You must be an English major."

Lizzie folded her arms. She was wearing an oversized sweater, so loose that the sleeves hung off her wrists. "Yep."

"Sometimes I think I should have majored in English ... or History."

"Instead, you chose what?"

"Accounting."

"Accounting. Well, that's uh .... practical."

"Oh thanks, now I feel bad."

"Hey, at least you'll get a job. I'm the one who should feel bad. Besides, it takes all of us to make this wide world. Didn't I just hear your guy sing about the diversity of jobs people do?" Jules was impressed she paid attention to Dylan's lyrics while talking with him.

After that, he sporadically ran into Lizzie on campus. They would walk together for a while, discussing the meaning of life. She would work a quote from Keats or Byron into the conversation, then Jules would respond with Dylan – his one-trick pony that she nevertheless enjoyed. An ember in his chest blazed during these spontaneous rendezvous.

He never asked Lizzie out or took any initiative to spend more time with her. He and Eileen were a couple, after all, and Eileen would never be okay with him having Lizzie as a friend, sharing poetry and song lyrics. He and Eileen met as teenagers, through youth groups at the Jewish Community Center. They attended different high schools and Eileen was a year older, so Jules was surprised when she asked him to her senior prom. That was their first date and the first time Jules slow danced with a girl. He responded to the shock of his own sexual energy by pulling his hips away, until Eileen leaned firmly into him, with her head fully relaxed on his shoulder. The following autumn Eileen went away to college at the University of Georgia. It was an easy drive for her to spend weekends in Atlanta with Jules as well as her family. They continued dating that way when Jules went to Emory.

The last time Jules saw Lizzie was the day after their graduation. She had called to say she had a gift for him. It was a book, a collection of English Romantic poems, of course. Thankful for the advanced notice, he had bought her Dylan's double album *Blonde on Blonde*. Her eyes teared up and she quickly kissed him on the lips. "I'm going to miss you, Jules. I hope you call me."

That was over a year ago, and he has never called. Now here is this girl Cathy, who also shows signs of liking him. Giving the desktop a decisive fist thwack, he picks up the phone and dials her number.

"Hello."

"Hi Cathy, this is Jules. We met at the beach?"

"Hi Jules. I'm so happy you called! I've been thinking about you." Her voice is effervescent.

"Really?"

"Yes, really."

"Um, would you like to go for a walk?"

"Sure. I can be ready in 15 minutes."

"Oh, I meant at a future time, but now's good. Now's great, actually."

They meet at a park near Cathy's apartment and stroll down a pathway. She's wearing loose shorts and a sleeveless top, with her hair in a ponytail. She gazes at the ground as they walk. "Remember I told you I've been thinking about you, Jules? Can I tell you what I've been thinking?"

"Sure." Where is this going?

"Well first, I'm not smart like you, but God did give me a good sense about people. I can tell that you have a good heart, Jules. But something's missing – maybe you're lonely sometimes, even though you have that girlfriend. I know how that is, to be lonely even when you're with someone. Also, I think you're not sure about your purpose in life."

Jules hesitates, then puts it back on her. "Do you know your purpose?"

"I know I'm here to spread God's love. That's the main thing, but I don't yet know what that means for me. Should I get a job at a church, or should I help poor people, or go to Africa, or something else."

They sit on a bench, facing each other. "Africa? Why would you go there?"

"You know, to do missionary work. That's kind of scary, though."

"Don't let fear hold you back, Cathy. You would be great at that, reaching out to new people. Didn't you tell me not to hide my light under a bushel?"

"Oh, Jules. You are so sweet. See, you do have a good heart."

"I guess. What did you mean about feeling lonely even though you have a boyfriend?"

"Oh, that's complicated. Matthew – that's his name – he's a good guy. He's polite and respectful and he's found Jesus, but I worry he doesn't understand me, I mean understand who I am. He's already decided things about me that I haven't decided, like I should want lots of babies, and that will make me happier than feeding the poor or healing the sick. Sometimes I think he loves his idea of me more than the actual me."

A knot grips Jules in his chest. Cathy is watching him. "Jules, are you okay?"

"Yeah, I'm fine. I ... I think you're wrong when you say you're not smart. You're very insightful."

She blushes at that, the light skin on her face and neck going pink. She studies her hands and rubs her thumbs together. "No, I'm not smart."

He pats her upper arm. "Hey, don't put yourself down. You're wonderful."

Cathy faces Jules and their eyes meet. He leans in, gives her a gentle kiss. She stiffens.

"I'm sorry. I should not have done that. I –"

"No, Jules it's okay. I know you mean well."

"We're both dating other people."

"Right. Besides that, you haven't found Jesus. You and I are friends. Let's keep it that way."

"Absolutely. I'm sorry I kissed you."

"No, don't be sorry. It was ... nice. Even though we shouldn't."

Jules stands up. "Let's keep walking. I want to hear more about Africa."

———

Friday evening at a movie with Richard is a respite for Jules. He has worked late every evening this week due to Paul

Perlman's endless demands, getting home after dark and missing his usual swim at the beach. When he suggested to Arnie they hire more accountants, Arnie refused, saying that wasn't in the budget plan and the higher expenses would anger Sydney.

Jules is seated in the fourth row, waiting for the film to begin and for Richard to return from the bathroom. His right knee starts bouncing. In addition to upsetting Sydney, Eileen would be ashamed if Jules disappointed her father. Co-mingling of career and courtship has always worked in Jules' favor, but now it's getting muddled.

"So, how's work going?" asks Richard as he takes his seat. "Have you figured out how to have fun as an accountant?"

"I'm doing the best I can, working my ass off!" Jules' voice comes out louder than he intended. "There's no time for fun."

"Whoa. I'm just asking a question. Are you okay?"

Jules turns to his friend, embarrassed by his outburst. "I'm sorry. I'm tense about work right now. I didn't mean to take it out on you."

"That's okay. I get it."

"Work is hard these days." Before Jules can explain, the house lights dim, and the film begins. The movie is more serious than Jules anticipated; over a long dinner, two friends share a long conversation about philosophy and life's purpose.

In the car on the way home, Jules briefs Richard on his date with Cathy.

"Way to go, Jules. I'm proud of you."

"Thanks for encouraging me to call her. I'm not going to see her again, though. We're way too different to ever get involved, and I'm too attracted to her to hang out as friends."

"You're not sorry you called her?"

"No, not at all. You were right; it was a good opportunity to stretch myself. Reminds me of the movie, when the two dinner companions discussed the roles we play in life, and how you need to break out periodically to stay authentic. How is that for you? Do you ever want to travel and leave it all behind, get a new perspective on life?"

"Not really," says Richard. "I love traveling for fun, but I don't need that to gain new perspectives. The dinner companions also agreed that you don't need to be a Jack Kerouac to pay attention to reality. You can do that sitting in your room."

"I guess, but isn't it hard to shift your perspective away from everyday life when you're in the midst of it?"

"Everyday life can be great. My every day is being married with Deborah. Sure, it's a routine, but it gives me so much."

"It's obvious you two love each other."

"Yeah, definitely...." Richard taps his fingers on the steering wheel as he trails off. "Here's the thing. It's more than love, and it's more than enjoying each other and getting along. We push each other to grow. I'm always introducing her to new music, not just rock but also classical and jazz. She's been taking me to art museums, which I've never done. So now I'm appreciating these incredible paintings, which are all about different perspectives on the world and on people – think Picasso and his out-of-the-box ways of seeing things."

"Hmm. Makes sense."

Richard continues. "So yeah, I know marriage can be a rut or a cage, but not for me. It's the opposite. Without Deborah I would be a smaller version of myself."

"I had no idea. If that's marriage, sign me up."

"Done." Richard grins. "When I make a toast at your wedding and mention this evening, only you will know what I'm talking about."

Jules smiles. He gazes out Richard's windshield at the sharp features of up-lit palm trees bordering the roadway. The view is crystal clear.

Jules is driving to his great uncles' house for his usual Saturday visit. Traffic on Highway 1 has come to a standstill. He peers at the RV ahead, reading bumper stickers from national parks thousands of miles away. He could travel. He could do it right now, simply continue north on this highway far beyond Miami, driving and driving all the way to Maine. How many days would it take? Who might he meet along the way? A beautiful New England girl with red hair and fair skin hitchhiking back to college after spring break? They would talk endlessly, then decide on a detour for her to show him her favorite clifftop overlook of the wild rocky coast. They would hold hands walking back to the car and later part ways with a gentle kiss in front of her dorm.

A blaring horn behind him jolts Jules from the daydream. He crawls ahead to close the bumper-to-bumper gap in front of him, then switches to conjuring a real-life image: making love with Eileen. Yes. One day they'll be living together, sharing their bed every night, wrapped in the comfort of each other's arms. They'll find ways to help each other grow, same as Richard and Deborah. He'll take Eileen to world-class aquaria, and she'll take him to.... where? She knows a lot about English literature, so they'll go to Shakespeare plays or something. He will call Eileen tonight to say he loves her and he's excited that she's coming to visit.

Traffic eases. Resuming speed, Jules passes a large billboard depicting Ronald Reagan as Superman in flight, wearing the full costume with bright red cape and Reagan's usual pasted-on smile. A caption reads *Our Hero, Our President!*

At summer camp, he and his 12-year-old cabin mates would thrill at receiving superhero comic books sent from parents through the camp mail. The boys laid on their bunks after lights out, reading by flashlight and trading comics. Everyone agreed the best superpower to have would be X-ray vision so you could see through the girl counselors' T-shirts. Now the best superpower would be flying. He would soar high above Miami, following the coastline while beholding the vast blue Atlantic.

He turns into his uncles' neighborhood on SW 13th Avenue and pulls to the curb in front of their house. He'd rather not drop in unexpectedly, but Izzy's refusal to pay a nickel to Southern Bell makes this the only way. He rings the doorbell, waits a minute, then rings again. He hears Max yell, "What?"

"Uncle Max, it's Jules," he calls through the front door.

"Who?"

"Jules, your great nephew."

"What?"

"Open the door, Uncle Max, it's okay."

The lock turns and the door opens a few inches. Max peers out. "What?"

"I'm Jules, it's okay."

"Oh...who?"

"I'm Jules. My mother is Esther, your niece."

Max squints and moves his lips without saying anything. The words finally come out. "The girl with the nice *tokhes*."

"Yes! That's right. That's my girlfriend. Uh, nice *tokhes*."

Max grins and opens the door wide. "Come in. Come in."

"Is anyone else at home with you?"

"I don't know." He calls out, "Anybody here?"

"This is Saturday. Davey must be at *shul*."

"Sure, sure, Davey's at *shul*."

"What about Izzy and Jack?"

"Nah, they don't go. Only Davey."

"I mean, where are they?"

"Who?"

"Izzy and Jack. Where did they go? Where are Izzy and Jack?"

"Oh, they're not here. Just me and the lady with the chicken legs."

Max described the chicken-leg lady during Jules' first visit. So, this is not a one-time hallucination. "Is she here often?"

"She keeps me company. She never says anything, but she understands me when I talk to her. She likes me – I can tell by the way she smiles." Max lowers his voice and moves closer to Jules. "She's skinny and flat chested and I don't think there's anything between her chicken legs."

"Does she have a name?"

"She's never said. I call her Darling and she likes that."

"That's nice." Who knows how long it will be before the other uncles return home. "Uncle Max, do you have paper and a pen? I'll leave a note."

"Where?"

"Let's go to the living room. We'll search together for some paper."

Max leads Jules towards an open rolltop desk made of dark walnut, matching the other furniture. Papers are scattered about. Jules notices a letter in the center written on medical clinic stationery. It's from the urologist, Dr. Jonathan Meltzer, asking Jack to come in on a specified date and time – the doctor must know the brothers lack a phone. The date is today, and the time is fifteen minutes from now. "Izzy and Jack must have gone to the doctor, right Uncle Max?"

"Yeah, sure. The doctor."

Jules decides to write a note for the absent uncles, saying he'll come back later. He searches for a pen and blank paper. The first four pens he tries are dried up. He finds an old pencil and leans on the desktop without sitting.

Max is watching him. "I saw you flying over the ocean. Me and my brothers were swimming, all of us swimming together."

Another hallucination. "You had a …. dream?"

"I don't know. Was it a dream? We were big fish, like Flipper."

"You mean dolphins?"

"Yeah, we were dolphins, but we could talk. I asked Izzy why we were swimming in circles, and he pointed to a big statue under the water, and it was our father down there staring up at us with his arms raised."

Jules reaches for the desktop to steady himself from a sudden vertigo. How could Max know details from his snorkeling trip? He finds his way to the desk chair, questioning the memory of his own dream from two weeks ago. Is Jules going crazy? Is Max contagious?

Max continues. "Our father is trying to say something, but he can't talk. What does he want to say?"

"That he loves you." Jules has no idea why he said that – it just came out.

A tranquility settles over Max's face. "You're a good boy, Jules."

"So, you were dolphins, swimming in circles."

"Yeah, and when I came up for air, I saw you, Jules. You were a big white ocean bird flying around."

Jules lets the image of himself flying above his uncles sink in. He crumples the half-written note. "Uncle Max, I think Uncle Jack needs me. I'm going to that doctor's office right now. Will you be okay here by yourself?"

"Me? I'm not by myself. Darling is here."

Pain shoots through Jack's hips with each step as he and Izzy shuffle from the taxicab to the front door of Doctor Meltzer's urology clinic. The pain is worth it – hearing from the doctor that it's cancer and it's bad will hurt Izzy. Jack is ashamed of wanting his brother to suffer, to pay for everything he did. It was a long time ago, and Jack should forgive.

When they finally make it to the front door, it's locked. A handwritten sign reads *Mr. Isaacson, please ring the doorbell.* So, the place is closed on Saturdays and the doctor is here only to meet with Jack. Izzy presses the button. Meltzer appears, unlocks the door and helps the two brothers inside.

The doctor leads them to his office and invites them to sit in the two chairs facing his desk. A stereo plays a lively Bach violin concerto; Meltzer turns down the volume. "Can I get you gentlemen anything to drink? I made coffee. Or maybe something stronger? I have bourbon and ice."

"I never heard of a doctor offering booze," says Izzy.

"Well, I'm a special person," says Jack. He smiles at the doctor, wanting to be sociable now that he is sitting, and the pain is less sharp. "Nothing to drink, thank you. It's nice that you invited us on a Saturday."

"I come in occasionally to work alone and get caught up on paperwork." He gives them a conspiratorial smile. "I like the quiet, especially with two teenage daughters at home always arguing with my wife."

"And I suppose Saturdays are a good time to have difficult conversations with patients like me. I think you have news for me."

Meltzer clears his throat. "I'm sorry that it's not good news, Mister Isaacson. The X-rays and blood tests confirm it's prostate cancer. Tumors have spread to your lower spine, hips, and shoulder blades. That's why you are having pain in those areas. We have good medicines to treat the pain."

"Ah, but no medicines to treat the cancer." So, the end is in sight. At least that will end the pain. Not just the physical pain. Jack is tired of his regrets, tired of replaying the past and obsessing over what might have been.

"We can try chemotherapy, but to be honest, the cancer is advanced, and the odds are not good. Plus, chemo has unpleasant side effects."

"I'm 84 years old." Jack gives Izzy a glance. "We all have to die sometime."

Izzy turns to Meltzer. "You can do surgery, right? Is this a matter of money?" Jack shakes his head. Of course, his brother tries to take control.

"The cancer has spread too much. Even if we remove the prostate, which is a tough surgery to go through, we would not be able to remove all the tumors. Your brother would suffer more."

"It's okay, Izzy." Jack turns to the doctor. "How much time do I have? Tell me straight."

"Hard to say. A few months, maybe less. The pain will get worse, but as I said, we can give you medicine for that so you can be as comfortable as possible. Consider moving into a convalescent center. I can recommend a couple where they do a wonderful job."

Izzy interjects. "Move? Leave his brothers?"

Meltzer continues to address Jack. "It may get to a point where you can't get out of bed to eat or use the bathroom. Your brothers will not be able to take care of you."

"What?" Izzy's voice rises. "We know how to take care of each other. We took care of our mother when she was sick.

And we moved her here from Brooklyn when you were sucking at your mother's teat, so don't tell me!"

Meltzer holds up his hands, palms faced towards Izzy. "Okay, okay Mister Isaacson. I'm sorry, I understand." He scribbles on a prescription pad, hands the note to Izzy. "Here's a simpler task. I want you to stop at a pharmacy on your way home to get pain medication for your brother. He'll need it."

Izzy accepts the prescription, then leans back in his chair. "Okay then. And... excuse me, I meant no disrespect of your mother."

When Jack and Izzy walk out, Jules is there in his car, waiting. Such a good kid. Jack shares the news with Jules as he drives. Jules nods but says nothing.

Jack gazes out the window as they pass a row of young palm trees. He and his brothers cared for their mother as her illness progressed, all the way to the bitter end when she had to be carried around the house. They were much younger and stronger then, and there were four of them to share the workload – now it would be an impossible situation. "Listen, Izzy, the doctor is right. You and Davey can't take care of me on your own, even if Max helps a little."

Izzy waves his hand dismissively. "Eh." Jack takes that as acknowledgement of an unpleasant truth. "You remember when Clare next door was taking care of her mother?"

"Sure, I remember Sarah being sick. She had cancer too," Izzy explains to Jules.

Jack pushes away the dread that comes with the memory of poor Sarah. She looked awful near the end, shriveled and pale and incoherent from the narcotics. "Clare set up a special hospital bed, and she hired nurses to come over every day for a few hours. They helped take care of Sarah by doing things Clare couldn't do herself."

"So?"

"So we could do the same thing. But I don't know, it might cost a lot."

"Don't worry about the money. I'll take care of it."

After a few minutes of silence, Jack says, "There's something else we got to do. Plan for after."

"After? What after?"

"After I go. You know, the funeral."

"Oy, Jack, enough already!"

"Just listen to me. We plan now so it won't be such a burden then."

"What's to plan? We got the plots."

"I know we got the plots. All four, next to Ma, may she rest in peace, at the Mount Nebo cemetery. I'll be the first to join her, thirty years later."

"Seems like it was yesterday."

"I want to pick out the casket."

"What's to pick out? It will be a plain pine box with a Star of David. Same as Ma's."

"I want to lay eyes on it. I want to know where I'm going. Plus, I want it special on the inside."

"Special?"

"I want it to be beautiful. And soft. Yes, lined with thick velvet. I've always loved velvet. I want a deep red velvet surrounding me head to toe."

"You plan to have a party in there?"

Jack's smile is wistful. After all this time, he still cherishes the velvet from his teenage days, working at Katzenbaum's Clothing. When he thinks of Howard and the times they spent in his workroom, his eyes become watery. If only he had listened to Howard.

Jules pulls into the parking lot of the drug store, and Izzy goes inside. Jules turns to Jack and starts to speak but chokes up when their eyes meet. "How can I help, Uncle Jack?"

"Thank you, but there's nothing for you to do." Jack peers at his great nephew. The boy is a mirror of himself as a young man, kind-hearted and cerebral and fearful of disappointing those who love him. "Actually, there is something Jules. Now listen to me. I'm an old man and we're family so I'm going to tell you. Don't live your life the way other people think you should. You got years ahead of you, but it goes faster than you think. You need to do what's in your heart or else one day you'll realize it's too late and you missed the boat. Then you got nothing. Look at me and my brothers. You love who you want to love! You hear me?"

"Yes."

Jack is not convinced. It will take more than a lecture to get through to his great nephew. "Here's what I want to do before I die. You must be curious how my brothers and I wound up living the way we do, four old bachelors in an old house wearing old clothes. I want to tell you how it came to be. You're young and have a long time to live. Maybe knowing our story will help you."

"Yes, I've wondered about your lives, Uncle Jack. I'd like to know more, but ... do you think I need help?"

There's the boy's self-doubt again. He's a smart kid, but he doesn't see what's what. "We all need wisdom in life. Courage too. I hope our story will give you a bit of both."

"Okay. When do we start?"

"As soon as we get home today. We'll sit in the back yard, away from my brothers' ears. This is between you and me, Jules. It's a long story, so we'll need several visits."

Chapter 8
Brooklyn 1921

DAVEY TREMBLES AS he leads Jack through the door of the Beth Abraham synagogue. They're here for Davey's first bar mitzvah lesson with Cantor Kugelman. Davey surprised the family a few months ago by announcing he wanted a bar mitzvah. Jennie keeps a kosher house and lights candles every Friday night, but the family never attends *shul*, even on the high holidays. Though the youngest of her sons, Davey would be the first to have a bar mitzvah.

Davey made the decision a few weeks ago, when Jennie took him and Lilly to the bar mitzvah ceremony of a neighbor boy, Shlomo Schlossberg. Davey was enthralled when the congregation joined together in reciting the strange prayers and singing the uplifting songs, everyone speaking to God in the ancient language. The service was orderly, slow paced and calming, a haven from the harsh bustle of day-to-day Brownsville.

Davey generally avoids being outside. The crowds are intimidating, jostling their way down the anonymous sidewalk. No one acknowledges him, except when a random bully passes by, usually in a group of older boys, and calls him "dumbass" or pokes him in the ribs, for no reason at all. He's less afraid when accompanied by Izzy or Jack. Nobody messes with Izzy, who protects him like a father. All Davey remembers of his real father is an angry face and a sour smell, but Izzy – sixteen years older than Davey – fills the role. Izzy runs the family, goes to work each day, and pays for everything they need.

After Davey announced he wanted a bar mitzvah, Jack bought him a children's book of bible stories. It reminded him of other books he loves, stories of escape from danger to safe, beautiful places: *Anne of Green Gables* or *The Wonderful Wizard of Oz*. His favorite bible story is the Hebrews fleeing from slavery in Egypt and traveling to the Promised Land, always under God's protection. God is strict, but if you follow his rules, he will take care of you.

When he declared at family dinner his bar mitzvah intentions, Izzy reacted immediately. "Ah, it's a waste of money. Why waste your time with that?"

"I'm Jewish, and I'm going to be thirteen."

"So what? We're all Jewish. Your brothers and I didn't bother with that. Why should you?"

Jennie spoke up. "Such a blessing one of my boys wants a bar mitzvah. Izzy, it's up to you, but it would make your poor mother so happy." She stepped towards Davey and embraced him. "My children are my pride. It's up to you, Izzy darling. You know best."

"Okay, Ma. So we'll have a bar mitzvah boy in the family." He slapped Davey on the back.

Jennie picked up Izzy's hand and brought it to her lips for a kiss. "Such wonderful sons I have. Now Davey, you will need to study and practice. Izzy, where will we do this?"

Izzy shrugged.

Jack said, "I'll talk with Charlie at the theater. I remember his uncle Zachary has a brother who's a rabbi."

"That's fine," said Izzy, "but let's find a *shul* that won't cost an arm and a leg."

It turned out Charlie's uncle Ezra was a cantor, not a rabbi, retired from a synagogue on Atlantic Avenue. After hearing about Davey, Cantor Ezra set things up with his successor, a young cantor named Bernard Kugelman. Cantor Kugelman agreed to give bar mitzvah lessons to Davey, on the condition that his family join the synagogue. Izzy balked at this deal until he learned that a widow with six children would not be expected to pay the regular dues.

Now, Davey watches Jack shake hands with the cantor, who is smiling warmly. Kugelman is clean shaven, wears glasses, and speaks softly. He could be in his mid-twenties, the same age as Jack.

"I'm so glad you came today with David to help us get off to a good start."

"We're four brothers who take care of each other. Our mother and sisters too." Jack hesitates, then says, "Excuse me, but I thought you'd be older."

Kugelman's smile is friendly. "Old cantors all start out young. With God's blessing, one day I will be an old man. You too, Jack. May he bless both of us for many years to come. Don't worry about your brother's lessons. I have already tutored many bar mitzvahs." He turns to Davey. "Are you ready to get started?"

"Yes." The cantor seems nice. Davey hopes he's a patient teacher and won't get angry if Davey is slow to learn.

"Wonderful, we have lots of work to do together. Jack, you are welcomed to stay or come back to pick up David in an hour."

"Thank you, Cantor. I... Davey, do want me to stay?

Davey glances at the cantor, whose calm eyes assure him everything will be fine. "No, that's okay."

"Alright, I have errands to run anyway. Wait here for me after the lesson." Jack leaves the teacher and student to themselves.

The cantor turns to the boy. "So, your brother calls you Davey. Does everyone?"

"Yes."

"I hope you don't mind if I call you David. You are named after a great king, the greatest in the Bible, who protected the Israelites from their powerful enemies and built the temple in Jerusalem." Kugelman pauses, then his face lights up. "In fact, your bar mitzvah will be on the Sabbath closest to Shavuos, when God gave Torah to all of Israel at Mount Sinai. A very special holiday but most people do not know it is also the birthday of King David. Yours is a special name and if you don't mind let us honor our ancestors by calling you David when you are in this synagogue."

"Yes. I mean.... no, I don't mind. But I don't want people thinking of me as a king."

"Ah, you are humble. God smiles. Humility is essential for a king to be great. David knew that he was God's servant.

He obeyed Nathan the prophet, who always reminded David that he must bow before God even though he was a mighty king of the people. The lesson for us is that we can be king over our own lives but must never forget that we are humble before God."

"But...how can I be a king? My brother Izzy is the boss in our house."

"Hmm, I understand." The cantor peers at the ceiling, then turns back to Davey. "Jack said that your brothers take care of your mother and sisters and each other. Does Izzy do that too?"

"Oh yes. He's in charge and he takes care of everybody."

"So, he is serving others. And you are too, so that means you can be a king." Davey is bewildered. He doesn't tell people what to do; he doesn't boss anyone.

Kugelman watches Davey's face, then continues. "Let me tell you something else about your bar mitzvah Sabbath. The Torah portion for that day teaches us that Moses climbed Mount Sinai and God gave him the law for the Jewish people. We will also be reading the Book of Ruth, a special story, with a very beautiful lesson about love for a mother." He goes to the bookshelf, opens a bible, thumbs through it, and marks a page with the attached ribbon.

"Here, David this is a gift for you. Your assignment for this week is to read about Ruth and her devotion to Naomi. Ruth does not resemble a king but her love for family makes her king of her own life. You think about that. Now let's get started with your Torah reading."

While Davey listens to his new teacher, Izzy stomps around the lumber yard parking lot, furious. It took four months to negotiate terms with Joe Galermo, coordinate with Lewis on behalf of The Brain, argue contract terms with that shyster lawyer, and close the deal. Izzy and his brothers spent another two months reorganizing Morgan's Lumber Supply to Izzy's liking, all while keeping the business open. The new sign was to be the final touch, except these cockamamie Russian contractors, Moshe and Meir Moskovitz, made a mess of it. Instead of saying "Isaacson Brothers" above "Lumber and Building Supplies," the big bold letters on top read "Brothers Isaacson."

"You idiot immigrants! People are going to think we don't speak English good. As if *we* are the immigrants! Who wants to do business with an outfit that can't even get its name right?"

Izzy's rampage draws Max from inside the store. He stands beside his older brother.

"We are sorry, Mister Isaacson," grovels Moshe in a strong Russian accent. "We fix it. You see. No problem."

"No problem? My boss and his boss are coming to check out the place this morning. They're going to think I can't run a business. I should go burn your house down. Where do you live?"

Moshe's eyes widen and his lips move, but no sound comes out. He glances at his cousin for support, but Meir is looking at his feet. Moshe mumbles, "When we are boys, Meir and I see mob burn down our village. Every house. That was pogrom of 1905."

"Eh!" Izzy slaps the air with an outstretched hand, palm down. He's not interested in old stories from Europe. "At least take down that sign for now. Pronto!"

The hapless cousins grab their ladder and tools, but it's too late. A fancy car pulls to the curb on the far side of the parking lot. It's a new Lincoln Model L, with a deep green hood and bright red wheels. Izzy recognizes Joey in the front passenger seat, wearing his tough-guy scowl. Lewis is in the back seat talking with an older man Izzy does not recognize – that must be The Brain.

Lewis emerges from the rear left door. He strides up to Izzy, smirking. "Hey *boychik*, what's with the sign?"

"It's a mistake, Lewis. You can blame these two good-for-nothings." He points to Moshe and Meir, frozen in place a few paces away. "Tell Mister Rothstein I'm going to fix it right away."

"Not so fast. He likes it. He laughed at first, then said it will be good for business, because it will stick in people's mind. Add 'the' in front, so it says, 'The Brothers Isaacson.' That will be classy, like Russian literature."

Max chimes in. "The Brothers Isaacson. I can use that with the customers. It will be great for laughs. 'The Brothers Isaacson will give you a price good.' Then they'll come back. Why go to some other lumber yard that's no fun?"

Izzy frowns. "Are you sure, Lewis? Do we want to stand out as oddballs?"

"The Brain is sure, so I'm sure. He's the boss and that's that. Plus, he's happy with the whole project here. You're doing good, *boychik*."

"Does he want a tour around the place?"

"No, he just wanted to lay eyes on his new investment. Now what will matter to him is the numbers, you know what I mean."

"Sure. Well, can I go meet him?"

"Nah, he keeps a low profile. It's better this way." Lewis shakes Izzy's hand, nods to Max, and marches back to the Lincoln. The car speeds away.

Izzy turns to Moshe. "Okay, you heard him. Add the word 'the' – that's capital T, small h, small e – in front of 'Brothers'. You understand?"

Moshe's head is bobbing enthusiastically. "Yes, yes, Mister Isaacson. We make it right. You see."

Izzy doesn't bother to acknowledge Moshe further. He signals to Max to follow him back into the store. He's still fuming, but the focus of his anger shifts to The Brain, who is so high and mighty he refused to say hello to Izzy, one of his most productive soldiers. Then he tells Lewis to keep the ridiculous sign as it is, without even asking for Izzy's opinion. The sign, and now the business itself, mangles his family's name. It's humiliating.

―――――――

After Jack leaves Davey with Cantor Kugelman, he strolls up Atlantic Avenue to the women's clothing store he noticed earlier. Inside, mannequins wear a broad assortment of styles and colors. Lapels are getting wider, and pleats are popular. Such a different world from the lumber yard, where his days are filled with two-by-four studs and rough, shabbily dressed men. The smell of lumber is not unpleasant, but joyless compared to the fabric on these new dresses. He drifts closer to a mannequin to breathe in the fragrance. A voice, suddenly nearby, startles him. "May I help you?" He jumps.

It's a young saleswoman, wearing a royal blue dress with a periwinkle collar and a hint of perfume. She smiles at him earnestly, showing no suspicion that a lone man would be in a women's dress shop sniffing mannequins. "Uh, no thank you. I'll look around on my own."

"Fine." She turns abruptly and is gone. Did Jack hear a hard edge in her voice? Did he say something wrong?

Last night was his fourth date with Leah. She is kind, thoughtful, and well spoken. She listens carefully when he explains his passion for fabrics and dressmaking yet understands the family commitments that keep him from pursuing clothing as a career. She aspires to be a teacher, and she shares his love of books. On her recommendation, he's reading *The Age of Innocence* by Edith Wharton, about a man who regrets his marriage because he was too afraid to marry his true love, who was unacceptable to his family and social circles. Is Leah his true love?

He's growing fond of her. When he kissed her last night, she was receptive, with lips soft and eyes closed. Finally, Jack enjoyed kissing a girl. But there's something ... missing. Leah leaned forward into the kiss with an urgency that Jack could not match. When he finally pulled away, he worried he had disappointed her.

This is so confusing. Leah would be a nurturing mother and a reliable wife, a person he could count on, and he would love being a father. Why is he not more excited by her? Does he expect too much? Is this how real love feels: a steady warmth, not a fiery blaze?

He leaves the clothing store and wanders the neighborhood. He pauses at an alley where boys are playing stickball, taunting each other. He passes a teenage boy and girl holding hands. At a delicatessen window two old, bearded men are sitting at a table, engaged in conversation. He envisions the men as future versions of Cantor Kugelman and himself, two old friends enjoying each other's company and debating the meaning of life. The men turn to stare at Jack, aware they are being watched. He hurries off.

When it's time to pick up Davey, Jack meets him outside the front door of the synagogue. "So how was the lesson?"

"It was great. Cantor Kugelman knows a lot of important stuff in the Bible. My bar mitzvah Sabbath will be on King David's birthday, so the cantor is going to call me David not Davey. David was humble, even though he was a king, which is like being the boss of a family like Izzy, but we can all be kings even if we're not the boss. And Ruth was a king, even though she was a girl, because she loved her family so much. He gave me this bible so I can read about Ruth."

Jack is happy his little brother has a passion to pursue. Though he doesn't share Davey's appetite for Judaism, Jack figures it's similar to his own enthusiasm for women's clothing. He resolves to protect Davey from Izzy, who will eventually try to pull their youngest brother into the family business. As they walk to the trolley stop, he puts his arm around Davey's shoulders and gives him a squeeze. "So, David and Ruth were brother and sister?"

"What? No, I don't think so. He didn't say that."

"Do you want to be called David? That is your real name, you know, like mine is Jacob, but I've always been Jack and you've always been Davey."

Davey takes a minute to respond. "I like it when Cantor Kugelman calls me David. But just him. Ma wants me to be Davey."

"Okay. So what else happened with the cantor?"

"We started the Torah part I'm going to read. Except it's more singing than it is reading. Cantor sang a little, then I copied him, then we sang together. Then we did more. At first it was hard because it's in Hebrew and I don't know the words, but the singing makes it easier to remember."

Jack smiles. "You're going to enjoy being a bar mitzvah boy."

On Monday Izzy sits in his office at the lumber yard, racking his brains for a new business idea for him and Lewis, something independent of the Rothstein organization that poses no competition or threat. It should capitalize on their business knowledge and be easy to manage while they continue their work for Rothstein. Though the benefits of working for him are too good – plus Izzy would never leave Lewis – he needs an outside venture to insulate him from the indignities of Rothstein's disrespect. He still burns whenever he glimpses *The Brothers Isaacson* sign.

It's time to close for the day. Izzy spins the combination lock on the Diebold safe. Lewis had instructed Izzy on exactly what safe to get, the same one used by The Brain's organization at other facilities. Izzy had balked at the $250 price tag, but Lewis insisted. The Diebold is massive, weighing over 600 pounds; it took four men to move it from the truck into the office. Then they cut a hole in the floorboards, sunk the thing four inches deep, and poured concrete around the bottom.

Izzy works the lock, then turns the handle with a satisfying click. He inserts the cash take from the day, stacked and bound in neat piles. Then he stows the real treasure, the counterfeit accounting books he's crafted since taking over the lumberyard business. The system of fake bills of sale from upstate lumber mills and fake invoices paid by phantom customers is working as Lewis planned. Izzy's books show thousands of fictitious dollars flowing through the business every week. He closes the safe with an unmistakable thud, fortified by its solidity and promise of treasure.

It's been a good day. He locks the office door and walks across the show room. Max has already locked the front door and is sitting at the counter waiting for him. He's reading a book of jokes, giggling. "Hey Izzy, what's the difference between a bad marksman and an owl with constipation?"

"Okay, what?"

"The marksman shoots but can't hit. Pretty good, huh?"

"Sure, hilarious. Let's go Max."

They walk towards the trolley stop on Flatlands Avenue. Izzy knows Max has been going with the same girl for a while. If Max settles down, he might get cured of his woman craziness, and take work more seriously. Izzy should check her out. "Are you going out again tonight?" he asks.

"Yep."

"With that same girl? What's her name again?"

"Ida. Ida Ichtenstein."

"You should bring this Ida to the apartment to meet Ma. She's a nice girl, right?"

"Oh… sure, she's nice."

"So bring her over; we can all get to know her."

In his room that evening, Davey opens the bible to the blue ribbon marking the Book of Ruth. He reads that Ruth was not born Jewish but married an Israelite who had moved with his family to her country. Her husband's father died and then her husband died, leaving Ruth and her mother-in-law Naomi to fend for themselves. Naomi told Ruth to leave and get remarried so she wouldn't be poor, but Ruth refused to leave Naomi's side: *Where you go I will go, and where you stay I will stay. Your people will be my people and your God my God. Where you die I will die, and there I will be buried.*

That's it! That's how Davey can fulfill his duty to the family without following his brothers into the brutal world of business. He will take care of his mother, staying home to make sure she eats enough and is warm and safe. He will always be there for her no matter what. Davey fills with relief – the Bible is alleviating him of the fear he's been carrying that one day he must join his brothers and the workaday hordes.

He reads on. Ruth stays with Naomi, remarries and has a baby, who becomes the grandfather of King David. Ruth is King David's great-grandmother. Davey's mind is racing. God wrote this story for him, that's why he's named after the Bible king! He will practice his bar mitzvah readings until they're perfect. He will be faithful to God because he's a king, a humble king, who chooses to be Jewish, same as Ruth.

Davey paces the room, electricity surging down his arms through his fingertips. He wants to share this new vision of his future with his family. The moment his trembling hand reaches for the doorknob, he is awestruck with a realization: his mother and his brothers are not who he needs to speak with. He sits back down on the bed, closes his eyes, and bows his head. For the first time in his twelve-year-old life, David Isaacson prays to God.

On Friday night Jennie is waiting with the family for Max to arrive. She hopes this girl he's bringing for dinner is deserving of her son. It's past time for at least one of her boys to get married. Jennie is not getting any younger, and the prospects for a grandchild are dimming. Bessie is having trouble getting pregnant, bless her heart. Izzy runs around a bit, but he's too busy with work to get serious with a girl. Jack finally has a girlfriend, but he's lukewarm, a mother can tell. Such a contrast to Max – he's crazy about this Ida. That's good, but young and woman-crazy can be a dangerous combination. The girl could be a temptress. After all, he met her in a dance hall, and last week, when Jennie and her neighbor Bunny Horowitz were on the roof together hanging laundry, Bunny told Jennie all about the conniving women these days who dance with unsuspecting men as a way to touch them – "you know what I mean" – and trap them and get them to buy things for the temptress. Then when she's gotten what she can, it's on to the next poor man. America is filled with loose women who don't care about decency or family or anybody but themselves. It's a sin against God and God will punish them eventually, but in the meantime, we have to live with it.

Max opens the front door and walks in, with Ida close behind. "Hey everybody, this is Ida. Ida, this is everybody. Here's my ma."

Ida is wearing a dress that exposes her lower leg all the way to her knees. Despite her disapproval, Jennie tries to be nice. "What a pretty dress."

"Oh, this is the latest fashion. My sister helped me pick it out." Ida turns to Jack. "Hi Jack. Been to any more dances lately?"

"No. That's Max's department."

Ida turns back to Jennie. "Max is a marvelous dancer, Mrs. Isaacson. What moves he makes!"

"That's nice."

Max points to Izzy. "Ida, this is my big brother Izzy."

She extends her hand. "Max has told me all about you, Izzy, your new lumberyard and what a good businessman you are. The family must be doing well."

"We do okay." Jennie hears ice in Izzy's tone. He doesn't like this girl sticking her nose in his business.

Max continues the introductions. "This is our baby brother Davey, and this is our sister Lilly, who turned nineteen last week."

"You're such a cute girl, Lilly. The boys are going to be falling over themselves to get to you." Lilly smiles uncertainly. What a thing to say to Jennie's sweet girl who is innocent in the ways of the world.

Max breaks the moment's awkwardness. "So, when do we eat, Ma?"

"Dinner is almost ready. Let's light the candles."

Jennie opens a drawer in the sideboard, a beautiful piece made of dark walnut that Izzy bought for her last birthday. She pauses at the lace head coverings; there are four that are frayed and yellowed and four that are white and new. The old ones were knitted in Lithuania by her mother, who gave them to Jennie for the voyage to America. She puts the least frayed one on her head, then hands two of the new ones to Ida and Lilly. Their heads covered, the three women huddle close around the two candles. Lilly lights them. All three close their eyes, wave their hands over the candles in a gathering motion to invite the Sabbath, and together recite the ancient Hebrew blessing: *Barukh ata Adonai* ...

At least this girl knows how to light the candles, that's something.

Over dinner Jennie asks Ida about her family. Her parents came from Minsk as a young couple, settled in Brownsville, and had five children, all girls. Ida helps her mother with the cooking and the washing and caring for her younger sisters. Maybe she could be good for Max after all, even if she is brash and outspoken.

Max adds, "Ida helps her father run his shoe store. He taught her how to keep the books. Since she has no brothers, her father wants her to run the store someday."

"Who ever heard of a woman running a business?" says Izzy.

"Why not?" says Ida. "There's no law against it, and I'm at least as smart as the average businessman."

Izzy shrugs.

After dinner Max leaves to walk Ida home. Jennie turns to Izzy. "What a mouth on that girl. What do you think?"

"She's a floozy. Max can do better."

"Or he could do worse. She is ... coarse, but that doesn't mean she's a floozy. She comes from a nice family."

"I guess, but Ma, why should Max settle for a girl who is okay but not great? He's barely twenty and this is the first girl he's gone with."

Jennie ponders this. Max does have time to meet other women, ones who are well mannered, who will give Jennie more confidence about their wifely and motherly temperament. And that revealing dress she was wearing, oy. On the other hand, Jennie needs a grandchild – she's tired of hearing Bunny brag on hers. Max might be her best chance.

When Max returns, Jennie and Izzy are still up. "What do you think of Ida, Ma? Isn't she great?"

"She's very ... friendly. That's nice. Listen to me my darling Maxie. You got to be careful about girls these days."

"What do you mean?"

"I mean, some girls are out to catch a man for the wrong reasons. For selfish reasons, such as getting ahold of his money."

"Ida's not that way, not at all."

"I'm not saying she is, but you should know these things, darling, and be careful who you go with."

Izzy says flatly, "She's too interested in our money, asking about our business."

"She was making conversation, that's all," says Max. His voice is pleading. "Ida likes me for the right reasons."

"Yes darling," says Jennie. "We just don't want you to get hurt."

Davey stands before Cantor Kugelman, chanting the Torah reading portion of his planned bar mitzvah. This is his first time going from start to finish uninterrupted. The Cantor smiles broadly.

"That was excellent, David. You are a quick learner with a promising voice. Now let's try something new. You know how to chant the Torah, so let's move on to a real song." He opens a hymnal and hands it to Davey. "This is the *Ein Keloheinu*, one of my favorite prayers. You can read the transliteration that shows how to pronounce the Hebrew. We praise God and thank God for there is no other that compares to our God. There are several tunes written for it, so let's try one that suits the register of your voice. I will sing a line, then you repeat it."

The cantor clears his throat, raises his pitch higher than usual, then slowly sings out: *Ein keloheinu, ein kadoneinu, ein kemalkeinu, ein kemoshi'enu.*

Davey's first attempt is broken and stilted. He is embarrassed and disappointed in himself. "That's okay David, take deep breaths and keep going." The cantor repeats the line, and they fall into a call and response pattern. With each repetition, Davey becomes smoother in tone and tempo. Once the cantor is satisfied, he moves on to the next line.

After they complete the song line-by-line, the cantor instructs Davey, "Now let's sing the entire prayer, together, and this time I want you to close your eyes. Focus on the sounds our voices make. Take a good full breath after each line." Midway through, the cantor gradually lowers his volume, so by the end Davey is singing solo. He is filled with the song and the mysterious words that are outside him and inside him at the same time. When he reaches the end, he opens his eyes and wipes them of moisture. The cantor beams at him.

"David, I want you to come by the synagogue tomorrow evening, can you do that? That's when our choir rehearses. We have men of all ages but no one quite so young as you."

"What is choir?"

"That's a group who sings together. A beautiful thing, you will see. Ask your brothers if it's alright. It will be after dark when we finish so I will bring you home on the trolley."

"Okay," Davey agrees without knowing quite what he is agreeing to. But he trusts his teacher and the euphoria lingering in his body from singing a prayer to God.

Max and Ida sit in the back row at the Pitkin Market Theater, waiting for the movie to start. All the seats this far back are taken by couples, recalling Max's days working at The Olympic. A uniformed usher walks by. Max is surprised he's an old man, bent over and moving with a limp. Their eyes meet and Max smiles. The old guy ignores him.

Since the night Ida came for dinner, Max has worried over his mother's view of her. She can't be right. Ida likes him for real, not for some sinister reason. How can he convince his mother and Izzy that Ida is okay? He must persuade Ida to act demurer around them.

She grabs his arm, turns towards him. "I'm so excited to see Rudy, he's *sooo* dreamy." Max brought Ida here for *The Sheik*, the new picture starring Rudolph Valentino in the title role.

"Oh yeah? What's he got that I don't have?"

"Well, let me look at you. He has beautiful eyes, you have beautiful eyes. He has a strong chin, you have a strong chin. He has an average nose, you have a nice big nose. You actually have him beat."

"You're a good liar. And a great girlfriend."

Ida giggles. "I am *not* lying. You do have a big nose. And I love it."

Max leans close and kisses her on the neck, in the soft part below her ear. He lingers there. "Oh Max," she whispers.

The lights dim and the organ player takes his seat in the corner. A man dressed in a tuxedo steps onto the stage. "Ladies and gentlemen, thank you for coming to the Pitkin Market Theater, the grandest movie house in all of Brooklyn. Before we start our feature presentation, starring none other than Rudolph Valentino, we have a special treat for you. Brooklyn's own Gabe Gellman, singing that hit tune *Love Nest*. Let's hear it for him!"

The audience responds with mild applause while Gabe strolls onto the stage. Max and Ida look at each other, laughing. "It's our *yenta* boy," whispers Max, "such a doll." Ida pokes him in the ribs.

To Max's surprise, this time he enjoys Gabe's singing, now that it's a good song. Hours later when he and Ida stroll up Pitkin Avenue, awash in the afterglow of the movie's romantic ending, Max sings out the lyrics:

Best of all, a room,
A dream room for two.
Better than a palace with a gilded dome,
Is a love nest
You can call home.

Ida wraps her arm around Max's waist. "Is that you want, Max? A love nest to call home?"

Before he can answer, two teenagers pass them on bicycles and shout, "Hubba hubba." Max yells back. "Jealous, huh boys?"

Ida giggles. "Oh, Max, stop it."

They cross Howard, pick up East New York Avenue and wander towards Lincoln Terrace Park. Max ponders how to explain that Ida should be different around his family, more modest.

In the park, they spy another couple on a bench, embracing. "That's why they call this kitzel park, you know" says Max. "Guys bring their gals here for a tickle."

"Then we better get to kitzeling, baby."

Max's body lights up when Ida talks coy and sultry. He's nuts over her – despite his family's interest, he wants an enchantress, not a shrinking violet. He grabs her hand, picks up the pace, and pulls her behind a tall hedge row. Their smooching gets heavy. Max whispers, "I'm so crazy about you. I think about you all the time." He reaches around her hips to hold her bottom. Ida lets his hands remain, then gently pulls away. "Not unless we're married. What kind of girl do you think I am?"

Max is breathless, his body crying for more. "Okay, let's get married."

"What?"

"You heard me. Will you marry me, Ida Ichtenstein?"

"You're proposing?"

"How many times do I have to say it?"

"Yes, my answer is yes! Oh, I'm going to make you so happy Max. Picture us together, doing whatever we want." Ida pushes her hips firmly against Max, encouraging the bulge in his pants. He's giddy.

Then he freezes. "Wait, I have to talk with Izzy and my mother. They might not go for this."

"What? What does Izzy have to do with it? This is between you and me." Ida's eyes bore into him as she takes a step back, her passion flipped from amorism to anger. "You can't live under your big brother's thumb forever, you know. You're twenty years old, it's time you stand up for yourself and be a man."

"Hey, I am a man. It's just that, well, it would be good if you could act differently around my mother, be more ... ladylike."

"What are you saying? Does she think I'm a tramp? Do you?"

"No, of course not." This isn't going well. How can he say this? "You know in the movie tonight, the way Lady Diana is headstrong and daring and beautiful? That's how you are, and that's why I'm so in love with you. But my mother is old-fashioned. She thinks women should be ... reserved and soft spoken."

"What about Izzy? Is that what he thinks?"

"Izzy is private about his business. It's best not to bring that up." Max ventures on. "And be sure to wear dresses that cover your legs and shoulders."

"This is too many rules, Max. I can't pretend to be someone I'm not."

"Just until we're married. Please, can you do that for me? For a little while?" He holds her right hand in both of his, brings it to his lips for a gentle kiss. "Once we're married, we can do whatever we want."

Ida's voice softens. "Okay. I'll be a good little girl. I'll show your mother I'll be her ideal daughter-in-law. But I'm not going to like it."

"Also, don't say anything about us getting married to anybody yet. If my family hears it before they get to know the new you, it will ruin everything."

"Geez, this is a complicated proposal."

"I guess so, but what counts is how we feel about each other, and I'm totally in love with you. That's not complicated." Max pulls Ida close to him. "Now, where were we?"

She smiles. "Right here." She kisses him deeply.

Jack walks through the front door of Katzenbaum's Clothing and Fabric Emporium, exhilarated by the scent of new fabrics. He's here for his bimonthly visit with Howard, a schedule they have maintained since last year.

Howard's brother Herman stands on the showroom floor, speaking to a young salesclerk. He spies Jack. "Jack! It's always good to see you. Howard told me you would be coming today. He says you're really helping him out. I appreciate that."

"It's nice to see you too, Mister K."

"How many times do I have to tell you? Call me Herman. You're not an employee anymore."

"I guess you'll always be Mister K to me."

"Well ... you'll find Howard in the workroom. You know the way."

Jack strides across the sales floor, ready for another day as Howard's apprentice. Jack now knows how to draw a dress pattern from a magazine photo of the finished product and how to cut the pattern for the seamstresses to follow. Howard has also taught him the details of fabrics — which are easier to reshape to a woman's figure and which are stiff enough for collars and lapels.

Jack knocks on the workroom door. Howard opens it, smiles broadly, and enfolds Jack in his arms. Jack startles for a moment, then relaxes into Howard's hug. Howard steps back. "Uh... sorry Jack. I'm just so happy you're here."

Jack resists an impulse to touch Howard again. "That's okay. I'm happy to be here too. What are we working on today?"

Howard shows Jack the pattern he's drawing. It's complicated, with mid-torso darts in front and back that create a slimming effect. Jack studies the drawing. "This will be difficult to sew. The seamstress will have to get all four angles exactly right without bunching the material. What if you offset the darts by moving the back ones two or three inches lower?"

Howard considers this. "Let's try it." He hands the eraser and pencil to Jack. "You do the honors."

Jack works carefully. It takes him fifteen minutes to complete the revisions. Howard studies the new drawing. "Jack, this is brilliant!"

"Really?"

"You're so good at this. I can't believe how much you've learned, only coming in here occasionally."

"I have an excellent teacher. Talented, but also patient and kind."

"I've become so fond of you, Jack."

What exactly does Howard mean? Does he think of Jack as more than a friend? Jack has heard the faggot jokes, laughed along with them, though they're not funny. He's spotted the disgust in people's faces when homosexuality is mentioned. No, Jack and Howard are not that way. "Let's cut the new pattern," says Jack.

Howard unrolls the brown butcher paper and cuts off a fresh piece. Jack traces the design onto it from the drawing paper. Then they each grab scissors to cut out the pattern, working from opposite ends towards the middle. Jack has his head down close to the paper, concentrating on each snip. He becomes aware of Howard's breath a few inches away. He looks up to find Howard beaming at him. Their eyes meet. Jack leans in, kisses Howard on the mouth. Their lips move apart for a moment then reunite. Howard's mouth is warm and tender – it reminds Jack of his mother's chicken soup, of all things. A wellspring arises within his body.

Howard slowly pulls away. "Jack."

"What ... what are we doing?"

"Love. I'm ... falling in love with you."

"No, you can't. I mean, I can't. I mean ... it's wrong, Howard."

"How can love be wrong?"

"You know what I'm saying," says Jack.

"Of course I do." Howard reaches out to hold Jack's hands. They stand together in a rich silence. Howard finally speaks. "Do you remember the offer I made last year at the Bushwick Deli? Would you reconsider?"

"To work here with you?"

"Yes, but not only that. You and I would ... see each other more. In secret."

Jack's mind races, imagining his family discovering such a secret. His mother would be devastated with shame. Izzy would consider it a family disgrace and cast Jack out like he did their father. It would be the same for Howard and his family. "If we were ever discovered, our families would shun us, disown us. We could even be arrested and put in jail. It's too risky, Howard. I can't live in constant worry that we would be found out."

"Well, I can't live without love, and you're the person I love."

Howard's avowal melts Jack's resolve. Could he be with Howard in a romantic way? His magnetic attraction towards Howard is undeniable now. How can he turn his back on that feeling and on this wonderful man? Could they be together without anyone ever knowing?

Howard is gazing at him. "Don't be afraid, Jack. Please."

Being asked not to be afraid ignites another eruption of fear within Jack. He's already reeling from the sudden intimacy with Howard, but now a crosscurrent of terror grips his insides. If they were caught, it would destroy his life. Howard's too. "I *am* afraid.... I can't lose my family, my job, everything. I can't let you take that risk either. And I can't hide in the dark."

"Either way, you're hiding."

"I guess that's right, but it's safer to hide myself than to hide the two of us together."

"Oh Jack." Howard wipes tears from his eyes. Jack embraces him in a hug. Howard shudders softly as he sobs.

"I'm sorry Howard. I can't do it. I want to, I want to be with you, but I can't. Please ... forgive me."

Howard laments, "There's nothing to forgive, Jack. This is who we are, and we live in a world that doesn't understand us."

Izzy waits for Joe Lefkowitz to drive him from the lumber yard to the bank for the biweekly cash deposit. Izzy has a soft spot for his old pal, and he's okay with being escorted, especially after he heard from Lewis that another of The Brain's "depositors" was robbed at knifepoint.

A car pulls up, with Joe in the front passenger seat and some goon behind the wheel. Joe now has his own tough guy to boss around. He climbs out of the car to shake hands. "Hey Izzy, how's it going? I'll sit in the back with you."

They both get in. Izzy carries a small satchel. Inside is $4,540, neatly sorted into bundles by denomination. The heft of all that cash sends a frisson through Izzy that he hides through casual conversation. "Hey Joe, got a stick?"

Joe grins. "Don't I always?" He pulls a pack of *Juicy Fruit* chewing gum out of his breast pocket and offers it to Izzy, who extracts a piece and hands back the pack.

"This here is Sammy." Joe nods towards the driver.

"Hey Sammy, how you doing?"

Sammy grunts. "Eh."

"He don't say much. So, how's the family?"

"Ma and Lilly are doing fine, and I got Jack and Max working at the lumber yard. Davey's gonna have a bar mitzvah."

"Is that so? Your ma making him do that?"

"Nah, it was his idea. Go figure."

"Yeah, go figure. Hey, I seen Max with the same girl out a few times around the neighborhood. She's a babe. Curves in all the right places, you know what I mean?" Joe winks at Izzy, then elbows him in the ribs.

"Ah, she's a floozy, alright. It's okay that Max wants a piece of that, but he's fallen for her, head over heels. She's got her claws in him, and I got to help Max realize she's up to no good." Izzy doesn't mention his other misgiving about Ida. Last week, after he returned to the lumberyard from an errand, he found that Max had brought Ida to The Brothers Isaacson to "show her around." In his office, Izzy discovered that his accounting books were not quite where he left them on his desk. He remembered that Ida knows something of bookkeeping from her family's shoe store. If she was rifling through his books – both sets were left out – she might get ideas about Izzy's phony business for The Brain.

"Hmm," says Joe. "You want I should get rid of her?"

Izzy stares at his old friend, alarmed. "What do you mean?"

"Oh, nothing rough. You know, I could show her a good time, get her drunk and then Max would see she's a tramp."

"No, she won't go out with you. She has her eyes set on Max." Joe's plan wouldn't work, but he has the right idea. Izzy could concoct a lesson for Max by plotting behind the scenes. Should he do such a thing? "Thanks anyway Joe. You're a real pal."

"Hey, we got to watch out for each other in this dog-eat-dog world."

A loud popping noise makes Izzy jump. Joe yanks a gun out from under his jacket. He scans the street in all directions.

"A backfire," says Sammy.

"You sure? How do you know?"

"Busy traffic and we just slowed. The guy behind me probably downshifted too hard. Everybody's acting normal."

Izzy's heart is racing. "Goddammit, Joey, you got me jumpy now. Put that thing away. What are you doing with a gun anyhow?"

"Hey, this is my friend. My pocket friend." He replaces the gun in the shoulder holster under his jacket. "I got to be sure nothing happens to you or to The Brain's money. That's my job."

They pull up in front of the East New York Savings Bank. Joe turns to Sammy. "Wait here in front. If a cop tries to chase you off, give him this." He hands Sammy a fiver. Joe steps out of the car curbside, looks up and down the sidewalk, then waves to Izzy to come on out. They walk in together.

"I'll wait here by the door," says Joe.

Izzy crosses the high-ceiling lobby, rimmed with marble columns and walnut paneling. As he passes the teller lines, Bernard Blumstein approaches. They shake hands. "Hello, Izzy. Nice to see you." He leads Izzy towards his private office.

Izzy has known Bennie since the early days on Pitkin Avenue. Bennie and Lewis were the same age and grew up together. As teenagers the older boys let Izzy and Joey play stickball with them in the alleys off Amboy Street. While waiting for turns at bat, Bennie would mock his immigrant father's accent and ignorance, always making Izzy laugh. Now he's a big shot working at a bank.

Bennie shuts the office door behind Izzy. "Here for another deposit? You're quite a businessman, Izzy. First the theater, now this lumberyard. What's your secret?"

"Keep sales high and costs low. It's no secret." Izzy will never divulge the real secrets of The Brothers Isaacson, though he figures Bennie knows that Lewis works for The Brain. It was Lewis who set up the lumberyard accounts at the bank so that he and Izzy are both authorized to make withdrawals. Is the bank in on the scheme, too? That would explain how Bennie got this job in the first place.

"What's the secret to being a big-time banker, eh Bennie?"

Blumstein lowers his voice. "Three things. Be good with numbers, don't steal even a nickel from the bank, and kiss the boss' ass at least once a day."

"You always were a smart guy."

"You're pretty smart yourself, but brains alone are not enough, sometimes you need brawn. It's good that Lewis' brother comes with you when you're carrying cash."

"Yeah, well. Lewis looks out for me and Joe both."

"Lewis looks out for a lot of us. Still, I worry about Joe. He acts the tough guy, but I remember Joey the boy, trying to prove himself. I hope he doesn't pick a fight he can't win."

Izzy recalls Joe's moment of panic in the car, waving that gun around. If he's carrying a gun, so are the guys who want to steal Rothstein's money. Bennie's right – Joe's tough on the outside, but he's not meant for violence. He might get hurt one day, hurt bad. "Oh, he'll be okay."

"Well ... you keep an eye out for your old friend Joey."

"Sure. In the meantime, I'll keep an eye on you as you count my money."

Bennie grins. "Okay, smart guy. Let's see what you got."

Back in the car on their return to the lumberyard, Sam takes an unfamiliar side street in Canarsie. They pass a row of houses under construction, a full block long. Half a dozen painters are working on scaffolds. They're a ragtag outfit, no uniforms or matching caps. Their truck is a jalopy with hand lettering on the doors: *A-OK Painting Company*. That's a lousy name for a business. If Izzy owned it, he would call it *Precision Painters* or *Professional Painters,* and the crews would look the part.

Izzy gets a flash: here's the side business for him and Lewis, independent of Rothstein. They would be their own bosses, and Izzy could manage it while still running the lumberyard. How hard can house painting be? There must be plenty of demand, with the economy booming and houses being built all over eastern Brooklyn. It wouldn't take much capital to get started and there's plenty of cheap immigrant labor. The hardest part would be managing the workers – Izzy would need someone to check on them throughout the day. That could be a job for Joey, away from the dangers of protecting Rothstein's cash shipments. There's plenty of thugs Lewis could hire for that, like Sam here.

Joey raises his chin. "Hey Izzy, what's got you grinning?"

"I got an idea, a business idea. It's good." Izzy claps his hands, rubs them together. "I hope Lewis thinks so too."

The sanctuary at *Beth Abraham* is full, as happens when a Saturday morning bar mitzvah service ends with a luncheon paid by the boy's family. Word has spread that Gurewitz's Deli will be catering, so everyone is anticipating high quality salami, corned beef, and pastrami.

Sitting in the third row, Abel Abramowitz is whispering with his old friend Elliot Eisenblatt, "God willing there will be none of that *schlock* bologna served last *Shabbat,* when the Grubenstein family hired Morton's Meats and Matzos to lay the spread. Even the chopped liver wasn't good."

"How can you make bad chopped liver? Even my wife, may she rest in peace, made good chopped liver."

"Morton's can make anything bad. At any rate, the boy's family today is doing well. I hear they own a lumberyard in Canarsie. That's a good business these days."

"What's the father's name?"

"The father is out of the picture. They say he drank himself to ruin and disappeared years ago when his eldest was not yet of age."

"So who runs the lumberyard?"

"The oldest brother, that's him in the front row with the crooked *tallis*. There's two other brothers who work there with him, then the bar mitzvah boy, he's the youngest. They say he's got a nice voice for one so young."

"I heard that before. Then the boy gets up to chant and sounds like a sick rooster who forgot how to cockle-doo."

Abel laughs. "Not everyone can be a cantor."

"But we can all be roosters. God willing."

"Ha! Well, God hears everything, whether it's from a cantor or a rooster." Abel gazes skyward. "He hears our thoughts too."

"That's right. And I say blessings on this bar mitzvah boy and his family. And on Gurewitz."

"Amen."

In the front row sits the Isaacson family, filled with thoughts not of God but of this world. Jennie worries about her Max, the way his head is turned around by that jezebel Ida. How can Jennie find him a nice girl, one who will be a good wife and mother? After the service, she'll ask Bessie's mother-in-law Golda for advice. She's the closest thing to a real *yenta* Jennie knows in Brownsville.

Max considers whether to elope with Ida, given the dim prospects of persuading Ma and Izzy that marriage is a good idea. His plan for Ida to act differently around them is not working – she tries, but can't pretend to be mild and meek. He was impulsive to propose marriage, but there's no backing out now. Their engaged status opened the door to full-on sex, the greatest joy Max has ever experienced. He loves her and he wants to get married. He has little money of his own – Izzy lets him and Jack save a bit of their pay for personal spending – but maybe eloping won't cost much. All he needs is a license and a courthouse ceremony, if that's okay with Ida. Maybe he can borrow a little from Pauly.

Izzy, sitting to his mother's left, adds up his costs for this bar mitzvah: the luncheon, Davey's new suit, the "donation" to the synagogue. At least it's less than Bessie's wedding three years ago. Besides, this is making his mother happy. She would also be happy if there's a falling out between Max and that Ida. How can Izzy convince Max to dump her and find a nice girl?

Bessie frets over her inability to get pregnant and the latest advice from her mother-in-law: eat honey with cinnamon before doing her wifely duty with Pauly. He's a good husband to her, and she owes it to him and his family to bear him children. She wonders whether a doctor could help, but going to that kind of doctor would be so embarrassing.

Lilly reviews her favorite baby names – Esther, Aaron, Sonia – and wonders how long she must wait before a man asks her to marry. She wants to have lots of babies to love, children that will love her, same as her mother has. Six is a good number. How will she find a husband?

Jack thinks about Howard. It's been three weeks since their kiss, that wonderful moment. Jack hasn't dared to meet Howard since then, though he yearns for him terribly. Was Jack too hasty in saying no to Howard's proposal that they "work" together? No, it's the right decision. Their love is forbidden, and seeing each other is too dangerous. Why has God made him this way, attracted to a man? Maybe he'll grow out of it – staying away from Howard will help.

The sole untroubled Isaacson is the youngest one, sitting to the side of the podium waiting for the bar mitzvah portion of the service. Not only is Davey confident with the material, he knows in his heart this is his special day. It will go exactly as God intends, the God of Abraham, the God of Ruth and David. When Davey is called to the *bimah* to read from the Torah, he will be in God's majestic hands.

The moment arrives. The cantor nods to Davey, who floats from his chair to the lectern. The rabbi hands Davey the pointer, the *yad,* to follow the text – touching the scroll with fingers would defile the sacred Torah. Davey recognizes the ancient Hebrew words from his lessons, yet this is his first sight of the special lettering, inscribed by hand with serifs and tails. He sings the reading using the traditional tune. Davey's voice fills the sanctuary, a boy-man's voice rich with the passion of faith being conveyed to all assembled in rhythmic cadences inherited from the ages. The congregation is rapt, held by the vibration of a thirteen-year-old boy singing three-thousand-year-old words. Even Abel Abramowitz and Elliot Eisenblatt sit in awed silence.

Davey holds the final note and looks up from the scroll. All eyes are on him. His body rises to the ceiling, and he peers down on the rabbi, the cantor, himself, and the entire congregation. He has completed his reading of the Torah. Though the rabbi is yet to pronounce it so, Davey is now a man, a full member of God's chosen people. He counts in the world.

After a few prayers to close the Torah portion of the service, the rabbi delivers his sermon. He has chosen the story of King David and Bathsheba and the Prophet Nathan, "because I know from Cantor Kugleman that our *bar mitvah* boy David is interested in his namesake, the great king of ancient Israel." He tells of King David's lust for Bathsheba, his sin against her husband, and Nathan's command that the king must atone for his actions and beg God for forgiveness. "Thus we are taught that even a great king must obey God. He cannot be selfish. He cannot take whatever he wants. He must think of others and do right by all who depend on him. And who depends on him? For King David, it is his people Israel. For a rabbi, it is his congregation. For every one of us, it is our family and our community. We must think first of others, not our selfish desires."

As he declares this last sentence, the rabbi eyes the Isaacsons in the front row, each of whom withers from a mounting, amorphous guilt over their sins and shortcomings.

Chapter 9
April 1981

THREE WEEKS AFTER Uncle Jack's diagnosis, Jules is running from the Miami airport parking structure towards the terminal building. Eileen hates to be kept waiting in public places. Months ago in Atlanta when he was late meeting her at her favorite restaurant, she was angry and called him selfish and inconsiderate. It was humiliating to be left alone, she said. Jules apologized, despite her excessive punishment for a small lapse. Now it's about to happen again. He picks up his pace.

At the gate Jules discovers the flight is late, so he is not. What luck! He paces for a few moments, trying to decompress. His armpits are wet. "I need to calm down," he says under his breath, heading to a nearby airport bar.

The bartender sports a well-groomed beard and a generous smile. "Want a beer? We have Heineken on tap."

"Perfect. Thanks."

The barkeep fills a chilled mug. "Appears you could use this."

"Is it that obvious?"

"The airport can be a tense place. Everyone's in a hurry and there's always travel snafus."

Jules takes a sip. "Ah, good cold beer. Thanks again."

"It's what I do. So… are you going or coming?"

"I'm meeting my girlfriend. I ran here thinking I was late, but it turns out her flight is delayed. So now I'm early."

"She's lucky to have you, rushing for her sake."

Jules smiles. "No, I'm lucky her flight is late. I would have caught hell."

"That is lucky. I heard a saying about luck. 'There is no one luckier than he who thinks himself so'." He moves down the bar to welcome another customer.

Jules ponders his own good fortune. He's lucky to have a good job and a good career, notwithstanding the recent challenges with Paul Perlman. He's lucky to have Eileen. They'll be hugging in a few minutes – he tingles at the thought. He pictures their intimacy in bed tonight. Is this visit the time to propose to her? They wouldn't get married before he moves back to Atlanta, but a long engagement would be fine. He takes a swig of beer.

Thirty minutes later Eileen steps out of the jetway and rushes into Jules' arms. He kisses her full on the mouth, lingering until she pulls away. "Jules," she whispers, "people are watching."

"Who's watching? I don't see anyone watching."

"Anyway, I'm so happy I'm here with you. You got a haircut."

"Oh … yeah."

"Looks good." The way Eileen's eyes appraise his features reminds Jules of his mother, inspecting his haircut the first time he was old enough to go to the barber shop by himself.

"Let's go. I need to pee."

He grabs her carry-on bag and reaches for her hand. Together, they turn towards the terminal walkway and join the flow of pedestrians. The bartender emerges from a storage closet ahead, then turns towards his bar, now behind Jules. In the moment they pass, their eyes meet. He winks at Jules.

———

In the car leaving the airport, Eileen chatters about plans she and Deborah made for the visit. "We're going to this shopping mall, it's supposed to be fancy with a Neiman-Marcus and it's called Bal Harbour, but you and Richard don't want to do that, so we'll go while you boys are at work and one of our sorority sisters moved here, Susie Slivovitz, so we want to see her, but she lives in Fort Lauderdale, but Richard says it's not too far to go for dinner, and Susie has a boyfriend, his name is Todd, Todd something, so we'll make it a three-couple date and that will be fun, though Susie told Deborah that Todd's kind of quiet, but that's okay because Richard is always talkative. Won't that be fun?"

Jules doesn't answer. He had drifted off at "Neiman-Marcus." Was that bartender right about luck as perspective? Why did he later wink when he saw Jules with Eileen? Did he think Jules was lucky to be with her?

"Jules!"

He jerks back to the conversation. "Huh?"

"Are you listening to me? I said, wouldn't it be fun to go out as three couples for dinner?"

"Yeah, that sounds good. Definitely." Jules is not sure exactly what he is agreeing to but is not about to ask Eileen to repeat herself.

"So Jules, what else do you want to do while I'm here?"

"There's a place called the Seaquarium. They have dolphin shows and an amazing Orca whale and you can get a close-up view." His mind's eye pictures the two dolphins on the snorkeling trip with Richard, sleek and strong and playful. "I would love to experience dolphins up close."

"Okay, let's do that."

"Really? I wasn't sure you'd be interested."

"It's sweet that you like fish and if it makes you happy, I want to go. If there's a gift shop I can get something cute for my niece. Allie is turning three next month and I'm helping Lorraine with the party. It's going to be a pink pony theme. Won't that be adorable?"

"They aren't fish. Dolphins and whales are mammals."

"Oh. Okay, I guess I knew that."

"Mammals breathe air, fish breathe water. Mammals nurse their young and almost always bear live offspring. Fish lay eggs and move on."

"Well thanks for the science lesson, Mister Brainiac." Eileen pokes his shoulder. "Tonight, you can give me a class on human anatomy."

Jules grins. "That's my favorite subject."

Several hours later, Eileen is asleep with her head on Jules' chest. He relishes the weight of her body pressing on his, the touch of her skin. By the moonlight seeping into the room, he takes in her beauty: brown-black hair falling over a bare shoulder, full lips slightly parted, lush eyebrows relaxed. Her breathing is soft and slow. If only she could be this quiet more often. He shouldn't complain, she loves him and is good to him. His family likes her, and she likes them. So what if she talks a lot?

Uncle Jack does not talk a lot, but his words carry weight. He told Jules to love whoever he wants, because life is too short not to. Jack must have been speaking from experience. Who was this woman, and why couldn't he be with her? Maybe she wasn't Jewish, and his family intervened. Whatever happened, Jack is now an old bachelor with regrets, lonely and ... unfulfilled. What if Jules ends up like that?

Now he is wide awake. He gently slips out from under Eileen. She sighs, then nestles into the pillow without waking. Jules heads to the sofa with a book, fidgets to find a comfortable reading position, gives up and tries pacing around the living room. Finally, he gets dressed and steals out the door into the warm, humid air that blankets Miami. Except for his own soft footsteps, the night is silent and still.

He walks through the apartment complex and follows a sidewalk into the local neighborhood of one-story bungalows with small front lawns and scattered palm trees. The moon casts a soft glow. The houses are mostly dark, though Jules ambles past a few with lamplight leaking from the edges of drawn shades. At one house the front window is open wide. The spectral blue-white luminescence of a television pours into the yard. He pauses half a step; no one is in the room.

In the next block a lone mockingbird sings plaintive notes while perched on a palm. Is it calling for a lost mate? Or one yet to be found? Its song could belong to Uncle Max, still hopeful for a woman despite – or maybe due to – his addled brain.

Jules turns a corner and a large black and white cat bounces towards him with an inquiring mew. He squats down and the cat rubs against his offered hand, purring. "Hey kitty, what's your name?"

"His name's Oreo but I'm thinking of changing it to Leonard." Jules stands up, startled by the gravelly voice coming from a nearby stoop, where a man sits with a lit cigarette. "Much more dignified, you know? Naming him Oreo was my girlfriend's idea. She had him before we met, but she's gone and left me with the cat so I figure I can name it whatever I want."

"Uh ... Leonard's a good name. Like Leonard Nimoy?"

"What, who's that? No, Lynyrd like Lynyrd Skynyrd. Keep on rockin', I always say." The man reaches into a small cooler next to him and pulls out a can of beer. "You want one?"

"No thanks." Jules is not about to ingest something offered by a stranger, though the guy seems friendly enough.

"Suit yourself. My name's Lee, by the way."

"I'm Jules. Good to meet you."

"Likewise. So yeah, my girlfriend moved back to her family in New Jersey. She finally decided she'd had enough of me. My own fault, honestly. I was cheating on her, and she knew it. I promised to stop but I didn't." He pops open the can and takes a long swig. "She was good to me, too. I guess I'm an idiot, but I don't know, she wasn't very smart, and it bugged me that she didn't understand me. Not that I'm the brightest bulb in the boat. Anyway, I can't blame her."

"How long were you together?"

"Let me think…. We met at a New Year's party to start 1977 and she left last March, so …" he counts on his fingers, "that would be four years, a little more I guess. Now I'm thirty-eight years old, living alone except for a cat named after a cookie. Who'd have thought?"

Lee pulls a deep draw from the cigarette as if he was smoking a joint.

"Well, Lynyrd is a great name."

"Yeah. And what the hell, there's always more fish in the sea. Ain't that right, buddy?"

"Definitely." Jules wants to get back to Eileen "Well, I'll catch you later."

"Yeah, okay. Hey, you live around here?"

"A few blocks away."

"Come over anytime, if you want a beer or whatever."

"Okay, thanks. Bye."

"Keep it real, amigo."

Jules turns back towards home. His pace is brisk now that he has a destination. Eileen is in his bed at this moment and will welcome him when he cuddles up. He transitions into an easy jog. More fish in the sea, ha! Jules pictures the actual fish he saw while snorkeling, then recalls Max's vision of his brothers as dolphins, right out of Jules' own dream. How could such an image have come to Max?

Jules' right foot suddenly gets caught, losing purchase. His body falls forward with momentum and lands hard on the concrete. He struggles to regain his breath and sit up, then takes stock. Instinct raised his hands to absorb most of the impact, yet his forehead hit the sidewalk hard enough to hurt. His palms are scraped and painful. His forehead is bleeding. He presses on the cut with two fingers, gets to his feet and takes a few tentative steps. He glances back at the sidewalk; he tripped on a bulge in the concrete. Jules curses himself for not paying attention to where he's going.

By the time he gets home, his forehead is no longer bleeding, just sore to the touch. Jules cleans himself up in the bathroom, bandages the wound, swallows two ibuprofen tablets, undresses, and slips into bed without waking Eileen. He gently spoons against her back, relieved to be safe and sound. She exhales a soft moan – such a sweet statement – then resumes her steady breathing.

Hours later, his eyelids are twitching in REM sleep. A mockingbird sings a lyrical message Jules strains to understand. He cannot make out the words because Eileen is chattering about a pink pony party for their daughter. What? When did they have a baby? Then Izzy appears as a young man with a dark moustache, wagging his finger at Jules and saying, "You messed up, Max. Now you got to pay, big time. I tried to tell you. You can't trust a pretty face." Jack is there too, not scolding but resigned to what must happen. Jules tries to protest that he is not Max, he is Jules, but the words are stuck in his throat – he can only emit breathy gulping sounds.

The next morning Eileen shakes Jules awake, inspecting the bandage and nasty knot on his forehead. "Did you fall out of bed and hit your head?" He tells her what happened. "Jules, you could have been seriously hurt. That's crazy, wandering around the streets in the dead of night. Why in the world did you do that?"

"I was thinking about my great uncles, and I couldn't sleep. Then later when I finally slept, I had a disturbing dream about them."

"They are disturbing."

"That's not what I mean. Anyway, it's no big deal."

"It is a big deal, walking alone in the dark, when all kinds of bad things can happen. I'm worried. What's going on with you?"

"Nothing's going on. I just couldn't sleep. Listen, let's have a nice breakfast before our day at the Seaquarium. I'll run out for bagels while you do your makeup and stuff."

Richard and Deborah arrive just after Jules returns. He welcomes them in with hugs. "I'm so happy you guys are joining us. I've been looking forward to this ever since Richard and I went snorkeling." Then to Deborah, "On the way back two dolphins followed the boat. They were leaping into the air, so carefree and beautiful."

A few minutes later they're on their way, munching on bagels in Jules' car. From the backseat Deborah asks, "So those two dolphins you saw, were they a boy and a girl dolphin?"

Richard giggles. "Definitely. What a *shmeckel* on that guy, big as a donkey's flopping around. You know when dolphins have sex, they do it underwater, so they hold their breath the entire time. Deb, remember last night? I had to come up for air."

Deborah does not miss a beat. "Oh honey, you were working so hard, you needed oxygen."

Jules seizes the opportunity. "Is it hard work, Richard?"

"Well, it's my husbandly duty. The Bible says I have to spread my seed."

"Oh honey, you're so seedsy."

Eileen groans. "Eww."

Jules catches them kissing in his rearview mirror. "Hey, don't be using my back seat for immoral porpoises."

Richard grins. "Oh my Cod! You're being so shellfish."

"What did you say? I'm not herring you."

Eileen breaks in. "Stop it, you two. You're giving me such a haddock."

Jules reaches out for Eileen's hand and squeezes it. "That's my girlfriend!" Eileen beams ear-to-ear.

The Seaquarium grounds emanate an amusement park vibe, congested with families and groups of teenagers. People swarm at booths selling miniature plastic sea creatures and shaved ice. The icy treat looks good to Jules – the heat and the crowd are stifling – but the waiting line is too long.

The foursome works their way to the dolphin tank and find a viewing window. Three dolphins are swimming in broad circles along the tank perimeter. As they pass the window, one gazes right at Jules. Though the tank is enormous, it binds the dolphins within walls of concrete, bounding a course that loops back on itself. The wound on Jules' forehead throbs.

Eileen, Richard, and Deborah stop to use a restroom. Jules waits outside, studying an exhibit on environmental threats to dolphins and other sea life. He learns that most tuna are caught with nets that ensnare dolphins, which often swim with the tuna schools. The netted dolphins drown to death. Under the heading *Things You Can Do to Help*, the exhibit encourages boycotting tuna until fishing practices change.

His friends return and a public address system announces the show will soon start in the main arena. Richard leads the way as they join a current of people. They find their seats up front on the second row. The air is hot and still with the south Florida sun beating down on the audience. People fan themselves with the park brochure.

An usher warns the first few rows that they'll get wet during the show. "If that's not what you want, now is the time to move into the back rows. We'll help you find a new seat."

Deborah frowns and turns to Richard. "I just straightened my hair."

Eileen calls to the usher. "Does the water smell fishy?"

"No ma'am, we keep the tanks very clean."

Jules knows this is not the time to remind Eileen they are mammals, not fish. "I paid extra for these tickets so we could get the best view." He turns to Richard for help.

"It's so hot and I'm sweating like a dog," says Richard. "A little splash will feel great. I doubt we'll get that wet."

"Dogs don't sweat, they pant." Jules is happy to change the subject.

Richard extends his tongue and mimics a heavy pant. "Arf." He licks Deborah on the neck.

"Richard, stop!" she squeals, giggling. "Down, boy." Richard whines and holds up limp wrists for paws.

The show begins. The announcer introduces the three dolphins as Huey, Dewey, and Louie. They do all sorts of stunts: wagging their heads as if nodding yes to questions, clicking and whistling, jumping in coordinated acrobatics. The crowd laughs and claps its approval, but Jules is uneasy. He loves watching the dolphins move, so speedy and sleek and graceful, yet this is a performance motivated by food rewards. These extraordinary creatures have been trained to do tricks as if they're circus dogs.

The announcer bids goodbye to the dolphins and then booms in a baritone voice, "Ladies and gentlemen, boys and girls, it's time for the star of our show! He's an Orca whale, weighing in at nine thousand pounds, more than the average elephant. He's a BIG BOY. Introducing ... BUBBA!"

On cue, the Orca emerges straight up out of the water to grab a ten-pound fish snack. He is impossibly large, an enormous black and white beast. His fall back into the water creates not a splash, but a tidal wave that soaks the first few rows of spectators. The water is shockingly cold, triggering screams and cackles all around Jules. He's relieved Eileen is laughing with Deborah.

Leaving the arena afterwards, Richard and the girls are ebullient, giggling about getting soaked. Jules tries to join the fun but keeps seeing the dolphin eyeing him through the viewing window.

Their clothes are nearly dry by the time they get to the car. On the way home, they stop at Wolfie's delicatessen for a late lunch. While Richard and Deborah are in the restrooms, Eileen and Jules munch on dill pickles and peruse the menu.

"I think I'll have the tuna sandwich," says Eileen.

"I read at the Seaquarium that tuna fishermen use nets that drown dolphins. One thing we can do to help is stop eating tuna."

Eileen frowns. "But we love tuna fish. You know tuna salad is one of my favorites."

She always shoots down his ideas. Why can't she be more open minded? "Well, I'm not eating tuna anymore. I didn't know better but now I do. I'm not going to eat things that kill dolphins."

"Jeez, aren't you holy?"

Jules raises his voice. "Dolphins are dying because we want to eat tuna. I'm not going to be a part of that. Think of those beautiful animals we just saw. We all have a responsibility to do what we can."

"Okay, if you don't want me to enjoy one of my favorite foods, I'll get a grilled cheese. Unless that hurts dolphins."

"You know what, eat what you want. I don't care."

"Fine."

They sit in silence until Richard and Deborah return. When the waitress comes, Jules asks for an egg salad sandwich on rye. Shooting Jules a glare, Eileen says, "I'll have the same, unless it hurts chickens."

The waitress hesitates, confused. "Uh, I don't think so."

"Never mind," says Eileen. "Inside joke."

"Not funny," mumbles Jules.

Chapter 10
Brooklyn 1921

IT'S A SLOW day at the lumberyard, the perfect time for Max to approach Izzy with the plan he and Ida developed. He silently practices his side of the conversation with Izzy. Ida has a cousin, Harvey Kaplan, who works at a construction company called Sokolov Homes. They're building lots of houses in East New York, and they need a salesman, somebody good with people. That's a perfect job for Max and it will be a good way to get more money into the family – the job comes with a big bump in pay. It won't hurt the lumberyard business, which is doing great and can keep going strong now without Max. Plus, The Brothers Isaacson might get a big new customer out of it.

Max expects his brother will hate the idea of him going to work elsewhere, but Max will keep at him, help him realize it's a good money-making idea for all of us. Then when everything works out, Izzy will soften his attitude towards Ida, and see that she is good for Max and good for the family.

He's ready for the face-to-face with Izzy. He won't let a negative reaction discourage him, even if Izzy starts yelling. Max knocks sharply on the office door.

"What is it?" calls Izzy.

"I've got an idea for you." Max opens the door, strides through, then recites his speech without a pause. Izzy frowns but doesn't interrupt. When Max is done, he adds, "Now Izzy, I know this is a lot, and it's sudden, and me going to work somewhere else might seem disloyal, but it's not. It's more money for all of us, so mull it over and don't say no right away. Okay?"

Izzy scowls at Max, who refuses to show fear. He stares back at his older brother. Finally, Izzy speaks, "Okay Max. I'll think about it. Now leave me alone so I can finish working on these invoices."

Max goes back to the sales floor triumphant. That went as well as he hoped. Once he starts working for Ida's cousin, Izzy will realize she's an asset. Max and Ida will get married, they'll have sex every night, he'll have a great job, and the whole family will be happy.

Izzy helps his mother into the apartment and eases her into the living room chair. He's worried. The doctor said she might have pneumonia. Her coughing lately has been awful, and she's not eating enough. He hates watching her suffer, hates that there's little he can do to stop it. In the meantime, he needs to get going for his appointment with Lewis. Izzy arranged for them to meet at Gurewitz Deli, away from Jack and Max at the lumberyard.

Davey emerges from the kitchen. "What did the doctor say?"

"It might be pneumonia. The best medicine is rest." Izzy turns towards her. "Okay, ma? You need to rest. Let us do for you." He helps Jennie put her feet up onto a stool and wraps a blanket around her legs. "How's that, ma?"

"Such wonderful sons I have, caring for your poor mother. But don't worry, I'm fine. The cough is almost gone."

"It was pretty bad for a while," says Davey. "Did you sleep better last night?"

"Yes, but I'm still a little tired. Tomorrow I'll be back to normal, God willing, and I'll take over again in the kitchen."

"Don't worry, I'll take care of the kitchen until you're better."

Izzy says to Davey, "Bring her a cup of hot tea with honey, and something to eat. Ma, how about if Davey heats up soup, puts in saltines?"

"No, *bubbellah*, nothing for me. I'm fine. You go rest."

Davey reaches behind his back to retie his apron. "I made strawberry Jell-O last night. Can I fix you a bowl?"

"So, I'll eat a little Jell-O." She pats him on the cheek. "Such a sweet boy, my Davey. One day we'll find you a nice girl, not like that one chasing poor Maxie. I just want all my children to be happy." Her gaze alternates between her two sons. "I'm so proud of you boys, my oldest as head of the family taking care of us, my youngest making meals and singing in the choir at *shul* on Friday nights. And last time, a solo no less. After the service the cantor said to me that he never saw such progress in a young singer."

"Ma, after you eat the Jell-O, I'll start on chicken soup for dinner. That will be good for you." Davey pulls a worn sheet of paper from his apron pocket. He glances at it, turns to Izzy. "We have all the ingredients here, except for carrots. Can you grab two bunches on your way home later?"

"Sure." Izzy kneels beside his mother, brings her hand to his mouth for a kiss. She beams at him. He makes her take two aspirin and a tablespoon of cough syrup, then heads out to meet Lewis.

Lewis is waiting for him at their usual table inside the deli. Izzy shakes out his raincoat, leaves it on the rack inside the front door. He barely noticed the rain during his walk from home – he's been mulling over how to get Ida out of his hair once and for all.

After brief small talk, Izzy says, "I got two things to talk with you about. First, I got a new idea for a side business for you and me. We can make good money, all legit. It will be good for Joey too." Izzy lays out his proposal to start a house painting company, with Joey as the crew overseer. He gives Lewis all the information he has gleaned on market demand, potential competitors, expenses, and projected profits.

Lewis nods, smiling. "I like it. I need to check with The Brain – I doubt he'll have any issue with me doing a side business, but we need to stay above board. In the meantime, you put together an estimate of how much we need to get started. Instead of using our savings, we can get a low-interest loan from Bennie."

"Will do."

"You said there's a second thing to talk about. What's up?"

"This one's personal. The girl Ida that Max is running with, the one I told you about. He thinks he's in love, but what he really loves is that thing between her legs. What she wants is his money. Our money. She's sticking her nose in my business, trying to get Max a job working for her cousin." Saying this aloud has Izzy fuming again. He's been aggravated over Ida since Max described her scheme. Plus, she might have studied his accounting books enough to realize that he keeps two sets. If she figures things out and spills the beans, it will ruin everything. "I can't figure out how to put an end to this. Any ideas?"

"I heard about your problem from Joey. So how's this for a plan? I'll pay her a visit with Joe and Sam. Tell her she needs to break it off for good with Max by telling him she's fallen for another guy. If she doesn't do that, we'll break her legs. Not that we're actually going to hurt her, of course, we'll just scare her really good. And I'll tell her she can't say anything to Max about me or you being part of this. She's got to say it's all because she loves somebody else."

Izzy winces. "When she breaks up with Max he's going to be hurt."

"Yeah, and that's too bad, but it's for his own good," says Lewis. "Pain today, gain tomorrow. Like an investment."

"I guess that's right. He'll get over it. Women love him – he won't have trouble finding a nice girl who will be good for him in the long run, a good wife he can count on."

"It's a good plan, Izzy. I'll have a talk with her in the next few days. I should threaten to hurt her family too." Lewis snickers. "This will be fun. I'll even threaten to hurt Max. Then I'll give her money to seal the deal."

Izzy lets out a sigh, shakes hands with his long-time mentor. "Thanks Lewis. I owe you one, big time."

"Nah, you do plenty for me *boychik*. Just keep The Brothers Isaacson rolling, not to mention this painting company idea of yours, and we're all happy."

On Saturday evening Jack sits on the living room couch, reading *Tarzan of the Apes*. Once a helpless orphan of English parents, Tarzan is a young man who knows nothing of human ways. Though his ape mother loves him, the ape community ridicules him and calls him Tarzan, which means 'white skin'. Jack sets the book on his lap and closes his eyes. Tarzan lives in a place where he's different than everybody, not only in the way he looks but also on the inside, the way he thinks and the way he navigates the jungle world. He will never fit in, despite his attempts to act like the other apes.

Jack pretends to be asleep, lest his mother or Davey ask him again what's wrong. It's been three months since the kiss with Howard, three months of refusing the person he loves, three months of confusion and anger and self-loathing. Jack strives to hide his inner turmoil, but it seeps through his mask. The other day, Max asked him why he's so sad lately. Jack denied it, said he's fine, but Max kept trying to cheer him up. Jack played along, though he suspects he's not fooling anyone.

The front door bursts open and Max stumbles into the apartment. Jennie startles from her knitting. "Hello darling. How was the picture show?"

Max starts to speak, then breaks down in tears and collapses onto the floor. Jack rushes to him, kneels besides his brother. Peering into Max's face, a stabbing pain arises in Jack's chest. It must be Ida – nothing else could affect Max this deeply. "Max, what happened? Speak to me."

Max shakes his head, gasps for breath between sobs. Jennie joins her two sons on the floor and puts her arms around Max, rocking him gently back and forth. Izzy and Davey come in from their bedrooms.

Izzy kneels next to Jennie. "It's that Ida, isn't it?"

Max nods his head. "She dumped me."

Jennie is confused. "Dumped you? What does that mean?" She looks at Izzy.

"It means she broke it off with him, she doesn't want him anymore, left him for some other fella."

"That tramp! I knew she was a good-for-nothing."

"Max didn't say there's another guy," Jack mutters, eyeing the subtle smirk on Izzy's face.

Max is breathing now. "There is ... another guy. She's in love with someone else. I can't believe it." He wipes tears from his cheeks. "I love her. I trusted her. I don't get it. We were so happy together."

Jennie releases her embrace, holds Max by the shoulders. "Don't you worry darling, we'll find you a nice girl. One who treats you right."

"I don't care about that. I'm done with girls. Izzy was right, you can't trust them."

Jack shudders. He knows how it hurts to be denied in true love, and this was true love. Ida has her flaws, but Jack is certain that her attraction to Max has been sincere. Her dumping him makes no sense. He studies Izzy's face, finds no compassion there, only ... vindication. "Izzy, come with me for a minute."

Jack leads his older brother into a back bedroom, then shuts the door. Keeping his voice down to contain his anger. "What did you do?"

"What do you mean?"

"You know what I mean. How did you get Ida to break it off with Max?"

"Are you crazy? I haven't said a word to her." Izzy is indignant, his voice rising, but Jack's not buying Izzy's denial. Not only is Jack sure about Ida's love for Max, he also knows the depth of Izzy's disapproval and his compulsion to control his brothers' lives.

"Then why did she do it?"

"Who knows why that kind of girl does anything? She's a floozy, no good for Max." He slaps his hand in the air, palm down. "Good riddance."

"They're in love with each other."

"Love? What do you know about love?"

Jack starts to respond but there is nothing he can say. Izzy continues, "Max wants sex, and he thinks he's in love. That's not love. Love is taking care of your family, making sure we survive, looking out for each other."

Jack seethes. "You ... you can't decide everybody's life for them!"

"I can, and I will, because I know what's best. Period." Izzy storms out, leaving Jack exasperated and alone. His outrage drains away, revealing the grief that lies underneath. He grieves for Max and for himself and for the loss of cherished love, stolen away. The pain is worse to think that, in Max's case, it might be their own brother doing the stealing. Jack can't be sure of that – he can't prove it – but his instincts point to Izzy. The same Izzy who denied Jack a career in fabrics and clothing, arrogant to think he's taking care of his younger brothers who don't know what's good for them. Jack's anger flares with frustration that he can't blame Izzy entirely for his loss of Howard. Jack and Howard are doomed, not only by Jack's family, but by a world that forbids their kind of love.

Chapter 11
May 1981

JACK WAITS FOR Jules to walk around the car to the passenger door – he can no longer get out on his own. Looking away, Jack allows Jules to lift him into a standing position. He then uses a four-post walker to shuffle to the nearest bench, while the boy lightly holds his upper arm.

This is their third visit to Bryan Park in the past six weeks, since Jack committed to tell Jules the story of his life and that of his brothers. During his first attempt, after Jack received the death sentence from his doctor, he realized that the storytelling would never work at the house, where it was impossible to be out of his brothers' earshot for more than five minutes. Now he tells them he leaves with Jules for a bit of fresh air.

Jack takes a deep breath. The air carries the scent of freshly mown grass and flourishing magnolia trees. Children scamper around a playground, their parents chatting nearby while keeping an eye. These children will be around for years to come, long after Jack is gone. He remembers kids from his own childhood days – now they're as old as him. Or dead.

"So where did we leave off?" Jack asks.

"You told me about the Olympic movie theater, your friend Howard inviting you to work again at the clothing store, and Max meeting Ida at a dance." Hearing his memories vocalized by his great nephew gives them life outside of himself, a power of their own. The time has come to talk about Howard. He hopes that Jules, being part of the young generation, will hear him without the condemnation and ridicule that Jack has feared for sixty years.

Jack read the newspapers about Harvey Milk in San Francisco, the brave leader – now dead three years – who encouraged homosexual men to stop hiding and tell others the truth about themselves. Jack was startled by that message, and by Milk's unabashed public stance. Does that only work in California? Are all young people truly more accepting? Jack gathers his courage.

But Jules has more to say. "You told me you said no to Howard because you had to stay with Izzy and the family business. You loved fabrics and dress design, but you did what you had to do and walked away from a career in clothing. Are you sorry that you did that?"

"More than sorry. I might have had a life doing what I love. I thought I didn't have a choice. Now looking back, I realize that wasn't true. I had a choice, but nobody to help me see that. And Jules, it wasn't only a career that I turned away from."

"What do you mean?"

Jack focuses on the magnolia trees. "Well, my friend Howard...."

Jules is quiet.

"Do you understand what I'm telling you?"

"You told me I should love who I want to love, not who other people think I should. At first I thought you were once in love with a non-Jewish girl, but the last time you described Howard I started to understand. He was the one you loved, wasn't he?"

Jack nods his head. He sniffles, wipes his nose with the back of his hand. If he had had more courage back then, he and Howard might have spent their lives together. Instead he chose a life that never expressed the truth of who he is. "I was afraid. If anyone found out, we would have become outcasts, even to our families. Howard wanted to take that risk, thinking we could keep it secret. But I couldn't do it. It's not like today, where people are talking gay this and gay that."

"I understand, Uncle Jack. I'm so sorry that you couldn't be with him."

"Howard was my one true love." Jack's voice breaks. He pulls out a yellowed handkerchief from his pants pocket and blows his nose into it. "You're the only person I have ever said this to. In sixty years. Now I won't be taking it as a secret to my grave. Thank you."

Jules casts his eyes towards the ground.

A heaviness lifts from Jack's body. There was no hint of judgment or rebuke from the boy, only compassion. Tension releases from his shoulders. No more hiding, no more pretending, at least when he's with his great nephew. Jack drops his face into his hands, relieved that no one besides Jules sees him weeping.

———

Back at the house, Jules is surprised by two visitors sitting with Izzy, Max, and Davey. He recognizes Clare Cohen, his uncles' next-door neighbor. The young woman with the prominent nose and high cheekbones must be her daughter Miriam, home from graduate school in California. Clare had described her as smart and practical. That fits. Her thick brown hair is tied back into a ponytail, and she wears no makeup.

"Hello, Uncle Jack," says Clare. "Miriam is back from school for the summer. I brought her over to visit."

Jack leans on his walker. "That's nice, honey. Sorry I can't talk. I need to go lie down."

Jules helps Jack to his bedroom. When he returns, Clare gets up to give Jules a hug. "It's nice to see you again, Jules," she says. "Your great uncles have told me how much work you've been doing around the house, and the yard looks great. This is Miriam, who I told you about."

Jules glances at her again and she smiles.

"I hope my mother didn't say embarrassing things about me."

"Just how smart you are." That was a dumb thing to say. How to recover? "I hear you're in California for graduate school. How do you like it?"

Izzy interrupts, frowning. "Why did you have to go so far away? What the hell is in California anyway? A bunch of hippies and queers. That's why Ronald Reagan is president. Those hippies didn't want him in California anymore."

No wonder Jack has never come out to his brothers. Jules wants to defend gay people to Izzy, but he freezes, afraid of an argument. His silence is embarrassing in front of

Miriam. She speaks up, in a cheerful tone. "I've met lots of wonderful people in California, Uncle Izzy. And, you know, gay people are everywhere."

Before Izzy can respond, Clare says, "I have an idea. Why don't you all come over for lunch? I'll make egg salad sandwiches. I already have the egg salad."

"Nah, we already ate," says Izzy.

"Maybe ... *ulp* Jules wants to go," says Davey. "Did you get ... *ulp* lunch, Jules?"

"No, but ...."

"Yes, come on Jules," says Clare. "I insist."

Jules follows Clare and Miriam into their house, which is clean and bright, with oak floors, colorful area rugs, and a white sectional sofa with fluffy cushions. It's another world from his uncles' dreary old house. When Clare goes into the kitchen, leaving Jules with Miriam at the glass-topped dining table, he says, "My mother told me how kind you and your mom are to my great uncles. Thank you for that. They're an odd bunch and they need help."

"They weren't always like this, though they were always a bit ... eccentric. I have fond memories of them from my childhood – they were my family next door. Especially Uncle Max, he was always bringing me little gifts, taking me places, and generally doting on me. Let me show you something." Miriam walks across the room and comes back with a framed black-and-white photograph. "Here I am with my mother and grandmother and the four of them."

She's a toddler in the photo. "Wow, they're dressed normally, and everyone is smiling, even Uncle Izzy. All four of them look so ... healthy."

Clare returns with lunch, pushing heaps of delicious potato salad and sauteed spinach on Jules to go with his sandwich. As they finish eating, the phone rings and Clare returns to the kitchen to answer it.

"It's nice that you spend time with Jack," says Miriam. "Before you arrived, Izzy was telling us they have four burial plots next to their mother at the Mount Nebo cemetery. That's Mount Nebo from the Old Testament, so it got me thinking about Moses."

Uh-oh, she's a religious Jew. Jules braces himself for a lecture. "Mount what?"

"Nebo is the mountain that Moses climbed at the end of his life to look out over the Promised Land. Pretty good name for a cemetery. Anyway, you probably know the story, how God forbid Moses to enter the Promised Land. Poor old Moses had no choice in the matter, in fact his entire life was about doing whatever God commanded. But I think we have all kinds of choices in life. What do you think?"

"Uh, I guess." He pushes his plate away. How can he get out of here gracefully?

"No, seriously. I'm curious."

"About me?" Wow, this girl is direct.

"About what's important to you." Miriam takes a sip of water. "Though honestly, it's for my own growth. The more I talk with people, the better I understand myself, but I can come on too strong, and not everyone is comfortable with me. I hope you don't mind me asking you questions."

Her sincerity is disarming. Jules lowers his hackles. "No, it's okay. So, your question… I'm not much into Judaism, at least not the religious parts. For me, it's the culture. I like

Jewish humor, Jewish food, Jewish sensibilities. I was raised in a Jewish community, went to Jewish summer camp, and all that stuff. Is that how it was for you?"

"Pretty much, but now I'm ready to explore whatever meaning I can find in the more spiritual parts of Judaism. I'm also interested in Buddhism."

A Buddhist Jew? "What do you mean spiritual parts of Judaism?"

"The places where we can connect directly with God, whatever God is. Without all the mumbo jumbo that absorbs so much attention in mainstream Judaism."

Jules loosens another notch. "So, you don't sit in the dark on Saturday because you forgot to the leave the lights on Friday afternoon?"

She rolls her eyes. "Or obsess over which fork touched a piece of chicken or a slice of cheese."

"Or recite rote passages in an ancient language that might have held meaning a thousand years ago?"

"Yes, back to meaning. If it's not ritual, what is important to you? Belief?"

Jules sits back, rubs an earlobe with his thumb. "Actions. What we do in life."

"Okay. You mean right and wrong?"

"Not exactly. When I was a kid, I thought God was always judging me, waiting for me to do something wrong so he could punish me. I left that behind years ago. Trying to make God happy by doing what we think he wants, which is impossible to know anyway, can't be what makes life meaningful. When I say actions, I mean being kind and responsible. Following through on commitments. Self-control."

"So, you're in control? You like to control everything?"

"Well, not everything." Boy, is she intense.

"Have you ever heard of Kabbalah?"

What now? "No."

"It's the mystical branch of Judaism. Been around a long time, but they never teach it in synagogues. It's a practice that encourages direct experience, such as meditation, to open your mind to God or whatever you want to call the essence of the universe."

"Meditation? As in Buddhism?"

"Exactly!" She does a small bounce in her chair, beams at Jules. "I was introduced to Kabbalah a few months ago at a Buddhist group in Santa Cruz. Knowing that I would be in Miami this summer, the teacher put me in touch with a rabbi here that does Kabbalah. I'm going to his class on Sunday. Would you like to come with me?"

"I don't know. I'm not into far out stuff."

"Oh, c'mon, give it a try. What have you got to lose? It's just one evening." She pokes his forearm playfully. "It might be fun. Think of it as an adventure."

She's so enthusiastic. Maybe it will be fun, or at least interesting. "Alright. I'll go."

"Yay!" Miriam claps her hands like a little girl. It's an endearing gesture.

"I'll drive. What time should I be here to pick you up?"

"Class is at seven, so be here at six-thirty."

"Okay, see you then." He stands up and Miriam walks him to the door.

"I'm going back over to my uncles' house. I'll try to convince them to let me paint the exterior." He steps onto the porch and glances back at her.

"Good luck." She smiles warmly and waves.

The next morning Jules is waiting in Arnie's office for a planned phone call with Sydney. He hopes Sydney is pleased with their performance and will approve hiring more accountants, so Jules can finally get his weekends back. The phone rings right on time. Arnie puts it on speaker. "Hello."

"Hey Arnie. Is Jules with you?"

Jules speaks up. "Yes, I'm here. How are you, Sydney?"

"I'm great, thanks to you two. I'm reading the quarterly report for your office. Billable hours are up 45 percent, and net income is up 35 percent. I knew that getting the firm into Miami was a good idea but didn't expect us to do so well so quickly. Way to go, guys!" Arnie grins at Jules, shoots him a silent thumbs up. Jules relishes the moment – all that work has paid off.

Sydney chatters away. "If you keep this up, you'll both get a nice end-of-year bonus. In the meantime, I'm giving you each a company car. Two Chrysler Lebarons, brand new. I got them from Al Jones – you know, our client Big Al who owns four dealerships here. He's going to ship them to you. The firm will cover the insurance, gas, the works. You like black? Yeah, black is a professional color. Now when you're visiting potential clients, they'll know that you're successful accounttants working at a successful firm. And Jules, you won't have to drive that old beater of yours anymore. Pretty great, huh?"

"What about Marty?" asks Jules.

Sydney's ebullience fades. "Who?"

"Marty Spiegelman, one of the Schlesinger guys. He's been here forever, and he works on the Perlman accounts with us. If I get a company car, at my age, he's going to feel slighted."

"Don't worry about that, Jules. He doesn't have to know the car you're driving isn't owned by you." Arnie shakes his head at Jules, scribbles a note to Jules: *He's rewarding you. Say thank you!*

"This is really generous of you, Sydney. I thought a company car was for older accountants. I never imagined I might get one. Thank you." Jules pictures himself driving a boxy black car that's made for the Bob Hope crowd – he might as well wear an ill-fitting suit. He loves his stylish, baby blue Mustang, but he can't turn down a gift from Sydney. He'll have to use the company car for commuting, then drive the Mustang for nights and weekends.

"Well, you're special, Jules. Isn't that right, Arnie?"

"Absolutely. And Sydney, this old accountant is honored. Thank you."

"You're welcome. Now I know you two have been working your asses off, and with these numbers we can think about hiring a junior accountant. Maybe two."

Finally, Jules will get help with the workload.

"I'll tell you what. If you can add two more business clients, we'll increase your budget. Deal?"

Arnie responds. "Deal. We'll make that happen."

Jules' relief evaporates. He must work harder to work less.

Early Sunday evening Jules parks in front of Miriam's house. He contemplates the Kabbalah session with mixed feelings. It involves a rabbi, and all the rabbis Jules knew in his childhood were severe, disapproving of Jules for obscure reasons and instilling an amorphous guilt. On the other hand, Miriam's enthusiasm over exploring a growth opportunity is inspiring.

She answers the doorbell wearing a peasant skirt, a batik blouse, and a long necklace with colored stones. Her wavy brown hair is loose and thick on her shoulders, framing her dark brown eyes. Is this the same girl he lunched with on Tuesday? He opens his mouth but can't get any words out. A compliment might make this into a date, and he's not unfaithful to Eileen.

"You okay?" she asks.

"Uh … yes, fine. Should we go?" This is not a date. Miriam is a family friend, and they're going to a religious event with a rabbi. Eileen would have no problem with this. She shouldn't anyway.

Miriam turns into the house. "Mom, we're leaving!"

"Okay, honey. Have a good time!"

They walk to the car. "Wow, an old Mustang. I love the color. Is that called baby blue?"

"Yep. I bought this car used when I was sixteen. One of the happiest days of my teenage life." They get in and Jules starts the engine.

"And now you're what, twenty-four?"

"Twenty-three."

"One year older than me."

"But you're way smarter."

"Ha! What makes you say that?"

"I don't know anyone else who's into Buddhism. That's pretty advanced." Over the past few days, Jules has pondered how Buddhism and Judaism could overlap. "Plus, you're in graduate school. What are you studying?"

"Environmental biology."

"Is that the same as ecology?" Jules pulls onto a boulevard lined with palm trees. In the center median are azalea bushes, flowering in splashes of pink and crimson.

"It includes ecology but is broader. Ecology is about the interrelations between organisms and their surroundings. Environmental biology also covers human impacts on natural systems. I'm thinking of a PhD dissertation topic in ecology, maybe on symbiotic species."

"Like flowers and hummingbirds?"

"Exactly. That's an important relationship and it takes so many different forms."

"Like the shape of a certain flower matches the anatomy of a specific bird species?"

"And you say I'm smart."

"What is it about ecology that interests you enough to go for a PhD?"

"The basic idea that everything is connected to everything else. It's a giant web of interaction and mutuality."

"Wow." Jules envisions the shimmering underwater net made by the sunlight when he was snorkeling. "Do you think people are part of that web?"

"Absolutely. We all affect each other. We're all connected, but usually in ways that are unknowable to us."

They are quiet for a few minutes. In the setting sun, the boulevard palm trees are casting long shadows across the road, as if Jules is passing ancestral ghosts standing guard. "It's interesting to consider how you and I are connected," he says. I mean, we haven't met until this week, but you grew up with my mother's uncles. They took care of you and your mom, and earlier in their life they helped my grandmother, who was raising my mother and her sisters by herself."

"Hmm. What does that mean for you and me?"

"I don't know, but it means something. Like you said, the web of connections can be unknowable."

Miriam stares at Jules. "You're going to appreciate Rabbi Michael."

"He's an eco-rabbi?"

"Definitely." She smiles at him.

A pang of guilt grips Jules. Eileen would not be okay with this. If she was here, the three of them would not be having this conversation. Actually, if Eileen was in Miami, Jules would not be spending time with Miriam at all.

Twenty minutes later Jules is sitting cross-legged on a floor cushion in a circle comprised of Miriam, Rabbi Michael Fine, and nine other people. The group is meeting at the home of Sophie and Jerome Fleishman, a middle-aged couple who appear to have just returned from a Woodstock reunion. Jerome is wearing a tie-dye yarmulke that matches his T-shirt, and Sophie's long gray hair is braided with blue threads. The room fits their hippie vibe, with its psychedelic artwork, jumbled bookshelves, and world peace knickknacks.

In contrast, the rabbi is dressed in slacks and a buttoned shirt and wears the classic rabbinical beard, full and dark. Everyone calls him Rabbi Michael.

He describes one of the many names for God. "This one is very ancient and sounded as 'Yahweh'." He produces a framed plaque which displays the name in bold Hebrew letters:

יהוה

"For those of us who have forgotten or never learned Hebrew, these letters, from right to left, are *yod, hei, vav, hei*. We will use these letters, this name for God, in our meditation."

Jules is dubious. Is this another way to recite old prayers that glorify God as "king of the universe?"

Rabbi Michael speaks in a slow, deliberate rhythm. "Now sit comfortably with your back straight, not slouched, so your breathing channel is fully open. Shoulders relaxed, hands open in your lap. Close your eyes. Pay attention to your breath. Take a slow breath in, then allow a slow breath out. In … out. Deep … slow. Focus on those words as you breathe: 'deep' on the in breath, 'slow' on the out breath. If your mind wanders, gently come back to deep … slow."

Jules attends to his breath and lets himself be guided by Rabbi Michael's voice, starting with an imagined stroll down a dark, pleasant corridor. He encounters the Hebrew letter *yod*, composed of gray granite. He reaches out to touch it and discovers it's vibrating, sending a warm energy up his arm and into his chest. Farther down the corridor, Jules comes across the three other letters in sequence, composed of living plants, clear water, and pure light. He inhales the plants' fragrance, drinks from the water, and holds the light in his hand.

Rabbi Michael's voice invites him to choose one of three doors at the end of the corridor. Jules enters a chamber filled with blue and green swirls, the muted echo of surf underwater, and the smells of seaweed and salt. The moving colors coalesce into shapes of swimming dolphins, encircling him with joy. He is filled with love for the dolphins, who acknowledge him with smiles and squeaks and whistles. He is one of them.

After a period of silence, the rabbi gently brings them out of the meditation. Jules slowly opens his eyes and scans the room as the rabbi suggests they try an interpersonal exercise. He divides them into two groups, then tells group A to position themselves randomly around the room and stand still with eyes closed. Jules is in group B.

"With everyone remaining silent, all of you in group B roam from person to person in group A, touching and stroking each one with loving care on their shoulders, heads, arms, feet. No touching between the neck and knees. Be especially gentle if you feel inspired to touch a face. After a while, we'll switch, and group B will receive from group A. Whether you're giving or receiving, do so with an open heart."

Jules hangs back, watching others in his group touch and caress the receivers. Miriam is in group A, but he first approaches Sophie, the hippie host. She smiles softly with eyes closed, standing still with arms hanging relaxed. Touching this woman, a stranger to Jules, sparks a love for Sophie as if she's his lifelong aunt. Next to her is an older man who Jules pats gently on his shoulders and arms. When he finally reaches Miriam, he touches her face lightly, with a brother's love. Does she know it's him? She at least knows that Jules is one of her 'givers.'

The groups switch and Jules stands still with closed eyes. The anonymous hands touching him are filled with acceptance and affirmation and ... a knowingness. They know him. He wants to cry out his gratitude but remembers to honor the silence. Did he let out a whimper? Tears are seeping from his closed eyelids. The hands tell him it's okay, there's no reason to be embarrassed, we love you just as you are.

Following Rabbi Michael's closing instructions on how best to "return to our day-to-day world," Jules and Miriam maintain silence while walking slowly to the car. Once inside and buckled up, they beam at each other.

"Wow."

"Yeah, that was amazing."

"I'm kind of speechless," says Jules. "But I have so much to say. Where do I start?"

"How about the guided meditation? Anything come up for you?"

"I saw dolphins!"

"I was in a forest filled with baby blue butterflies."

"I can't believe that was a Jewish thing. Religion has always been flat and dry for me. I've never met a rabbi like that, encouraging us to have our own experience."

"Right. Michael is unconventional, but not unique. I'm getting to know cool people in Santa Cruz who are exploring ways to make Judaism a spiritual practice that is personally meaningful. Buddhism too. There's lots of commonality."

"Can we go somewhere to talk for a while? I'm too energized to go home."

"I know a place that makes fresh smoothies and vegetarian sandwiches," says Miriam.

"Sounds perfect."

A few minutes later, Jules parks in front of the Jamaica Juice Joint. They order at the walk-up window, then take their mango smoothies to an outside patio, enclosed by tall shrubs. Jules finds a relatively clean picnic table. He wipes the benches with napkins to make places for them to sit, across from each other. Another couple is sitting at a nearby table. The evening air is warm and humid.

Miriam sips the smoothie. "So, Jules, I haven't heard about your work."

"I'm an accountant. It's kind of embarrassing."

"Why?"

"It's so ... mainstream, especially after tonight."

"That doesn't matter, not if you enjoy it. Do you?"

"Well, the money is good. I wouldn't be honest if I didn't admit I like that part. I grew up in a family that didn't have much, or at least not enough to satisfy my parents. They argued often about money, and I hated that." Jules peruses the table surface. There's an illegible gouge where someone tried to carve their initials. He looks at Miriam. "I became determined to have enough money in life." Is this too personal for a non-date? No, it's okay – Jules has shared this with Richard and other friends.

"How much is enough?"

"I ... don't have a number."

"C'mon you're an accountant! 'How much' is a basic question."

There's Miriam's directness again. "You're right. Okay, 'enough' is not living in lack. It's being able to pay for smoothies or a concert or a camping trip without sweating the costs. On the flip side, 'enough' does not mean free to buy a Mercedes or diamonds or every luxury you might desire."

"Hmm, good answer. Okay, what else do you like about accounting?"

"I love numbers, and how they relate to each other when everything is in its proper place. Credits are balanced by debits, assets by liabilities. Adding or subtracting in one place always creates a change in another place."

"It's an ecological system?"

"Yes! I never thought about it that way. Everything relates to everything else. But it's different than the natural world, because an accounting system is one you totally control. Is that bad, do you think?"

"Bad? Why?"

"Because control is a big part of it."

"Right, you told me the other day that you like being in control."

"Yes, but not over people, that's not me at all. It's control over things. I arrange things, put them in order." Jules again peruses the gouge in the picnic table. It's ugly. "I can't stand chaos and clutter." He glances at Miriam. Why is he sharing so much about himself? "You must think I'm an uptight weirdo."

She laughs. "No weirder than me, if controlling how things are organized defines weirdness. Besides, tonight you went through a meditation session where you let go of control. You were open to a different kind of consciousness." Her face is soft. She's not judging him. "I guess that's right." Is that what meditation is, a surrendering of control? It wasn't hard, and it was so ... relaxing. "Anyway, thank you for helping me find deeper inspiration in accounting. The timing is good – I just registered to take the CPA exam. I've worked at an accounting firm long enough to qualify. There's lots of studying to do, so being inspired will be a motivator."

"So accounting is perfect for you."

"I thought it was, but these days I'm not so sure. I mean, accounting itself is good, but the reality of the job is a different story." Should he explain how his work products are not grounded in order and balance but filled with arbitrary numbers to satisfy a big client? No, that's confidential. "Plus, the hours are so long that I'm not able to go swimming or be out in nature."

"Maybe this is a phase you have to go through. Don't give up on something you really want."

"What I want right now is to spend time exploring south Florida outdoors. I've been here six months and haven't even been to the Everglades."

Miriam bounces in her seat. "I love the Everglades! Want to plan on a Saturday canoe trip?"

There's that girlish zeal again, breaking through her earnest intellect. "That would be great." How to make this not a date? "Okay if I invite my friend Richard? You'll enjoy him, he's funny and smart. I'll need to carve out a Saturday when I don't have to go to the office."

"Sure, bring your friend, but yikes, you *are* working too much. How did you end up moving to Miami, anyway?"

Jules takes a sip of his smoothie. He has been waiting for a natural opportunity to bring up Eileen, to let Miriam know where he stands. "I was working at the accounting firm in Atlanta and my boss offered me a transfer to our new Miami office, saying it's a great opportunity to prove that he didn't hire me because I'm his daughter's boyfriend."

"Wait. You work for your girlfriend's father?"

"Yep. He doesn't have any sons and I think he wants to make me a partner one day."

"Would you want that?"

"Definitely."

"How long have you two been dating?"

Does Jules hear a deflation in her voice? "Six years. We started in high school." He thought that telling Miriam about Eileen would be righteous, but instead he feels apologetic.

"And now you're doing long distance." She nods, purses her lips. "Yeah, that's hard. How's that going for the two of you?" Miriam absently pulls out a necklace from beneath her collar. She fiddles with the pendant – it's the Hebrew word *Chai*, 'life'.

"Well, I miss her. Though when she came here to visit a few weeks ago, we argued a lot." He shouldn't be saying this, it's disloyal. "Not a lot, actually. We had a silly argument over tuna fish. It was my fault. I still need to apologize to her." Jules considers how he will raise this with Eileen. He was wrong to be arrogant about it, but his intention of protecting dolphins was noble. He's talked enough about Eileen for now.

"Anyway, when you say long distance is hard, I'm guessing that comes from your own experience. Is that your situation?"

"It was. It's over now, though my former boyfriend is in denial. His name is Marcus. He's in medical school in Augusta, Georgia. That's a long way from Santa Cruz. We tried to keep it going all last year, but it doesn't make any sense. We're going to be apart for at least another three years. Besides, I think we want different things in life."

"What do you want?"

"Stimulation, adventure, meaning. He already wants to settle down, move back to Savannah where he grew up, and have kids. I might want that too someday, but that's in the distant future. Graduate school is my priority right now."

"Marcus aligns with Eileen. She wants to be married, have kids, live close to her parents in a big suburban house like theirs."

"And you don't?"

"I thought I did, but I'm having doubts. Like you said, maybe I'll eventually be ready for all that, but not now."

"Does she know that?"

"No. I've been afraid to bring it up." Jules is again surprised by what he's saying. Why is this coming up now? Is it Miriam's intense candor, her way of boring in on life's big questions?

She continues. "What's changed? Where are these doubts coming from?"

"I think living in Miami is effecting me."

"They say the tropical air will do that."

"Ah, Kabbalah breath. God blows the breeze."

Miriam grins at that. "Clever, you are."

Driving back to Miriam's house, Jules takes the same route he uses to visit his uncles. "It's not just the Miami air. I think my doubts are related to my great uncles. They're odd and eccentric, sure, but also ... lonely. I don't want to be like them when I'm old, full of regrets."

"Nobody wants that." She reaches towards him with her left hand and gently pats his shoulder. Thanks to her distinct mix of compassion and curiosity, he has revealed a lot of himself tonight.

"Thank you, Miriam, for ... everything. You're an amazing person."

She smiles at Jules. "I'm glad you noticed."

When he pulls up to the curb in front of her house, Miriam quickly says, "Don't walk me in. Let's say goodbye here."

"Alright. I'll call you soon, if that's okay."

"Definitely. Goodnight Jules."

"Goodnight."

She closes the car door and walks towards the house. Jules watches her from behind, her silhouette surrounded by moonlight.

Chapter 12
Brooklyn 1928

AS BAD LUCK would have it, just as Max turns the corner onto Pitkin Avenue, he spies Ida walking across the street in the opposite direction, hand-in-hand with her little girl. He looks straight ahead, refusing to acknowledge them. Seven years after she betrayed him, he is still angry. He heard how she got married right away, to a *shlimazel* named Hymie Himmelstein, the guy she dumped Max for. How could she get married so fast to someone else? The stone in his gut burns.

The afternoon he and Ida first had sex haunts him. They were in her bedroom – her family was gone from their apartment – and Ida let Max unbutton her blouse and unhook her brassiere. Contrary to her usual sassiness, she suddenly became shy, utterly alluring to Max. She gave herself over to him quietly and he instinctively honored her trust, forcing himself to go slowly when entering her. It was wonderful. So were their next two trysts, spread over the following week.

Then she rejected him. Was his lovemaking inadequate? If he didn't do it right, why did she kiss him over and over after each coupling, professing her love? There was no hint of the betrayal that would devastate him a few days later.

She got married so fast, she must have been two-timing him with Hymie the whole damn time, and that shyness she showed in bed was all part of her act. Max learned that Hymie and his family lived in her building, and that he and Ida had known each other since childhood. He was said to be meek and mild, unlike Max. Turns out she wanted a guy she could easily control.

His gut stone grows heavier. Max has never fallen for another girl. He's gone out with plenty and gotten into heavy necking with a few, but he's kept his heart closed. Women can't be trusted, and he refuses to get hurt again. So, he'll just have fun, joke around, maybe get lucky with sex.

Max pushes his way through the crowded sidewalk, heading to the Gurewitz Delicatessen. Since Izzy moved the family to a house in New Lots three years ago, Max comes to the old neighborhood only to pick up meat from his brother-in-law Pauly, who now runs his family's business and always has special cuts for his in-laws. Now Max is in no mood for Pauly's friendly chatter. Rather than complete his errand, he turns around and heads to a trolley stop, empty handed.

On Sunday Izzy gets up early and starts the kettle for tea. He treasures these quiet mornings when everyone is sleeping. Less than a mile away, it's another world from the old place in Brownsville, incessantly filled with street noise and apartment neighbors moving around and shouting. After moving the family to Bradford Street three years ago, he still savors its solidity and comforts: two stories, a red brick exterior and lots of windows. All four brothers have their own bedroom, while Jennie and Lilly share the master. Compared to the cramped tenement flat on Bristol Street where they grew up, this is a mansion. He pays for all that comfort, of course, with a mortgage of $140 per month. Izzy is uneasy being in debt, but Lewis convinced him it's a good investment. Plus, he has money in the bank and even the stock market.

It's warm inside, despite the early November cold snap that blew into New York last week. The frigid air smacks Izzy when he opens the front door to retrieve the morning paper from the stoop. Having the *Brooklyn Daily Eagle* delivered is a luxury, but they can afford it and the family enjoys it. Jennie reads the society page, Jack follows the Dodgers, Max likes the comics, and Izzy reads the business section.

When Izzy sits down with his tea and unfolds the paper, he is stunned by the headline news: "Arnold Rothstein Murdered." He was shot last night at a high-stakes poker game in a Manhattan hotel. The *Eagle* describes him as "a nationally known gambler and sportsman," with no mention of his widely rumored kingpin role in bootlegging operations throughout the mid-Atlantic states. Lewis and his pals must have connections at the paper. Thinking of Lewis, Izzy rushes through the article and is relieved to read that no one else on the scene was hurt.

The relief is momentary. Izzy's mind races with questions as he paces around the living room. What does Rothstein's death mean for the lumberyard? Who owns it now? What about all that cash sitting in the safe that Lewis had him stash? Is Lewis in danger? They don't call the mob "Murder Inc" for nothing. Is Izzy in danger?

He leaves a note for the family, grabs his long coat, scarf, and earmuffs, and hurries out the door. Cloud cover hangs low, sharpening the wind's bite as he rushes through the twelve blocks to Lewis and Joey's house. Izzy usually enjoys the uncrowded, litter-free sidewalks in this neighborhood, but today he takes little notice of his surroundings. What's going to happen with Rothstein suddenly gone? A power struggle within the organization may explode in violence, or Lewis may fall out of favor, jeopardizing the lumberyard operation. Izzy picks up his pace.

He climbs the steps to the Lefkowitz house and knocks on the front door. Joey answers, with the security chain attached. Upon spying Izzy, he relaxes. "Come on in."

"You doing okay, Joe?"

"Sure. Lewis is on the phone in our office room. Come on into the kitchen, I'll make you tea while we wait."

When they walk through the parlor, Izzy is surprised by a woman lounging on the sofa, dressed in a silky bathrobe. Joey points to her. "This is Daisy. Daisy, this here is my old pal Izzy."

"Pleased to meet ya," says Daisy, glancing up briefly from her magazine. Her nipples protrude through the robe.

Lewis enters and invites Izzy and Joey into the office. He turns to Daisy. "We got to talk business. Be a doll and make us a pot of tea, will you?"

Daisy perks up. "Sure, baby. I'll call you boys when it's ready."

As Lewis closes the door behind them, Izzy says, "That gal wants to do for you."

"Hey, I can't help it if dames fall for me."

"You mean fall for your money."

"Ha. Speaking of money, you're here because of The Brain?"

"I saw the news in the morning paper. I'm worried, Lewis. What happens now?"

"We keep going, that's what happens. Nothing changes for the lumberyard."

"How can that be? Everything belonged to him."

"Not exactly. Everything belongs to the organization. He was the big boss, but we got lots of smart guys that keep things running. Guys like Meyer Lansky. We call him The Accountant. The Brain made him second-in-command a year ago. I already spoke to him on the phone today. We're all going to stay calm, not do anything hasty, and keep the business going."

The phone rings. Joey picks it up, "Yeah?" He offers it to Lewis. "It's him, Mister Lansky."

"Izzy, I got to take this. I'll join you and Joey in the parlor in a few minutes."

Joey and Izzy take seats in the parlor. "Joe, you and I go way back. Tell me, you think everything is okay? Are you worried about tough guys throwing their weight around?"

"Not as long as Lansky's in charge. He's friends with another big shot named Lucky Luciano. Luciano's also focused on what's good for business."

"He's Italian?"

"Sure, we got Italians, Irish, even Pollacks. It's the old Sicilians you got to watch out for. They want to boss everybody, and they put revenge ahead of making money, so you got to know how to work with them. Me and them get along fine. A couple of times I've helped them out."

Daisy emerges from the kitchen, carrying a tray with four tea mugs. "Where's Lewis?"

"He's on the phone. You can bring those over here."

She frowns and sets the tray on a table next to Joey. Her robe falls partially open.

Joey sputters. "Jeez, girl, your tits are showing. Cover up!"

Daisy scowls. "You're jealous that all you're getting is a peek."

Lewis emerges from the office and announces he needs to leave for a meeting. Joe will drive and they can drop Izzy and Daisy home on the way. Daisy goes upstairs to get dressed.

Lewis turns to Izzy. "Like I said, we just keep going, same as always. Everything will be fine. You can relax, *boychik*."

"Okay Lewis," says Izzy, though he's far from okay. He hates uncertainty. This Lansky, the new boss, might not approve of the painting business Izzy started with Lewis. Rothstein gave it the okay, but that was before Izzy grew it into a good money maker independent of the organization. Plus, he uses the lumberyard as an operational base for parking trucks and storing paint supplies. Will Lansky demand a piece of the paint company? Izzy is a nobody, a powerless nobody. All he can do is trust Lewis that they are safe, their business is secure, and everything will be alright.

Six months later, Jack sits on the living room couch, reading *Howard's End*. The title drew him to the book, though it's not about a person named Howard. It's about English society and the strict codes of behavior expected of the characters, whose desires for love and fulfillment are thwarted by the judgement of others and of themselves.

He wonders what his Howard is doing right now. It's been seven years since they've seen each other. At first, Jack forced himself to stay away, afraid the attraction would be too strong to resist. By the time he thought it safe to visit Howard, so much time had elapsed he felt embarrassed to show up. Occasionally Jack ventured up Bushwick Avenue, surreptitiously walking by the Katzenbaum store from the opposite sidewalk, visualizing Howard inside at his workroom table.

After Jack turned 30 two years ago, he finally gave up on trying to make it work with women. No matter how lovely the girl or how strong her interest in him, he couldn't rouse a romantic attraction. He has grown to accept his lot in life – here he is spending another Saturday evening at home with the family. Jennie is knitting, Izzy is reading the newspaper, Max is thumbing through comic books, Davey is in the kitchen, and Lilly is waiting for her beau, Ralph Rubinsky, to arrive for their date. She turns on the radio. It's Fats Waller, singing "Ain't Misbehavin". Lilly sings along, then says to her mother, "Isn't that song romantic? It reminds me of the way Ralph kissed me on our last date."

"You be careful not to let him do more than kiss," says Jennie.

"I know, Ma. You told me a thousand times. Don't worry, Ralph's a gentleman."

Izzy snickers.

Lilly turns to Jack. "I'm going to the bathroom to check my hair. Will you get the door if Ralph comes?"

"Sure, sweetie. I'll make your fella feel at home." Jack is happy for his sister. She and Ralph have been going out for six months now, and she's in love. Ralph is a dream come true: strong and handsome and always nice to her, according to her descriptions of their time together.

Jack hears a firm knock on the door. He answers it with a welcoming smile that evaporates when he glimpses Ralph's face. "Your eye is all swollen!"

"Ah, it's nothing. You should see the other guy. I won a thousand dollars last night."

"Great. Come on in."

Jack leads Ralph into the living room where the family is lounging. "Hello, Missus Isaacson."

"Hello, Ralphie. Oy, what happened to you?"

"Ralph won a thousand dollars last night in his boxing match," Jack announces.

Max perks up. "Hey that's great Ralph. So, you beat that Irish guy, Kid Kelarney?"

"Yeah, I knocked him out in the fourth round. You wouldn't know he was the same guy who beat me last year. I've been training hard, so I was quicker than him on the jabs. By now I must have boxed with every welterweight in New York."

"That's three wins in a row, right?"

"And five out of the last six. My manager says I could go all the way."

Izzy slaps the air. "He says that to all the palookas."

"No, that's wonderful," says Jennie without enthusiasm. Lilly emerges from the back of the house. She gives Ralph a peck on the cheek. "Okay, we're going out now."

"Be back by midnight," orders Izzy.

After they leave, Jack says to his mother, "They've been going out for a while now. You think they'll get married?"

"She could do worse," says Jennie.

"She could do much better, too," Izzy exclaims. "He's a prizefighter for God's sake. There's no future in that."

Jack erupts. "You stay the hell away from her." He'll be damned if he allows Izzy to mess up his sister's love life.

Izzy stands up. "Don't you talk to me like that. And don't curse in front of Ma."

Jack stands up too. "Don't think that because you're good at running the family business, you know anything about people in love. You can't run Lilly's life. I won't let you."

Izzy takes a step towards Jack, who instinctively leans back. Jennie raises her voice. "Boys! You stop this. Stop right now."

Jack returns to the chair, turns towards his mother. "Okay, Ma. I'm sorry I used foul language. I just want Lilly to be happy. Don't you think she would be happy married to Ralph?"

Jennie nods. "He's nice to her. And it's good that someone will have her." She turns to Izzy. "Your little sister's not too bright, God bless her, and she's already twenty-five.

She wants children and that's fine. Boxing is not a good living, but don't worry, Ralphie will settle down. Maybe you can give him a job at the lumberyard."

Izzy sighs. "Maybe."

Jack presses on. "So, it's agreed, nobody interferes between Lilly and Ralph." He stares hard at Izzy. "If they want to get married, we give them our blessing."

Izzy shrugs. "If Ma says so, then okay."

Izzy, Lewis, and Joe head to a lunch meeting with two Italians connected to Meyer Lansky. When Lewis explained to Izzy that Lansky wants them to explore joint business possibilities in the construction industry, Izzy suggested they use the opportunity to talk up their painting business. He also insisted Joe attend the meeting, in case there are any doubts about labor reliability. They're to meet with a guy named Sal Vittorio, who works for Lucky Luciano. Lansky and Luciano are old pals who worked together under Rothstein.

They enter the restaurant and find Sal with another well-dressed man sitting at a corner booth in the back. After introductions and small talk, Sid proclaims, "Lunch is on me. They got the best mortadella and meatball sandwich in New York. You know mortadella? It's pork sausage made with olives and black pepper and Italian spices."

"Sounds good," Lewis declares on behalf of his party.

When the waitress comes over, Sal orders M and M sandwiches for the table. He offers her a five-dollar bill and winks. "And doll-face, bring us a round of your special seltzer water, you know what I mean."

Lewis gets down to business. "So, my boss and your boss want us to work out new business arrangements. You guys are booming in the construction business and we're doing great in lumber and other materials. That's where Izzy here comes in."

Izzy leans in. "We also got a big painting business, ready to work on those houses you're building."

Lewis nods. "We do money management too. With banks eating losses in the stock market crash, credit will dry up and construction companies will be desperate for cash. So our bosses think we can work together and make more money for all of us."

Sal grins. "You said the magic words – more money. We like doing business partnerships, anything that makes more moolah."

The waitress brings the five beers, each in a colored water glass. They all clink glasses. "*Saluti*," says Lewis in his best Italian accent. "*L'chaim*," says Sal. Izzy discreetly slides his glass to Joe.

They discuss the ins and outs of money laundering, price fixing, and kickbacks, testing ideas on where they can partner. Izzy explains he can make house painting an all-cash business, creating more opportunities for laundering.

The waitress brings the sandwiches, each piled two inches thick with mortadella sausage, meatballs, and provolone cheese. Joe digs in. "This is delicious!" he declares with a full mouth of food, "those kosher-eating Jews don't know what they're missing."

"That reminds me of a story," says Lewis. "A priest and a rabbi happen to sit next to each other on a train. The priest leans over and says, 'Excuse me, but I've always been curious about your kosher laws. Have you ever eaten pig?' The rabbi says, 'I have to admit that once I ate a ham sandwich. I was traveling and there was nothing else to eat. But I've always been curious about your celibacy rules. Have you ever broken your vows?' The priest says, 'One time, there was a woman who was desperate for me. I succumbed to temptation and had sex with her.' So the rabbi says, 'Hell of a lot better than a ham sandwich, huh?'"

The table erupts in laughter. With all the hysterics, it takes a moment for Izzy to realize something is wrong. Joe is silent, grabbing his own throat. An unchewed slab of mortadella must have gone down the wrong way. "Joey, you okay?"

Joe shakes his head. "Jesus, he's choking!" says Sal. "Give him water."

Lewis puts a glass to Joe's mouth. Joe slaps it away, spilling water on himself.

"Hit him on the back." Lewis slaps Joe, hesitant at first, then harder. Joe remains mute, his eyes wide with fear and his mouth agape.

Other diners gather around the spectacle. A man says, "You got to get him upside down then slap him on the back." Joe weighs two hundred pounds, so it takes everyone to turn him over and hold him vertically with his head near the floor, draped by the tails of his jacket. Joe's gun falls onto the floor with a thud; Sal kicks it under the table, out of sight. Lewis strikes his brother's back repeatedly.

A cook rushes in from the kitchen. "Lay him on the floor onto his side." Joe is now limp, his eyes closed and his jaw slack. The cook points to Izzy. "You have small hands. Push your fingers way down his throat, then dig out the blockage." Joe's face is turning blue.

The intimacy of moving his hand inside Joey's throat unnerves Izzy, but he persists. "I feel it, must be the tip of the meat stuck in there, but I can't get ahold of it. Everything's too slippery."

The cook hands him a fork. "Try to dig it out. Go deep."

"That might cut him inside."

"Don't worry about that! He's choking to death." Izzy works the fork to hook the blockage but cannot get any purchase. He tries again and again.

An old woman mumbles a prayer in Italian and crosses herself. Lewis sits on the floor and cradles his baby brother's head. "No, no, no," he mumbles. "This can't be happening." Izzy sees in Joey's face the trusting boy who followed him everywhere when they were kids. His ever-busy mind goes blank. He does not register the approaching ambulance siren nor the long faces surrounding them nor the spasms of Lewis sobbing.

Izzy and his family trudge towards Lewis' house to start *shivah*, the week of mourning. Joey's death hangs on Izzy like a lead necklace. It was Izzy who convinced Lewis to bring Joey to the restaurant meeting, and it was Izzy who failed to pull the meat out of Joey's windpipe.

Izzy enters first, followed by Jennie carrying a potato kugel casserole. The house is full of people, chatting in hushed tones. Several women are busy in the kitchen. Lewis sits in the parlor with his two sisters and his parents, Irving and Anna Lefkowitz. When Anna spies the Isaacsons, she stands to hug Jennie. "Oy Jennie, a mother should not live to mourn her own son. What have we done to deserve this *tsooris*?"

Anna turns to Izzy. "He always talked about you, his best friend since you were children. He looked up to you, and I know you watched out for him. Oh God, how could this happen?"

Izzy is speechless. Anna does not blame him, yet he feels worse. He shouldn't have let this happen. Lewis groans, "Ma, it was an accident, Joey choking on a sandwich."

"An Italian sandwich! That what happens when you eat *treyf*." Anna breaks down, drops her face into her hands. "He was such a good boy, always doing for me."

Joey's sister Blanche approaches. "Thank you for coming, Izzy, and for bringing your entire family. I know how much Joey loved you, in his way." Her eyes well up. "It's such a shock to all of us. One day Joey is fine, horsing around with my little boy, his nephew. Three days later, we're putting him in the ground. Lewis is beside himself. I've never seen him so unnerved."

"Well, they're brothers," Izzy can barely get out the words.

"He feels responsible."

The weight on Izzy grows heavier. He moves towards Lewis and Jack, standing in the corner. He laments, "What a year it's been. First, Arnold Rothstein gets killed. Then Lilly runs off to get married to that *shlemiel* Ralph. Then the stock market goes to shit. And now this."

"Shut up, Izzy," flares Lewis. "Don't compare my brother dying to all that."

Izzy is thrown. "Sorry, Lewis, I didn't mean anything."

Lewis starts to respond but breaks into a muffled sob. Jack steps in and embraces Lewis, who succumbs into Jack's arms, weeping.

A voice near the front door calls out, "The rabbi is here!"

Irving hurries out of the parlor and returns with the rabbi who officiated at the graveside, an old graybeard with hunched shoulders and long thin fingers.

"Everyone, this is Rabbi Rabinowitz." Irving announces. "He will lead us in the *Kaddish*."

The men gather in the parlor while the women migrate towards the periphery. The rabbi intones the ancient Hebrew prayer while the assembly murmurs along: *Yitgaddal veyitqaddash shmeh rabba…*

Izzy does not join in. Poor Joey is gone, and it's Izzy's fault. If only he could turn back the clock and make it right. But he can't. There's nothing he can do.

Chapter 13
June 1981

JULES DRIVES TO his uncles' house during his lunch break. Behind the wheel of the stodgy LeBaron, he's an old man on his way to visit four other old men. When he exits the air-conditioned behemoth, the midday heat and humidity beat down on him. He loosens his tie and unbuttons his shirt collar, but already he is sticky with sweat under his arms and across his back. He trudges through the heavy air towards the house.

Davey answers the front door with his breathy pseudo-voice. "Jules ... *ulp* it's nice you ... *ulp* came. Jack will be happy to ... *ulp* see you."

Jack is lying in a hospital bed set up in the living room. Izzy and Max are reading the newspaper in the easy chairs, now squeezed together to accommodate the bed. Max peers at Jules. "Who's that?" he asks Izzy, who responds with an "Eh" and a dismissive hand slap in the air. "Come on in, Jules."

A middle-aged woman in a nurse's uniform finishes reading a chart and steps towards Jules with an extended hand.

"Hello, I'm Nurse Fernandez," she says with a Cuban accent. "I'm here to check on Mister Isaacson. Please call me Leticia."

"¿Como esta? My name is Jules. I'm their great nephew." He turns to Jack, who is gazing at Jules. Jack is even worse than last Saturday. His eyes bulge, and the skin on his face is pale and shrunken. Jules makes out the contours of his skull.

"How are you feeling, Uncle Jack?"

Jack blinks, answers slowly with a slight slur. "Who me? I'm fine."

"Are you in pain? Does your back hurt?"

"Oh no, she gives me pills for that. But this is no way to live, laying around waiting to die while everyone does for me."

"Shut up, Jack," says Izzy, more as a plea than a command.

"It's true. You're spending all kinds of money and I'm going to die anyway." Jack lets out a soft moan. "Face facts. Better you the spend the money on Max. He's going to need help."

Leticia interrupts in a commanding voice. "Mister Isaacson, let's sit you up a little." She operates the electric bed and adjusts the pillows behind Jack's head. "There, now you can visit better with your great nephew." Jules, afraid he might start crying, tries to hide his despair behind a smile, for Jack's sake.

Davey chimes in. "He's an ... *ulp* accountant. A ... *ulp* good boy."

"It's wonderful you are here, Jules. I've been working as a nurse for thirty years and the best part is the love of families for my patients. What breaks my heart are the patients who are alone, who have no one, but here Mister Isaacson has you and his three brothers." Jules wipes his eyes, aware that Leticia is watching him. She continues, "So Jules, you must be about my son's age. How old are you?"

"Twenty-three."

"He's twenty-six. He sells cars at the Mercedes-Benz dealership on Dixie Highway. I also have a daughter a little younger than you. She goes to Northwestern in Chicago. Why she wanted to leave Florida, I don't know, but she's graduating and will be home soon for the summer." Leticia rummages through her purse and pulls out a photograph that she hands to Jules. "Her name is Carmen. I call her Carmelita."

Jules politely peruses the photo. It's a studio headshot. The girl is beautiful, with long black hair and a white flower behind her ear. "She looks very nice."

"Maybe you would like to meet her?"

"Oh ... thank you, but I have a girlfriend."

Max pipes up. "I have a girlfriend too!"

Leticia ignores him. "Que bueno. Is it serious?"

Izzy does another air slap and mumbles, "Eh," with a frown.

Jules replies to Leticia. "Sort of."

"Uh-huh. Sort of serious. Young men these days don't know what they want. My son is the same way." She shoots Jules a disapproving frown. He shrinks from her gaze.

Leticia turns towards Jack. "Okay, Mister Isaacson, it's time for me to go check on other patients. I will see you tomorrow morning." She checks her watch, turns her attention to Izzy. "It will be time for another pain pill in forty-five minutes. You remember, a white one every four hours during the day, then a blue one at bedtime. He can have an extra white one if the pain gets bad. But no extra blue ones."

"Yeah, yeah, I know," says Izzy. "The blue ones are morphine."

Jules hears Jack whisper to himself, "The blue ones are morphine. The blue ones are morphine."

The following Sunday Jules tries studying for the CPA exam. He plans to take the Georgia exam in September, when he'll be home with Eileen and his family during the Jewish New Year. Jules was a confident test taker throughout college, with a knack for standardized exams, but the CPA material is extensive, the scope is broad, and he needs many study days to prepare. There are multiple sections to the exam, broken down by topic, and he has purchased corresponding self-study guides.

As he opens the material for "Ethics and Professional Responsibilities," he visualizes Paul Perlman banging his fist on that ridiculous television commercial. Professional? It's not professional to overvalue an asset in one place and undervalue the same asset in another place. That's just ... making stuff up. His legs start to bounce on the balls of his feet under the table. He looks up, scans the living room, then returns to the text to reread a paragraph.

His thoughts wander to Uncle Jack and his deep regrets about choosing the wrong career. Jack did what others expected of him rather than what inspired him. He listened to his family, did what they wanted. Jules' father also struggled, in a different way. Instead of devoting himself to his safe career as a pharmacist, he pursued risky business ventures, all of which failed. Was he aware of the risk, and went for it anyway? Jules has never asked his dad about that — it's too sensitive a subject — but now there's an urgency for Jules, driven by his own doubts. Jack's story shows one path; does his father's past offer a different lesson?

Jules picks up the phone. His dad answers, surprised to hear from him. Jules skips small talk and gets to the heart of it. "I've been thinking a lot about work. Mom's Uncle Jack has been telling me about working for the family business and how he wishes he had made other choices, lived his life differently."

"That's how life goes."

"Well, I don't want my life to go that way, mourning for what I could have done otherwise."

Dad clears his throat. "Is there something else you want to do? Besides working at Sydney's firm?"

"Not really. I mean, I don't have anything in mind. I just don't want to look back one day and regret bad choices I made." Jules pauses. "Do you ever think about that?"

"For myself? I wish I had more money. I knew I'd never get rich as a pharmacist, so I tried different things — the motorcycle shop, the pinball arcade. None of it worked out, but I didn't lose much until I invested in that big homebuilding project, and the Nixon recession killed me."

"That's when you had to declare bankruptcy."

"Yeah." He lets out a long sigh. "That cost all of us in the family. There were times I couldn't pay for everything your mother wanted for you guys, and that broke my heart. I felt like a ... failure."

"Dad, do you think I'm on the right path, being an accountant, working at TEB?"

"You have a great thing going. Don't do what I did Jules. Stick with your profession, and make plenty of money as a CPA. If you want side investments, that's fine, but be careful."

"It's not just the money."

"Then what is it?"

"I want ... purpose, meaning."

"It's *work* Jules. Work is about making money. That's the purpose. You want meaning? You get that from your family and your community. Maybe your religion. One day you'll have children, and you'll be filled with meaning."

Work with no meaning? Jules sees Uncle Jack weeping on the park bench, face in his hands. The acrid smell of his great uncles' house permeates his nostrils.

"Jules? You still there?"

"I'm here."

"You okay?"

"Yeah, I'm fine. Thanks for talking, Dad."

Jules briefs Richard on their way to pick up Miriam for a Saturday canoe trip in the Everglades.

"You know what Kabbalah is?"

"A dish that combines shish kabob and challah bread?"

"Ha-ha. It's Jewish mysticism. Miriam took me to a meditation led by this funky rabbi."

"Wait, was this a date?"

"No. Well, not at first, but then it sort of felt that way."

Richard sits up straight. "Okay, this is getting interesting. Did you go anywhere else?"

"Afterwards we went to a smoothie place. We talked about lots of things. Ecology, accounting, God, what we want in life."

"Oh, this was definitely a date."

"No, it wasn't."

"Okay ... Does she know about Eileen?"

"Yes."

"That's good. No secrets."

"Right, no secrets. In the meantime, I know Eileen wants to get married, but I'm not ready for a mortgage and children and all that. On the other hand, I don't want to lose her." Jules sighs. "I don't know what I'm doing. I'm pretty confused."

"Hey, you're a complex guy, it's okay to be confused. You should talk with Eileen, straight up. Look, I'm married to Deborah, and we're having too much fun together to settle down with a house and a family. You and Eileen could do same thing."

"I guess. I do need to talk with her, see if she's willing to wait for me to get ... I don't know ... get more ready."

When they pull up to Miriam's house, she emerges from the front door carrying a day pack, ready to go. She reaches the car as Jules and Richard are getting out. She gives Jules a quick hug and extends her hand to Richard. "I'm Miriam. You must be Richard."

"That's me. I've heard great things about you. Ready for an adventure?"

"Always! Let's hit the road."

The landscape opens to the horizon as they leave the Miami region, heading west across the vast wetlands. Jules pops in a cassette of Neil Young's *After the Goldrush*. From the back seat, Miriam says, "Oh, I love this album. Definitely top ten."

Richard agrees. "What would you say are the top ten rock songs of all time?"

Miriam doesn't hesitate. "*Mister Tambourine Man*, definitely number one."

"Yes. It's *the* perfect song – music about the soul of music," says Jules.

Miriam gazes at him then starts to speak, but Richard interrupts. "It's an amazing song and I put it in the top ten but not number one. How about *Time*, on *Dark Side of the Moon*? I love that sense of life racing by, so you better enjoy every moment while you can."

The conversation switches to movies and outdoor activities they have each enjoyed. Jules is flying high, delighted to be spending time with two great friends.

At the national park, the outfitter's attendant directs them into a flatwater canoe. Miriam is the most experienced canoer, so she takes the stern seat. Jules sits on the makeshift middle seat. "You muscle men can be our power strokers up front," she teases, "I'll steer."

They paddle off into the wetland waterscape, starting with shady mangrove forests where each tree rests on an astonishing tangle of above-water roots. In other portions, the route opens into freshwater sloughs, where they are surrounded by fields of sawgrass. They pass clusters of bald cypress and small hammocks of dry soil with hardwood trees.

Breezes rustle the foliage, creating a gentle murmur and carrying a fecund smell like a fresh bag of potting soil.

Jules is awed by the natural beauty of this vast, rarified place. He is peaceful and exhilarated at the same time. He gazes at the blue sky and the watery horizon, recalling his recent snorkeling adventure, hiking in forest preserves, even strolling through urban parks – places where nature has nourished his soul.

The water is black. Miriam explains that the color comes from the tannins in decomposed organic matter. The outfitter staff said most of the route is less than three feet deep, but Jules cannot make out a bottom through the dark water. He tests the depth by plunging his paddle vertically into the swamp. Sure enough, he hits soft, thick mud. When he pulls the paddle up, however, the blade is covered not with mud but with a dense conglomerate of ooze and small worms writhing in the sun. He shows Richard.

"Wow, the bottom is made of living worms!"

"Look carefully," says Miriam. "There are eelworms, nematodes, tiny crustaceans, plus zooplankton and bacteria too small to see – lots of low food-chain organisms. With all this water and sunlight, the Everglades are a highly productive ecosystem, lots of biologic activity. These are the creatures that eat the decomposing organic matter and become prey for small predators. It's all a big recycling loop."

"How do you know all this?" asks Richard.

"Summer day camps when I was a teenager. I always went for the science programs. They brought us to the Everglades, the beach, the museums and planetariums." Jules imagines her as a teenager, hanging with the science nerds in high school – definitely not Eileen's crowd. Eileen would not be comfortable here, travelling in a canoe above a watery blanket of slimy creatures. She'd be grossed out. That's okay, he respects the ways he and Eileen are different. It makes for a healthy, symbiotic relationship.

The canoe emerges from cypress assemblages onto open water and full sun. Miriam checks the map. "It's exactly a mile across this stretch. Good thing the park service installed these posts to mark the trail. Otherwise, it would be easy to get lost."

Jules scans the waterscape. "This must be the flattest terrain on earth."

"Distance to the horizon is limited only by the curvature of the planet," says Miriam. "That's five miles."

"I think about the early European sailors," says Jules. "When they watched a ship approaching from the horizon, the top of the mast always emerged first. Strong evidence for a round earth, but they were stuck in a world view where the earth is flat. Then came Columbus, who everybody thought was crazy, crossing an unknown ocean just to fall off the edge of the world."

Miriam nods. "I wonder how we get stuck in our world view. What is right in front of us that we don't see?"

"Mostly stuff about ourselves," says Richard. "We don't know our own blind spots or our own potential. We don't understand how much we're influenced by what other people think and say and do. I see that all the time with my investment clients."

"So, your job is to help people get beyond themselves," offers Jules.

"Right. But I can't push too hard. Not everyone wants their assumptions challenged."

It's dinnertime when Jules pulls up to Miriam's house. All three hop out of the car, and Jules opens the trunk so Miriam can retrieve her things. "Thank you, boys, this was a great day. It was fun getting to know you, Richard. I get why Jules likes you so much."

"Well, he's kind of an idiot. Even if he is a great guy."

Richard and Miriam hug goodbye. She turns to Jules and hugs him warmly. "Listen to your friend. You *are* a great guy."

As their hug ends, Jules suppresses an urge to kiss her. He steps back. "This was an awesome day. Thank you for being our nature guide."

When Jules gets home, he finds a message from Eileen on the telephone answering machine. She doesn't say anything new, just asks him to call her back. He's too tired for a conversation. Instead, he heads to the shower.

Chapter 14
Brooklyn 1935

IZZY SITS AT his desk in the lumberyard office, distraught over the latest rejection letter. The Brothers Isaacson was not awarded the contract from Roosevelt's Works Progress Administration for the new post office in Flatbush. He was outbid by an outfit in Queens, same as the previous WPA opportunity that he lost. He yearns for the good times before the Depression dried up the construction industry and the demand for lumber. That makes it harder to concoct phony sales for laundering Lansky's money, so he must rely on real sales, where WPA projects are the only game in town. His once thriving painting business is mothballed. No new houses are going up, and people who already own a house don't have the money for a fresh coat of paint.

He blames Herbert Hoover for doing nothing in the first years of the Depression, when business ground to a halt. Izzy would have lost the lumberyard if not for Lewis providing money to keep him afloat. Lucky for everyone that Franklin Roosevelt is a genius, inventing the New Deal and the WPA construction projects all over Brooklyn: the Naval Yard expansion, new high schools, subway lines, libraries, Brooklyn

College, all sorts of public projects that need lumber. Despite the opportunities, however, Izzy keeps losing out to competitors. He'll have to lower prices and squeeze profits.

On top of that, he has new expenses for the family. Lilly now has two little girls; after she married that bum Ralph, he moved her to Hicksville Atlanta, and now he drifts from city to city boxing in small-time matches that pay peanuts. Davey may need surgery for that lump on his throat. Jennie's doctor says the family should move someplace warm like Florida, because her asthma is getting worse, and she's had pneumonia twice during the past two winters. How would Izzy make a living in Florida?

He used to have so much! If only he had not played the stock market and not kept so much at Bennie Blumstein's bank, which failed four years ago. "That's what I get for trusting fat cats who play us all for suckers," Izzy mumbles out loud. "Never again."

A gloomy cloud follows Davey into the doctor's office. A nurse invites him and Jack to wait in the easy chairs facing the mahogany desk. This is a fancy room in a fancy Manhattan medical clinic, adorned with walnut wall panels and a red Persian rug.

Davey fidgets as he waits for the doctor. He tells himself God will not let anything bad happen to him. Davey is faithful and devout. He keeps kosher at home for the family and he sings praises to God in the choir every Friday night. Last year, a young woman named Naomi joined the choir, adding a beautiful alto voice. Davey chats with her during breaks at rehearsals, mostly about their families and their love of singing. After he introduced her to his mother following the Friday night service several weeks ago, Jennie pronounced her to be a nice girl. "She's modest and soft-spoken, so what if her features are plain. She would be a good match for you, my darling. You should ask her out." He has been gathering the courage to ask Naomi for a date. He envisions marriage with her – they would live with his family, so he can keep caring for his mother.

Doctor William Wyatt walks in briskly, shakes hands, and sits behind his desk. He gets straight to business, his eyes on Davey. "The biopsy of your throat confirmed my suspicions from the X-rays and physical exam. The tumor on the larynx is malignant and must be surgically removed. This will be a total laryngectomy, where we remove the vocal cords. We can schedule it next week, the sooner the better. You're a young man of twenty-seven years in otherwise good health, Mister Isaacson, so your chances of recovery are excellent."

Davey tastes stomach acid erupting into the back of his mouth. His worst fear is coming true. "My vocal cords?" He puts a hand to his throat. "Then I won't be able to speak!"

"That's not quite right. Patients who have this surgery learn to speak without their vocal cords. We call it esophageal speech. Your speaking will not be normal, but people will understand you. Your voice will be muted, less strong, and limited to lower frequencies."

"I sing in a choir."

"Your singing days are over, Mister Isaacson."

Davey's eyes fill with tears. This doctor is harsh and arrogant, no matter that Jack said he comes highly recommended, among the best in New York.

Wyatt offers Davey a tissue. He pulls out an anatomical illustration of the trachea and neck. "You will breathe through a stoma, that's a small hole where your trachea – that's your windpipe – will be connected."

Davey tries to study the diagram but it's too hard to focus through his tears. He gingerly touches the front of his neck. "Here?"

The doctor reaches across the desk and touches Davey's neck in the exact spot. His fingers are rough and uncaring. "There."

Jack kneels beside Davey's chair, his arms around his baby brother. Between sobs, Davey manages to ask, "I'll breathe through that hole? Not through my nose and mouth?"

"That's correct. But you will eat and drink normally after healing from the surgery."

"This is terrible. Horrible." Davey wraps both hands around Jack's forearm.

The doctor is unmoved. "Dying from cancer is far worse, and that's what will happen without the laryngectomy. You do not want that."

Davey buries his face in his hands. "Why is this happening? Why is God doing this to me?"

"I know it sounds bad right now, but many patients get through this just fine and live a long life. You will adjust to your new circumstance. All my patients do."

But all his patients are not chosen by God. His hands still covering his face, Davey prays. *I do all the right things, God. I take care of my mother as I promised you. I obey the commandments, I go to shul, I'm a good Jew. Why are you punishing me? Why?*

Hunched over his desk in the lumberyard, Izzy is poring over material and labor cost estimates. The numbers are dismal. He finally won a WPA contract, this one for a high school in Bedford-Stuyvesant, but he bid so low to beat his competitors that he will barely break even.

Lewis walks in. "How are you *boychik*?"

"I've been better. This business is not what it used to be."

"Well, I have an idea for a new venture. But first tell me how Davey is doing, poor kid. It's been what, three months since his surgery?"

"That's right. He's healed up from the operation, and now he's eating and drinking pretty good. The doctor says the cancer is all gone, so that's good, but Davey is miserable. He can't speak — all that comes out is raspy gulping sounds. Doctor says that will get better with practice."

"What about singing?"

"No, that will never come back."

"He's always been such a sweet kid. It's a goddamn tragedy."

"He refuses to leave the house. He's embarrassed by the hole in his throat and he's afraid people will want to talk with him, and he won't be able to speak."

"Is he at least going to that synagogue he likes?"

"No. He doesn't leave the house."

"You should get him to go. Religious Jews love suffering. They'll welcome him back right away."

Lewis is speaking from experience – Izzy watched each step unfold. After Joey died six years ago, Lewis spiraled badly. He drank incessantly and made reckless business moves that almost got him thrown out of the Lansky organization. His parents and sisters finally dragged him to their synagogue on Yom Kippur, made him observe the fast and told him to atone for his sins. He cried throughout the service, grieving for Joey. Congregants flocked to him, hugged him, told him that we Jews have always suffered and that's why we must stick together. He started attending services every Saturday, got sober, even met a Jewish girl and got married. Her name is Rebecca.

Lewis stayed on the wagon for a year but eventually lost interest in Judaism, as well as monogamy. His return to drinking was gradual at first but accelerated rapidly. Izzy tried to stop him, to no avail. Lately he sees Lewis with a beer by midmorning and a tall glass of straight bourbon at dinner.

The stink of stale alcohol exuding from Lewis' body reminds Izzy of his father, dead and gone; it's the smell of decay and incompetence and self-indulgent wallowing. Despite the stench, however, Lewis continues to function as Lansky's lieutenant, maintaining his confident demeanor and business savvy. Yet the booze has taken its toll – his hands shake, little veins show on his nose, and his cynical view of the world has hardened into an unrelenting bitterness.

"So, Lewis, what's your business idea?"

Lewis pulls a flask from his coat pocket and takes a swig. "You know in business you have to adapt. You keep changing as things around you change, like we did with the end of Prohibition. Booze went legit and prices tumbled, so we moved into other lines of work. Now New York is changing again. The governor appointed that sonofabitch Thomas Dewey as special prosecutor to go after our organizations. He's focused on the Italians, but it's a matter of time before his stooges start snooping around Lansky's operations. He's smart and aggressive. He might even get through the layers of shell corporations we built that protect the lumberyard."

The specter of going to jail and losing everything terrifies Izzy. His family would starve. "Are we in trouble, Lewis?"

"Not for a while. It will be hard work for Dewey to get through our system, but Lansky reads the writing on the wall. So, we're going to shut things down in New York. It's time to move operations to other cities."

"What cities?"

"Las Vegas for one. There's good money to be made in legal gambling. Lansky has plans for a big hotel-casino there. Another is Miami. We'll build a hotel right on the beach."

Izzy frowns. "Will enough people go to these places? During a Depression?"

"Rich people already go to Miami on vacation. It's sunny and beautiful and people love to gamble, always have and always will, same as they always love booze. We give them what they want. Besides, this Depression will not last forever and Lanksy is thinking about the future."

"Is gambling legal in Florida?"

"Not casino gambling, but they're working on that. They already have legal gambling on horse racing, and everyone knows that attracts tourists and money to the state. Even if they don't legalize casinos, we'll go underground like we do here in New York. So – here's the opportunity for you Izzy. Move your family to Miami and work for us in money management, same as you've always done. I'll get jobs for Jack and Max at the hotel."

Leave New York? The only home Izzy and his brothers have ever known? Disrupt everyone's life and move a thousand miles away to a strange city? He tries to picture life in Miami but draws a blank. "What about the lumberyard?"

Lewis takes another swig from the flask. "We'll close it, before Dewey has a chance to find it. Time to move on."

"But…we don't know Miami. Who's who and what's what."

"So, we'll learn. Lansky already has a network there to get us started. Besides, what have we got to lose? You said yourself the lumberyard is dwindling, and the longer we stay in New York the more we risk a subpoena from Dewey's snoops. To top it off, the Miami weather will be good for your ma's health."

"You'll be there too?"

"Sure. I'll buy Rebecca a house in Miami and live like we're always on vacation. She'll love it, no more New York winters."

Izzy takes a moment. Lewis is right – the lumberyard is a failing business, and Florida will be good for his mother's health. He rubs the back and side of his neck, gains confidence by the feel of his own strong sinews. He takes a deep breath, lets it out. "Boy-o-boy, this is big, but okay, Lewis. I trust you, always have. You've never steered me wrong."

"And you've always been quick on the uptake for new ventures. I know I can count on you, *boychik*."

From the kitchen Davey hears a knock on the front door. Jack answers it, and Davey recognizes the voice of Cantor Kugelman. Davey does not want to see him; he doesn't want to see anybody. No doubt the cantor came to persuade him to return to synagogue. That's not going to happen, now that Davey's a freak with a ghastly hole in his throat. He's incapable of conversing anyway, so what's the point? He overhears Jack and the cantor talking.

"Cantor, it's so good of you to come all this way."

"For our David, I would go to the ends of the earth. How is he?"

"He's healed up pretty good, but he has no voice. He's been down in the dumps. I know spending time with you will cheer him up. Come have a seat on the sofa and I'll get him. My other brothers are out right now but our mother is here."

Jack leads Kugelman to the living room where Jennie is darning socks. "Ma, it's Cantor Kugelman, here to visit Davey."

"Hello, Missus Isaacson. How are you?"

"Cantor, so nice you are here. Come, sit." Jennie waves him in, points to the easy chair. "Oy, such *tsooris* in this house. My poor baby boy, so young to have an operation. Now he breathes through a hole in his neck. Have you ever heard of such a thing? The poor darling tries to speak but we can only understand a few words."

Realizing he cannot keep hiding in the kitchen, Davey enters the living room. "David, I'm so happy to see you!" Kugelman opens his arms and embraces Davey, who smiles weakly and points to his throat.

"I know, you can't speak right now. They tell me it will get better."

Jack says, "Ma, let's leave Davey and the cantor so they can visit. Come with me in the kitchen, we'll make a pot of tea."

Davey pulls out a small notebook and a pencil. He scribbles a note and hands it to Kugelman. *How are you?*

"Me, I'm fine. Everyone at shul has been asking about you. We miss you. I hope you will be coming soon to Shabbat services."

I can't talk to anyone.

"That's okay, everyone will understand. They will be happy just having you there. Besides, many of them already consider a conversation to be an opportunity to do all the talking."

They will stare at my stoma, the hole. It's awful. Davey visualizes the horror on Naomi's face when she stares at him breathing through that disgusting hole. He will not be able to talk with her. It's futile now to ask her out, much less imagine marriage. How could anyone want to be with him, deformed and disgusting?

"At first, yes, that's how people are. But they'll get used to it."

Davey bows his head, let's out a plaintive sigh. *I'll never again be able to sing all those beautiful prayers you taught me.*

Kugelman nods and puts his hand on Davey's shoulder. *Why did God do this? Why give me a singing voice, then tear it away?*

"I don't know why, David. Bad things do happen in this world. They always have, even to good people like you. Think of the story of Job from over two thousand years ago. He endures terrible loss. His children are murdered, he loses all his possessions and wealth, and he gets a horrible skin disease with ugly sores all over. He agonizes over why God is doing this when Job has lived an upright and righteous life. But he does not curse God. His faith is shaken but he never gives up on God. In the end he is richly rewarded."

If I remain faithful, will God return my voice?

Kugelman sighs. "I must tell you there is a harder lesson that Job teaches us. God is too immense and unknowable for us to understand everything he does. When bad things happen, we should not take that to mean we are being punished for wrongdoing on our part. God is divinely just, yet God is also beyond our comprehension. I believe he will reward you, but in ways we cannot yet know."

Davey puts down the notepad and closes his eyes. God won't return his voice. Davey is foolish to ask such a question. He imagines attending Sabbath service, unable to say prayers aloud. Davey scribbles another note.

I can't be with people. I'm too ashamed.

"David, listen to me. I know you. I know how good you are. And I know that you belong at synagogue. You are one of God's chosen people, no matter how you might suffer."

Kugelman gazes at the ceiling, then returns to Davey's eyes. "We all suffer David, every one of us, each in our own way. So, we take comfort in God and in each other. Come to synagogue this Shabbat; I promise you will feel better."

Davey does miss *shul*, the touch of the *tallis* wrapped around his shoulders, the familiar rhythm of each prayer and hymn. Cantor Kugelman, who Davey has trusted without fail since he was twelve years old, is promising he will feel better. He lets out a breath of resignation, nods his head while writing.

Okay, I will come. Please explain my situation to the choir members ahead of time.

The cantor smiles. "Yes, I will do that."

The next evening Jack sits on the living room sofa with his nose in a book, *Brave New World*. It's different from anything Jack has ever read, not so much a story about people as a fantastic vision of the future, where everyone is happy because they are given a drug that removes all fears and troubles. No one in the society is different, so no one is outcast.

His mother shuffles in from the kitchen, followed by Izzy. She gingerly sits next to Jack, breathing heavily through a slight wheeze. Her bouts of pneumonia have taken a toll. "Are you comfortable, Ma?"

"Yes, darling. I'm fine. Your brother has something to say." She nods at Izzy, who is standing beside her. Whatever this is, Izzy and Ma have already come to a decision.

Izzy clears his throat. "I got a big thing to discuss with the family. It's time for us to move to Florida. To Miami." Max and Davey, playing checkers at the card table, sit up straight. "We need to get Ma to a warmer place – her doctor keeps saying that. I don't want her to spend another winter in Brooklyn."

"But how?" sputters Max. "It will cost so much."

"Don't worry about that. I got a new business lined up there with Lewis. He knows people there already. There will be good jobs for all three of us. Maybe Davey too."

Jack is dumbstruck. Leave Brooklyn for an unknown city, for an unknown job that might be worse than the lumberyard? At least working there is easy, even if it is uninspiring. "What about the lumberyard? We've worked so hard to build it up all these years. Especially you, Izzy."

Izzy shakes his head. "The lumberyard's not doing good these days. With the Depression, nobody wants to buy lumber because nobody is building. If it wasn't for the WPA, we'd have already gone under." He shrugs, lets out a sigh, then peers into his mother's face and smiles. "Think about Ma, she'll have warm fresh air to breathe, all the time."

"You're always taking care of me, darling. All of you boys. What did I do to deserve such wonderful sons?"

Jack's thoughts turn to Howard Katzenbaum. Though Jack has not seen him in years, he draws comfort from knowing Howard lives in the same city. A move to Florida means zero chance that Jack will ever run into him.

After a moment, Max speaks up. "We've always lived in Brooklyn. This is our home. We don't know anything about Florida. Are there even any Jews living there?"

Izzy is hesitant. "I asked Lewis how many are in Miami. He said a few thousand, but that will grow once people realize what a paradise it is."

"A few thousand?" says Jack. "There are two million Jews in New York. It's safe here. You know they hate us everywhere else. It used to be Henry Ford with his rag of a newspaper. Now these days it's that *shmuck* priest Charles Coughlin on the radio."

"Don't worry so much," says Izzy. "Listen, I'm not crazy about this either, but think what happens if we don't move. The lumberyard closes and we're all out of work. Think we can get jobs in the middle of a Depression? And Ma's health gets worse with every year we stay here. Let's not put her through another winter."

Davey scribbles a note and hands it to Max, who reads it aloud. *"Are there synagogues there? Kosher grocers?"*

"Yeah, sure," says Izzy. "Anyplace with Jews, even a few thousand, is bound to have synagogues and Jewish food."

Davey's frowns as he writes a response. Max reads it. *"No one there will know I used to sing. That will be good. Less pity in people's eyes when they look at me."*

Jack turns to his mother. "What do you think, Ma?"

"I'm getting to be an old woman, always cold. It would be nice to live in a warm place. As long as I have my darling sons, I'll be fine."

Max nods. "At least I'll never have to worry about running into Ida there. I'll be happy knowing that I won't ever lay eyes on that woman's face again."

After fourteen years, this is the first time Jack has heard Max mention Ida's name. He's not surprised that she's a sore subject for his brother, but he's startled by the severity of Max's bitterness.

The move may be the best thing for the family, but not for Jack. Could he possibly stay behind? With his family gone, he'd be free to work at Katzenbaum's, but ... that assumes there's still a place for him there, which is foolish, all these years after Howard's invitation. Even if he could work there, then what? Live by himself? Pine away for Howard while being around him every day? They still couldn't be together. As for other jobs, Jack has no experience beyond cashiering, and nobody's hiring with the Depression. No, it's not realistic to think of staying in Brooklyn. "Okay, I'm for it, but it won't be easy. We're leaving civilization and moving to the wilderness."

Davey makes a raspy sound from his throat, writes a note, and hands it to Max. *"The ancient Hebrews had to live in the wilderness before they found the promised land, the land of milk and honey."*

"That's right," says Izzy. He brightens. "Miami will be a paradise. We'll bask in the warm sun, even in January. Ma will get better, and we'll have good jobs. We'll buy a nice house with a yard and maybe plant an orange tree. Sound good?"

Jennie responds. "Whatever you think, darling. You know best."

Izzy knows best? The notion torments Jack. Izzy has everyone else fooled, but not him. Izzy has no idea what's best for Jack. Yet he has no choice but to follow Izzy a thousand miles to a new job, a new house, a new life.

Six weeks later, Izzy sits at his office desk, staring at the empty Diebold safe. The lumberyard business is permanently closed. Izzy fills the last box of documents to be destroyed, as Lewis has instructed. Lewis also told him to empty out the safe and leave it closed, "in case there's a fire." When he asked if they were going to torch the place for the insurance, Lewis only said, "You don't want to know."

So that's the end of The Brothers Isaacson Lumber and Building Supplies. Izzy refuses to be sentimental, refuses to mourn the end of a business that brought wealth and good times. Same with the family house, now up for sale. Everyone is packed, and the movers will be emptying the place tomorrow. The next day they're all taking the train to Miami.

Things will be good there. Lewis will get Izzy and his brothers settled into new jobs, where there's no threat from a big-time police investigation. His mother will thrive in the sunshine, and they'll all have a nice place to live. Enough of Brooklyn – it's time to get out of this crowded, dirty city.

Izzy jumps when the phone rings. "Hello, Isaacson here."

"Izzy, this is Meyer Lansky." Why is he calling? He always communicates through Lewis.

"Yes, Mister Lansky. What can I do for you?"

"I'm afraid I have bad news, very bad news. Lewis was arrested yesterday by Thomas Dewey's task force. My insider at NYPD told me they threatened him with alcohol withdrawal if he didn't rat on our organization. You know Lewis, he couldn't make it through a day without booze. He was loyal though, and must have known he was trapped, so he chose the only way out. Lewis hung himself in that police cell last night."

"What? Lewis is dead?" The floor slips out from under Izzy.

"I know it's a shock. Despite his boozing, Lewis was a good man and one smart guy. I'll always be grateful for that kind of loyalty and bravery, and I'll take care of Lewis' people, including you and your brothers. Listen, everything should go forward as planned in Miami. The one change is that you'll have a new contact person. His name is Harold, he's a good guy. Call him when you get there."

Izzy's hand shakes as he writes down Harold's phone number. "Lewis and I go way back. We were kids together in Brownsville. I can't believe he's gone."

"I'm going to miss him too. This is a tragedy, a terrible tragedy." Lansky pauses. "Now if you need anything that Harold can't do for you, then you call me directly. I'm serious about taking care of everything. Okay?"

"Yes, sir. Thank you." Izzy hangs up the phone, his hand still shaking. Goddamn booze, that's what killed Lewis. Izzy should have done more to get him off the drink. He tried a couple of times, but Lewis reacted fiercely, yelling at him to butt out. He should have stood up to Lewis. Now it's too late.

What about the planned move to Miami? Should Izzy cancel the whole idea? But what then? The lumberyard is finished, there's no work to be had in Brooklyn, and Lansky would be unhappy. There's no viable alternative, but without Lewis the Miami plan is a roll of the dice, and Izzy has never been a gambler.

Chapter 15
July 1981

JULES COUNTS TEN people gathered around Jack's gravesite at the Mount Nebo Cemetery: Mom, Uncles Izzy, Max and Dave, Clare and Miriam, the rabbi and two old men from Dave's synagogue, and the hospice-care nurse Leticia Fernandez. The rabbi eulogizes Jack's life in dry tones: he grew up in Brooklyn, worked in the family businesses, cared for his mother, moved to Miami, blah blah blah. Nothing about his love of fabrics and clothing, his thoughtfulness and insight, his lost opportunities for fulfillment. The rabbi is going through the motions with no attempt to honor the real Jack.

As the group recites the Mourner's Kaddish, Jules watches the casket being lowered into the ground. Jack was grateful that he would not be taking his secret to the grave, but only Jules knows Jack's truth. How can he honor his great uncle's life?

Jules stares at the family tombstone, proclaiming ISAACSON in large letters. A smaller plaque shows that Jennie, "Beloved Mother" is buried here, with birth and death years 1870 – 1948. In addition to Jack's grave, there are three plots where Izzy, Max, and Dave will one day lie.

"Where's Jack?" Max suddenly asks. He looks around, confused. "Where's Marcia?"

Miriam steps next to him and holds his arm. "It's okay, Uncle Max. It's me, Miriam. I'm right here with you."

Max peruses her face, then smiles, "Hi, Miriam. You're such a darling girl." Witnessing their interaction softens Jules' grief. His chest opens deeper, as if a floor melts away to reveal a spacious basement.

The rabbi concludes the service by announcing *shivah* at the Cohen house. He shovels a bit of ritual dirt into the grave and hands the shovel to Izzy. He then invites all attendees to follow suit. Everyone fulfills this final act of love for Jack Isaacson with their own hands.

Two hours later, Jules sits at Clare Cohen's dining table with Mom, Miriam, and his three great uncles. Clare puts out a potato kugel casserole, fresh from the oven, along with sliced brisket. Mom helps by placing plates, silverware and water glasses. Jules is at home, mourning with the people who knew Jack best.

Clare says to Izzy and Dave. "I was thinking. It's now been 46 years that we've been neighbors."

"We moved here in 1935," says Izzy. "So that's right. You and your parents were already in your house. The neighborhood was brand new, with half the lots still empty."

"Of course, I was a little girl, so I don't remember that. I would have been three years old."

"I ... *ulp* remember," says Dave. "You ... *ulp* were adorable. Your mother and father were ... *ulp* wonderful people, may they rest in peace."

Clare turns to Jules. "After I grew up and got married, my husband and I moved to Tampa. He was a pediatrician and we moved there for his work. That's where Miriam was born. He died of lung cancer when she was a toddler, so I moved back here to live with my mother. My father had died by that time, from a heart attack. So, we were three females who were not handy around the house. Your great uncles were a godsend, helping us with home repairs, gardening, all the things a man usually does."

"There's no reason a woman can't do those things," Miriam states.

"You're right, honey, but I didn't have the aptitude or the time. I was busy raising you, working, and caring for your grandmother. Besides, I had four strong, lovely men living right next door. I will always be grateful for your generosity, Izzy and Max and Dave."

"Eh, it was nothing," says Izzy. "We did a little here, a little there."

"From the sound of things, the four of you did much more than a little," Jules says. "You sustained a widow and her child over many years." He points to Miriam. "Here sits the amazing result."

Miriam smiles. "Max especially was always doing things for me. He took me to the playground and to Disney movies. Sometimes Jack came too. We always went to the Woolworth's diner for ice cream. I remember the big counter and the bright red stools."

Esther says, "I remember that Woolworth's. The uncles took me there too, back in 1951 when I came to visit by myself from Atlanta. I was fifteen. I looked up to Clare; she was a year older than me."

Max blurts out, "Neapolitan!"

"That's right, Uncle Max," says Esther, "we always got Neapolitan ice cream."

"We did too!" says Miriam. "Same diner, same ice cream, but fifteen years later."

"Neapolitan is the best," Izzy pronounces. "You get all the flavors for the same price."

"I still love it," says Miriam, "after all this time."

The next day in his great uncles' living room, Jules watches Esther and Clare persuade Izzy it's time to move Max into the Jewish Nursing Home. Izzy protests, but the two women make a formidable pair. They remind Izzy that Max wanders the street after dark, getting lost, telling strangers that someone is trying to steal money from the house. Next time he might step in front of a car or be found by somebody who is interested in their money. Last week he forgot a pot on the hot stove – they're lucky Davey caught it before a fire started.

Izzy starts to speak, then pauses and turns to his baby brother. "What do you think Davey?"

"I think ... *ulp* Esther and Clare are ... *ulp* right. A few days ago, here ... *ulp* in the living room, Max asked me when ... *ulp* we are going home. He didn't ... *ulp* know where he was. He was ... *ulp* thinking of our house in ... *ulp* Brooklyn, in New Lots."

Izzy slaps the air as if a fly is annoying him. "That was 45 years ago." He frowns, slowly shakes his head. His shoulders slump in resignation. "Okay."

Jules speaks up. "I'll help with the move and getting Max settled."

Davey wipes his eyes, stifles a groan. "We ... *ulp* were four brothers ... *ulp* living together for so ... *ulp* long. Now we'll be ... *ulp* only two." He hurries towards the back door.

Jules stands too. "I'll go with him."

When Jules reaches the back patio, Davey is sitting in the one of the aluminum folding chairs where he and Jack would play checkers. "Is it okay if I sit with you?"

Davey smiles weakly. "Sure. Sit."

Jules sits in Jack's chair. The green fabric, worn and faded, sags with Jules' weight. How many times over the years did Uncle Jack sit here? The scent of rotting leaves hangs over them. Jules and Davey watch the clouds moving briskly across the sky, in contrast to the still air at ground level. Jules pictures his great uncles as amorphous billows of vapor, blowing into and out of view. Jack is gone, Max is leaving, and not much time remains for Izzy and Dave. One day it will be his turn to go – Jack said it happens sooner than you think. "Uncle Dave, can I ask you a question about ... Judaism?"

Davey looks at Jules. "Sure."

"Do you think God tells us what to do?"

"Yes. God ... *ulp* says to keep kosher, so ... *ulp* I keep kosher."

"Does he tell you why?"

"Because meat and milk ... *ulp* should not go together."

"Why don't they go together?"

"Because ... *ulp* you cannot cook a calf in ... *ulp* its mother's milk."

This is going nowhere. Jules needs a different approach. "I'm trying to decide whether I'm on the right track, being an accountant and ... everything. Maybe there's something else I'm meant to do. I'm not sure, and I don't want to make the wrong choice. Can God help me?"

"God ... *ulp* always helps us."

"But can he help me decide what to do? Has God helped you that way?"

Davey sighs, returns his gaze towards the sky. "When I was ... *ulp* your age I sang in the choir at ... *ulp* shul. God gave me a wonderful ... *ulp* voice and I knew in my heart ... *ulp* that I was doing ... *ulp* exactly what he wanted me ... *ulp* to do. But then my ... *ulp* voice was ripped away ... *ulp*. Ripped out!" He touches his throat. "After all these years, I ... *ulp* still remember that ripping ... *ulp* every time I open my ... *ulp* mouth to speak." His face hardens into a bitter frown.

Davey's abrupt change in demeanor rattles Jules. "I ... that must have been terrible for you."

Davey looks again at Jules, as if he's surprised Jules is there. "So, I ... *ulp* go to *shul*, I say the ... *ulp* prayers, I keep kosher." He shrugs. "That's that."

That evening Jules answers the phone. "Hello?"

"Hi, honey." It's Eileen. "How was the funeral?"

"Pretty sad. There were only ten people."

"Uh-huh." She sounds distracted.

"Is everything okay?"

"Well, not really. It's probably nothing, but my period is late."

"How late?"

"Five days."

"What? But you're on the Pill."

"Well, occasionally I forget. I missed a day last month, around the last time you were here visiting."

"Eileen, that is so ... irresponsible. How can you forget?"

Eileen raises her voice. "You think I want to be pregnant?"

"So why did you forget to take the Pill?"

"Hey, don't blame me. If we weren't sleeping together, this wouldn't be an issue. You could use condoms, you know. Don't lecture me about responsibility."

"Okay, okay. I'm sorry. But what if you are pregnant? You would get an abortion. Definitely."

"Easy for you to say. This is my body."

"Sure, but there's no doubt about it, right?"

"Don't tell me what to do."

Jules swallows his rising panic and tries to speak without raising his voice. "Eileen, I am not ready for a baby. No way."

Silence.

"If you're pregnant, there has to be an abortion."

Eileen clears her throat. "Wow."

More silence. His heart is pounding in his ears.

Finally, Eileen says, "It's my decision. But we're getting ahead of ourselves. We don't even know that I'm pregnant."

"How do we find out?"

"I'll get a pregnancy test. Not one of those you do at home; I hear they're a big mess and complicated to do. I have a friend who got a test at Planned Parenthood downtown – I'm not saying who – and she said it was easy. She's going with me."

"That's good. I don't want you to go there alone. If she can't go with you, I'll come to Atlanta and take you there."

"Thank you."

Jules does not know what else to say. Eileen changes the topic. "So how are you doing? How's work?"

"Honestly, I've been feeling bogged down. I have to suck up to this awful client, and the hours I'm putting in are relentless. Sometimes I want to ... float away."

"What does that mean?"

"To let the water gently nudge me. Not to always be bound to a plan."

Eileen says nothing. She must think he's a flake. He shouldn't have brought this up. "You know what? I'm just tired. Don't mind me, I'm fine."

As soon as Jules says goodbye and ends the call, the fear returns. He's ninety-five percent sure Eileen would get an abortion. An unplanned pregnancy would destroy Eileen's vision for her future: an elaborate wedding and then children, but only in that order. She plans her life and takes control of things, but her reaction just now raises doubt in Jules. He recalls his dream of drowning, being weighted down underwater like that statue of the helpless Jesus.

―――

Thirty minutes later the phone rings again. Jules expects it to be Eileen. "Hello."

"Hi Jules, it's Miriam."

Should he bring up the conversation with Eileen? "Hi Miriam, how is everything?"

"Great, actually. I heard from the biology department at Santa Cruz. They want to hire me as a teaching assistant this fall."

"Hey, that's fantastic! What's the course?"

"Introduction to Environmental Biology. It's part of the basic sophomore sequence in biology. I'm excited but a little nervous."

"Nervous? Why?"

"I want to do a good job, but there's so much I don't know."

"You'll be great. Those sophomores will be lucky to have you help them learn. And your enthusiasm for ecology will inspire them – you already inspire me. That's way more important than knowing all the facts off the top of your head."

"Thanks, Jules. I …. I'm going to miss you."

"There's always the phone. We can talk anytime. And you still have a few more weeks in Miami."

"Well, not anymore. I need to get back there soon to meet with the instructor and go over the curriculum and plan out the lab sessions. There's tons to do."

"Oh." This is disappointing. "How soon?"

"Soon. As in two days soon. I still need to book the flight, but I plan to leave on Friday."

"Wow, that is soon. Um, I want to say goodbye in person. Can I come over tomorrow evening?"

"Yes, please do. Jules, is anything else wrong? You sound kind of ... off."

"I heard from Eileen tonight. She's five days late on her period."

"Oh. Well, that happens. No need to jump to conclusions."

Jules blurts out, "Miriam, I'm scared to death. I guess I shouldn't be and maybe I'm a coward, but I'm not ready for this." His voice is shaking.

"Listen Jules. It's okay to be scared, or however you're feeling. But women get late periods all the time. I do. Try to find that inner place of peace and calm."

"Right. Kabbalah breath." Jules imagines Miriam smiling at that.

"Exactly. Get quiet and breathe. Do it now. And in bed tonight. I'll see you tomorrow, okay?"

"Okay. Thanks Miriam."

The next day Jules drives straight from work to Miriam's house. He spent two tedious hours that afternoon on the phone with Paul Perlman's bookkeeper, explaining why her shortcuts create distortions in the company's general ledger. Though the corrections he prescribes will not impact Perlman's taxes or apparent credit worthiness, Jules worries that

Perlman will be calling him with a new loud and threatening complaint.

Miriam answers the door, smiling. His spirits lift. "Hi."

"Hi yourself. Hey, I need to get out of the house. Want to go for a walk?"

"Sure."

They stroll the neighborhood in the low-angle sunlight. Everything – trees, houses, her face – is lit in a soft orangey yellow. Miriam's beauty is untainted by makeup.

"So, I heard from Marcus today," she says.

"How was that?"

"Not easy. He's still trying to convince me that we're a couple."

"What did you say?"

"That I do have feelings for him but we both need to let go. Our lives are too different, too far apart, and moving in different directions."

Jules shakes his head. "Poor guy, he must be miserable. What about you? Have you let go?"

"I think so. I have love for him still, but I don't consider him my boyfriend anymore. I always believed the Beatles, you know, all you need is love. But it takes more than love to be in a relationship."

"Such as living in the same city? Or more generally, timing?"

"Right, what you both want in life and when to make those changes."

What does that mean for Jules and Eileen? As if Miriam is reading his thoughts, she asks, "Have you heard any more from Eileen?"

"Not yet. She's getting a pregnancy test on Saturday."

"That's good." She gazes towards the horizon, then continues. "Sometimes it helps to think through the worst case, so I'll ask you, what happens if the test comes back positive?"

"I swim away in the ocean and never come back."

"Jules!"

"Sorry. I'm pretty sure she would get an abortion. But she got really angry when I suggested that. Talk about timing, I'm nowhere close to being ready for a baby."

"So why was she angry?"

"I think because I assumed she would get an abortion and then I insisted on it."

"I would be angry too. It's her choice to make, obviously. More than anything, she needs your support and love right now. She doesn't need you telling her what to do."

"Well, I do love her, but I guess she heard my panic and took it for a lack of love."

"Your fear makes perfect sense, Jules. It's okay to be afraid. Try not to judge yourself for how you feel."

Jules lets that sink in. They walk in silence for a while. He recalls the meditation with Rabbi Michael, the three doors at the end of the corridor. Is one door an accounting career at TEB? That's not the one he chose during the meditation. Instead, he ended up in the water with dolphins around him. What does that mean? And what about the third door, where does that go?

"Miriam, can I ask you something? Do you ever think God is guiding you?"

"Only in subtle ways I can't directly discern or understand. There's no voice from above saying, 'Miriam, thou shalt do this and not that'."

"Okay, but you do make decisions. For instance, you decided to go to graduate school in California."

"Yeah, it was my decision but how do we make decisions anyway? We find ourselves in situations, we hear all kinds of things from people, we read all kinds of information, we have our likes and dislikes, and we somehow pull all that together to make choices. Maybe that's how God works, if God is the totality of the universe and all its interconnections."

"That makes sense to me, though honestly, it's not helpful in a practical way."

"What helps me when I'm stuck on a nagging question is getting quiet and going within. Let's stand still for a minute, right now."

Jules takes a deep breath. Then another. On the third exhalation a loosening permeates his gut. A stagnant pool that has been upwelling within him breaks through a sandbar and flows into the current. Jules takes in the soft sunlight illuminating the world. "I think it's time for me to make meditation a regular part of life."

Miriam smiles broadly. "It helps me to be in a regular group, like the Buddhist meeting I go to weekly in Santa Cruz."

They continue walking the neighborhood, circling back towards Miriam's house. Jules wanted to use this time together to celebrate Miriam's progress in graduate school, not to wallow in his troubles. "Thanks for all that, Miriam. I'm sorry to dump so much on you."

"Not at all. I'm honored that you open up, sharing what's really going on with you. It's totally familiar to me, being in fear and confusion and asking these kinds of questions."

"I'm going to miss you. Spending time with you these past few weeks has been the best part of living in Miami."

"I'm so happy we got to know each other, Jules. We'll talk on the phone, right?"

"Absolutely. Listen, sorry I'm so complicated."

Miriam faces Jules. "Right, you're not simple. You're complex, interesting, and good-hearted. Plus handsome."

"I think you need glasses."

"No, I can see just fine."

She steps a few inches closer and smiles. He holds her hands, gazes into her eyes. Should he kiss her? He wants to, but –

Before he can decide, she leans in, gently touching her lips to his. When she pulls away, Jules wants to say something meaningful, but all he manages is, "Will you call me when you get to Santa Cruz?"

"I will. Goodnight, Jules."

"Goodnight, Miriam."

On Saturday afternoon Jules is home, expecting the phone call from Eileen. Restless, he tries to study for the CPA exam but cannot focus. He cleans the fish tank, then the bathroom. He wants to go for a swim but needs to stay near the phone. He tries meditative breathing but is unable to settle his mind, which is racing with scenarios involving Eileen. He recalls a science fiction story he read years ago, where a man walks through a door into an endless corridor and discovers to his horror that the door locks behind him and there are no exits.

Finally, the phone rings.

"Jules, it's me," says Eileen, her voice breaking. "I'm pregnant."

"Oh."

"I scheduled the abortion, for Monday." She is crying now. "I can't believe this is happening."

Jules breathes a quiet sigh. "I'll be there with you. I'll get on a plane to Atlanta as soon as possible."

Eileen sobs. "I don't want everybody knowing. How do we explain why you are suddenly visiting?"

"I'll tell everybody that I miss you and want to spend a few days with you. Which is true."

She sniffles. "Do you really want to be with me? Or are you coming to make sure that I go through with it?"

A knot grips Jules in his stomach. He almost asks whether she is reconsidering but remembers not to let fear rule him. "Eileen, no. I support whatever you want to do. And yes, I want to be there by your side."

Eileen does not respond. The silence goes on too long, until Jules says, "Okay, listen, I'm going to call the airline now. I'll be on the first flight out tomorrow morning. Okay, honey?"

"Okay."

"I love you."

She hesitates. "Bye, Jules."

Chapter 16
Miami 1958

IZZY IS AT the rolltop desk, writing monthly checks for the mortgage, water, power, and telephone. He ponders how they can lower expenses. The mortgage will be paid off in seven years; that will be a big help. He could get rid of the phone; they can do without it. He could cut back on the monthly spending allowance he allocates to each brother. Jack and Davey won't mind – they hardly spend anything on themselves beyond bus fare – but Max pours through his allowance as if it's water, going to movies all over the city. How many movies does one guy need to watch, anyhow? Max will fight any cutback, that's for sure. These days Max gets angry whenever Izzy questions how he spends his allowance. Izzy sighs.

He moves on to bank account statements. Their sole income is his social security, thanks to FDR. Soon Jack will be old enough to collect as well. Then there's interest on the bank accounts. It's not enough to keep up with their expenses, but he has built up a good nest egg, so he can cover the difference for years to come. Regardless, he hates watching the numbers ebb downwards. He must keep the family's expenses low to make their nest egg last for many years to come.

Izzy pictures all the money that went through his hands during his heyday with the Brothers Isaacson lumberyard. Then came the high-paying jobs at the Floridian hotel on Miami Beach, thanks to the Lansky organization. Lansky had invested in the hotel expecting that casino gambling would become legal in Florida. That never happened, so the tenth floor was converted into a secret casino, available exclusively to reliable patrons. It was a good money maker, and Izzy was given a job managing those books. The Floridian hired Jack and Max in other parts of the hotel, Jack as a cashier and Max as a concierge. The hotel thrived for years, until the war when tourism plummeted. By the time the tourist business picked up again, other big hotels were built on the Beach and the Floridian couldn't keep up with the more modern competition. When the hotel finally closed in 1947, that was the end of steady work for the brothers. They sometimes did odd jobs around Miami but basically relied on their savings for sustenance.

Max and Davey come in from the back porch, where they were playing checkers. "Hey Izzy, Davey reminded me we're painting the outside of the house next week. Does Jack know?"

"Sure. We all need to be here Monday and Tuesday to get the job done. Maybe Wednesday too. I already got the paint."

"Let's do ... *up* Sarah's house too," says Davey.

"That's a good idea," says Izzy. "I'll ask her what color she wants." A few weeks ago, the brothers painted one of

Sarah's bedrooms, converting it into a nursery. Her daughter Clare is moving back from Tampa with her baby, Miriam. Poor Clare recently lost her husband to lung cancer, only a year after her father died.

"It will be nice to have Clare around again," says Max. "I remember when ... *ulp* she was a little girl. Now ... *ulp* she's a mother."

"She's still our substitute niece, as far as I'm concerned," says Max. "That's a good thing for a bunch of bachelors with no children." At this, Izzy is hit with a pang of remorse. Did he do the right thing with Ida, back when Max was barely twenty years old? He was protecting Max, sure that a better woman would come along, but that never happened, and Max eventually gave up on dating a decade ago. Now he's glum and restless, running off to movie theaters or who knows where. Izzy decides not to reduce Max's allowance, or even bring up the subject.

Jack walks across the lobby of the Fontainebleau Hotel and parks himself in his favorite easy chair. The lobby is enormous, filled with white marble floors and columns, huge glittering chandeliers, beautiful wall murals, and the famed staircase to nowhere. It must be the grandest hotel in America outside of New York.

Jack wears his treasured white linen suit, perfect for Miami Beach, with a powder blue shirt and matching breast pocket handkerchief. Last year he convinced Izzy the brothers all needed new suits – they could not continue to rely on dress clothes bought in Brooklyn thirty years ago. Izzy objected at first, "Only Davey needs a suit, to go to *shul*."

"His suit is becoming threadbare," said Jack. "We can't have our brother going to synagogue dressed as a poor *shlump*."

"Okay, but the rest of us don't need it."

"Izzy, you never know when we all might need a good suit, maybe for a funeral. If we have to rush at the last minute, it will cost much more."

Jack found a buy-one-get-one-half-off sale at a good men's store, so they all went together. With the salesman's help, Jack searched out a good navy-blue suit for each of them. Then he spied the white linen suit. "You don't need that," said Izzy.

Rather than argue, Jack enlisted Izzy. "Why don't you negotiate with the salesman for a deep discount on this one? We're already buying four, that puts you in a good position. These linen suits are not easy to sell. Tell him we'll walk out on the whole deal unless he gives you a break."

Izzy rose to the occasion and left that store pleased with himself. Wearing the suit now in the Fontainebleau lobby, Jack smiles at the memory.

He comes here to admire the latest women's fashion. Most of the guests are wealthy New Yorkers and the women bring their newest clothes to their Miami vacations. The Fontainebleau lobby is a place to be seen, with women parading through to catch people's attention. Jack notices that this year the tide is turning away from billowy skirts and towards slimline, tapered dresses. Bold polka dots and large buttons are in, as are bright reds and emerald green.

Dominant fabrics are poplin and polyester blends, though silk continues to be stylish.

Two men walk by. One catches Jack's eye, slows his pace for a moment, then turns and approaches Jack. "Could it be? Jack! You recognize me?"

"Howard! I can't believe it!" Incredulous, Jack stands and they shake hands. Howard's warm smile lights him up from within, just as it did so many years ago. "It's so good to see you. You look great."

"It's been so long, decades. You've held up well. Handsome as ever." Howard turns towards his companion. "This is my friend and business partner Eliot. Eliot, this is Jack Isaacson. He worked at our store in Brownsville when he was a teenager. I wasn't much older."

Eliot smiles broadly. "Good to meet you, Jack."

"So, you're partners and friends? That's wonderful. How long have you known each other?"

Howard and Eliot share a glance, silently communicating. "We go back nearly thirty years," says Howard. "Eliot and I must have met shortly after you left the store... the second time."

The old pang of regret, so familiar to Jack, tightens in his stomach. This time, in Howard's presence, he's ashamed. He fights the urge to apologize, to beg Howard for forgiveness. Instead, he changes the subject. "So, you're here in Miami on vacation?"

"Yes, we've been here over a week. Tomorrow we go back home. How about you?"

"I actually live in Miami. My entire family moved here in 1935."

"That's wonderful," says Eliot. "I would love to live here. So glamorous."

"Well, we don't live in fancy Miami Beach, we live in the city proper. But it's nice, and I don't miss the New York winters. Are you still in the clothing business?"

"Oh yes," says Howard. "We almost lost the store during the Depression, but thanks to good decisions by my brother Herman, we survived. After the war we expanded and opened stores in Manhattan and Queens. Then Herman died ten years ago from a heart attack."

"Oh ... I'm sorry to hear that. Your brother was a tough boss to work for, but he always treated me well."

"Thank you. Eliot and I have been running the stores ever since. And we bought a house together. It's on Long Island. Tell me about your family. Are you married?"

"Nope, I'm not ... the marrying type." Jack winks. "I live with my brothers."

"Do they all dress as well as you?" Eliot grins.

"Ha! Let's just say I'm the clothier for the family."

"We're on our way to lunch," says Eliot. "Come join us, Jack."

"Oh, thank you, but I don't want to intrude." Though it's heartwarming to run into Howard, Jack fears the stored grief and self-condemnation that more time with Howard will evoke. His worst times these days are when he imagines what his life might have been, how his loneliness could have been prevented.

"You wouldn't be, not at all," says Howard. "It will be a pleasure to catch up after all these years. C'mon, the hotel has a nice café for lunch."

"No, I need to get back home to my brothers. Maybe next time you're in Miami, we can plan ahead. Let me give you my address." Jack pulls a pen and notepad from his jacket's inner pocket, scribbles, tears off a paper, and hands it to Howard. "It's wonderful to see you. I wish you well, both of you."

"Okay then, next time. Take care, Jack." As they shake hands, Howard pats Jack warmly on the shoulder.

Jack scurries across the lobby and exits out the front doors. He asks one of the bellmen to hail him a cab, in case Howard and Eliot are watching. He doesn't want them to catch him walking down the street towards the bus stop.

He settles into the back seat of the cab, relieved to be hidden from view. The urge to flee from Howard and Eliot was overwhelming. All these years, while Jack was living and working with his brothers, Howard and Eliot have been together, working in fabrics and clothing and now living in a house that belongs to the two of them. The two of them!

Jack recalls the love he once felt for Howard, the attraction and yearning that swirled in his heart and his body. He never truly loved another. Sure, there were a couple of brief encounters, but those were more about sex than love. The first time was during the war, at the Miami Army Air Corps training facility. Jack had gone to work for the army as a civilian – he was too old to enlist – because he wanted to contribute to the war effort against the Nazis. They were rounding up Jews all over Europe and the Japanese had attacked America, so Jack did what he could. He went to work for the quartermaster, issuing and fitting uniforms to the thousands of soldiers being trained to fight the air war.

That's where Jack met Roy, a young draftee from Houston. Roy was lean-bodied, with delicate blond eyelashes and long fingers. He spoke softly with a lilt to his southern accent. Jack suspected that Roy's sergeant at basic training knew he would be a disaster as a fighting soldier, so had him assigned to quartermaster duty. Though twenty years junior to Jack, it was Roy who initiated their relationship, giving Jack discreet but unsubtle clues about his interest. They had sex together twice in the supply room, which had a locking door. It would have continued, except for a rumor that another homosexual couple had been caught in the act on base. The two unfortunates were court-martialed and thrown in military jail, where they were probably beaten for their homosexuality. Panicked, Jack immediately cut off things off with Roy. That was not much of a loss – though he liked Roy well enough, the young man never captured Jack's heart.

Jack's reverie is interrupted by the cab driver, asking if SW 12th Avenue is the best route to his destination. "Yes, that's good," Jack responds, then returns to his silent contemplations. He is happy for Howard; at least his old flame is in a loving, lasting relationship. As the car glides past the pastel houses and palm trees, Jack considers his own life and imagines what might have been, what so palpably is not.

Max sits in the center of row D at the Lyric Theater. The curtain closes on the matinee feature and the house lights come up. Max always sits for a few minutes after the film ends to let it sink in before he rejoins the day-to-day world. This is an especially good habit for today's movie, *Attack of the 50 Foot*

Woman. It was great – a giant sexy gal goes on a rampage. Yep, that's what happens when a woman gets power: she destroys everything.

Max has been coming to the Lyric for years. When he and his family moved to Miami in the mid-1930s, the theater hosted vaudeville acts, and Max delighted at the stand-up comics. After the war, he brought dates to the Lyric to enjoy big-name musicians, mostly jazz and blues. Now the big theater only shows movies. Occasionally he convinces Jack to come with him, if it's a big musical with colorful costumes, but usually Max comes alone. He did bring Davey to *The Ten Commandments* two years ago and *David and Bathsheba* back in 1951. Izzy never comes.

Max enters the lobby and chats briefly with the ushers, who know him as a regular. They understand that he worked as an usher many years ago at a fancy theater in New York. Today, he teases them about their little vests and how measly they are compared to the full-length uniform with hat that he used to wear.

He walks out onto NW Second Avenue towards the bus stop. The Lyric is in the heart of Overtown, Miami's original Negro neighborhood. He notices another storefront boarded up and worries that the area is declining. Max remembers Second Avenue as a thriving place in the 1930's and 40's, filled with shoppers during the day and revelers at night. There was so much nightlife that the thoroughfare became known as "Little Broadway." It was a great place to bring dates, where they could dance in the clubs, listen to concerts or simply stroll the avenue. It was easy to find girls at the Floridian hotel where he worked as a concierge. There was a large staff of cocktail waitresses and chambermaids and desk clerks, no end of opportunity for an outgoing guy. Those were fun times, though he was careful never to fall for any gal, never to risk the pain and humiliation that love brings. The memories raise an old emptiness within him, one that he used to fill by spending time with women. Now he's not interested, even for the prospect – increasingly remote – of sex. It's not only the fun that Max misses. The hotel gave him a sense of purpose and a daily connectedness with people. He hadn't expected to be a 57-year-old bachelor with no job.

The bus arrives. It's a short ride east to downtown, where he can transfer to a southbound bus to go home, but when he hops off the first bus, he decides not to go home yet. Instead, he enters another of his regular destinations, the Red Flamingo bar. The place is half full, mostly with guys who just got off from work in a downtown office. He sits at a small table near the stage, orders his usual two glasses of seltzer to fulfill the bar's two-drink minimum for stage shows. He doesn't care that they charge him the mixed drink price. Like his older brothers, he never touches booze.

A girl steps onto the stage, wearing a scanty outfit with sequins and feathers. Recorded music starts up with the old bump and grind, and guys hoot and holler from their tables. She removes each item of her clothing with exaggerated seductiveness. The old thrill courses through Max's body, like the time they gave him morphine after he fell off the roof and broke his forearm. The drug is thrilling and sedating at the same time. He drinks in the visual details of the stripper's nude, writhing body, an image he will recall tonight in bed.

On Saturday Davey walks the two blocks from his bus stop to the synagogue. He makes this journey every day of the year, always in the early morning. The prayer service never changes Sunday through Friday – the liturgy is so familiar he can recite the entire ceremony verbatim. Sabbaths are less formulaic, varying with the Torah reading and the rabbi's sermon.

He prefers the weekday service, with its absolute predictability. He belongs to the small brotherhood of worshippers who wrap themselves in *tallis* and *tefillin,* and don't bother with small talk. Each man is there for ritual, not for chatter.

Saturdays are crowded and boisterous. People come to catch up with friends, whispering long conversations during the service. Extended families sit together, with squirmy children moving from lap to lap. Restless teenagers pretend to visit the restroom, then linger and mingle in the lobby. Children stare at his throat stoma; he returns their attention with a gentle smile.

Adding to the hubbub today is a bar mitzvah. As the boy reads from the Torah, Davey recalls his own bar mitzvah and the ecstasy he felt being close to God. That was over thirty-five years ago. He had assumed that rapture would continue throughout his life, not end in his mid-twenties after throat cancer. Now, when he prays the Mourners Kaddish towards the end of the Shabbat service, he not only grieves the loss of his dear mother but also the empty place within him that was once filled with transcendent joy.

The best part of Saturdays is all the wine that flows. Most people sip from one-ounce paper cups, following the traditional prayer at the luncheon. Davey knows where to get a full-size glass and how to get a hefty refill. He sits with two other middle-aged men who are also weekday regulars. All three drink full helpings of the sweet wine. He suspects people judge, but he doesn't care. After all, it's for the blessing.

The wine permeates his consciousness with warmth and serenity. No wonder that since ancient times, Jews celebrate wine, proclaiming it in prayer as a blessing from God. Maybe God cares about Davey after all. Maybe this wine-induced peace is his weekly Sabbath reward for being a devout Jew all these years, even after throat cancer left him with a hole in his throat and another in his heart. He rises from the table, goes for a third glass.

―――――――

The next week, Max is on a ladder in front of Sarah and Clare's house, brushing paint onto the roof eaves, when a woman steps out of a cab in front of his house next door. She is youngish, maybe mid-thirties, with stylish dark brown hair and a pants outfit. She treads lightly to his front door and knocks.

"No one's home," he calls out. "We're over here working. My brothers are in the back."

"Oh."

He climbs down and walks towards her. Her face is vaguely familiar. "Hello."

"Hello. I'm looking for Max Isaacson."

"Well, it's your lucky day," he smiles. "You found him."

"Oh. Oh, my goodness." She stares at Max. "My name is Marcia Greenbaum. I'm sorry to drop in unexpectedly, but I wanted our first conversation to be in person rather than by phone. It took me a while to find you. I live in Chicago."

"What brings you to Miami?"

"You. I mean ... I'm here to find you."

"What? Why?"

"Could we sit down somewhere?"

Max hesitates. Why would a strange woman travel from Chicago for him? He can't imagine. She appears harmless enough, and pleasant. "Okay, come on in the house. I'll get us iced tea."

In the kitchen Max pours two glasses of tea from a pitcher and invites Marcia to sit with him at the table.

"Thank you," says Marcia. "After coming all this way, I'm kind of nervous."

"Don't worry. I don't bite."

She takes a breath. "My mother died from breast cancer last year. Her name was Ida Himmelstein. I think you knew her as Ida Ichtenstein."

Max tightens. The old knot in his gut returns. "Yes, I knew her. That was a long time ago."

"When she knew she was dying, she told me an astonishing story. She said my father Hymie – he died five years ago – was not my biological father. He never knew, no one knew. She told me about you, how you two had plans to marry. And she said that .... that you are my father."

"What?" Max raises his hands in front of himself as if he's pushing something away. His mind is racing.

"I know this is a shock. It was for me too." Marcia speaks quickly. "I wasn't sure I should come, but the more I thought about it, the more I wanted to see you. Just to get to know you, that's all. I'm not here to ask you for anything else, I swear. Hymie will always be my father, of course. He raised me and took care of me and loved me. If you want me to leave, I will, and I won't bother you anymore."

Her nervousness stirs compassion in Max. She seems sincere. Why would she make up such a story? Even if she did not, her mother might have lied to her. "Ida left me. She dumped me for Hymie."

"She said her biggest regret in life was that she broke up with you. She loved you and wanted to marry you, but someone forced her to break it off. He threatened to hurt her and her family if she didn't. He forbade her to tell anyone. He even threatened to hurt you too. She was very scared – this man Lewis was in the mob."

"Lewis? Why would Lewis do such a thing?"

"You know him?"

"I did. He's long dead."

"Oh. Well, she didn't know why either. But she cursed him up and down, lying on her deathbed. Anyway, she explained that she found out she was pregnant with me right after she broke things off with you. She was in a desperate situation, so she rushed to marry Hymie, who she had known since childhood."

Max shakes his head, trying to loosen a rusted gear. "That's quite a story." A story from Ida. "Excuse me, but how do I know this is true? Either way, Ida lied to me."

"There's no proof, so we can't know for sure, but I don't have any reason not to believe my mother. She said she didn't want to take this secret to her grave, that's why she shared it with me." Marcia becomes quiet, slowly wrings her hands. "But after she died, I started thinking that she wanted me to make amends to you on her behalf. I can't know that was what she wanted, but I'm convinced that you're owed an apology. I ... I'm sorry this happened to you. And to her."

Max sits in silence for a minute, trying to process it all. Did Lewis really do this? Why would he? What could he have had against Ida and him? Has Max been angry at the wrong person all these years?

Izzy walks in. "I came to check on you, Max. You're loafing on the job?" He turns to Marcia. "Who is this?"

"This is Marcia. Marcia, this is Izzy, my oldest brother. Marcia says that we're related. She travelled from Chicago to tell me this."

Marcia repeats the story. Izzy glares at her, folding his arms tight across his chest. "What kind of bullshit is this? This must be a con to get money from us. You need to leave."

Max is not surprised at Izzy's reaction. "No Izzy. She doesn't want anything, just to get to know me."

"And for you to know me." Marcia's voice is shaking. "I have a daughter named Dawn. She's ten years old." Marcia reaches into her purse, pulls out a photo and hands it to Max. That's for you to keep, if you want."

"I have a ... granddaughter?"

"Yes. She's a healthy and happy girl. I got married to a wonderful man named Harry. He's a good father."

Max stares at Izzy. "Why would Lewis force Ida to break up with me?"

"How would I know why? This cockamamie story can't be true!" Izzy storms out of the house, passing Jack and Davey at the front door. They come into the kitchen with paint-splattered hair.

Jack looks at Marcia and turns to Max. "What's going on? What's wrong?"

"This is Marcia. She says I'm her father." The full story is repeated, this time Max does the telling.

Jack and Davey sit down at the table. Jack speaks in a hushed voice. "Is this true? Can it be?" He turns to Max. "Did you and Ida .... when you were engaged ... you know?"

"Yes, we did. I remember. I've always remembered that. We were in love." Max wipes tears from his eyes.

Davey studies Marcia's face. "She reminds me of ... *ulp* our sisters. She could ... *ulp* be an Isaacson."

"Yes, I see that," says Jack.

"This means you are both my uncles." Marcia is crying with her face in her hands. "I'm sorry. It's just that ... all these years of living and we didn't know each other. It's heartbreaking."

"I didn't know," says Max. "I didn't know. If I had, everything would have been different. I would not have abandoned you."

"Oh no, you didn't abandon anyone. Please don't think that. None of this was your fault. I didn't come here to make you feel bad. That's the last thing I want."

Izzy comes back into the room. "We have a house to paint. Let's get back to work."

Max shakes his head. "Izzy, you're being crazy. This young woman came all the way from Chicago to meet me. She's family, Izzy. Family! Let's visit, I want to hear all about her and her little girl. And listen, we should pay for her trip."

"Oh no," says Marcia. "I couldn't."

Izzy slaps the air. "We don't know this story is true."

"Look at her face, Izzy," says Jack. "The family resemblance. She has Ma's eyes."

Izzy hesitates. Max can tell he doesn't want to look at her. "It all makes sense, Izzy, except why Lewis did this. He hardly knew Ida, but you did, and you never liked her, and you and Lewis were partners."

Jack points an accusing finger at Izzy. "You knew, didn't you? You and Lewis were in on this together, scheming to force Ida to break up with Max."

"No. No Max, I ..." All the brothers are glaring at Izzy now. Marcia averts her eyes.

"I don't understand," says Max. "How could you have done that to me?"

Izzy drops his head. "I was trying to protect you. I thought it was for your own good, Max. I didn't know she was pregnant."

An anger rises from deep within Max, pushing through accumulated layers of sorrow. His own brother did this? "For my own good? You think this life I have is good? No woman to love, no child to love. Living with you three all these years, when I might have had a family of my own?"

"I ... I wish I could take it back. I wish things were different." Izzy clears his throat. "And Marcia, I'm sorry to you too."

Max is fuming. "Well, you can't take it back. Things are what they are, what they've been for thirty-five years." He stands up, paces in the small kitchen. "I'll tell you what you can do. You can stop bossing me around and controlling my life. Those days are over!"

Everyone is silent. Max is steeled by his own outburst. "I want to know my daughter and my granddaughter. Marcia, I know that the man who raised you will always be your father and that I'll never replace him, but I want us to be in touch. We can write letters, we can talk on the phone, we can make visits, whatever works best for you. Next time you can bring your little girl and your husband here for a Miami vacation, and we'll pay for everything. Right, Izzy?"

Izzy says faintly, "Yes, that's right."

The battle won, Max relaxes. A tidal wave of grief washes over him. The old wound in his heart, the place he has guarded since he was a young man, is torn open. The pain comes no longer from betrayal by his long-ago betrothed but from the irretrievable loss of what might have been.

Chapter 17
July 1981

JULES HOLDS EILEEN'S arm as they walk from the clinic to the car. He focuses on his breath. The knot in his stomach, persistent since he learned of the pregnancy, has dissolved. He helps her in and closes the door. When he gets behind the wheel, he turns towards her. She is glaring at him. "You happy now?"

"No, I'm not happy. I'm …" Jules is not sure what to say. "How do you feel?"

Her eyes fill with tears as she yells, "How do I feel? I feel like shit, that's how I feel!" Her mouth quivers in an angry frown.

"Does it hurt?"

"Not physically."

Jules speaks gently. "Well, how were the doctors and nurses in there? I hope they were nice to you?"

Eileen nods. "They were great, actually. Very caring. No more questions, Jules, I'm too tired. Let's not talk. I just want to go home and crawl into bed."

They drive the thirty-minute trip to Eileen's house in silence. Jules wants to comfort Eileen, but he fears that whatever he says will upset her. He reaches to hold her hand and is relieved that she lets him.

When they arrive at Eileen's place, she says, "Don't come in."

"Are you sure? At least let me help you get out of the car."

"No, I'm fine, Jules."

"Well, I'll call you tomorrow. I'll come over."

"Sure, you do that." She hurries out.

The next morning, Jules rings the doorbell at Eileen's house, worried that she's still angry. Eileen's housemate and long-time friend Susan answers the door, giving Jules a disapproving frown. "Hi Jules."

"Hi Susan. Is Eileen here?" That's a dumb question – Eileen is expecting him.

"Come in. We're in the kitchen."

Eileen is sitting at the table with her other housemate, Linda. Three sets of breakfast dishes are yet to be bussed. Jules senses he's interrupting but does not wait for an invitation to sit in the unoccupied fourth chair. He gives Eileen a feeble smile. "Good morning, honey." Susan and Linda make themselves scarce. "Did you get a good night's sleep?"

"I did. I'm sorry I was so bitchy yesterday. I know you were trying to be helpful, but I was so upset by this whole thing. Not just upset, Jules. Devastated. I still feel devastated, though I've calmed down."

"Are you regretting your decision?"

"No, it's not that. I made the right decision. I'm upset that you never gave any consideration to the alternative. You didn't even imagine the possibility that we could start a family now, get married and have a wedding before I started showing."

Jules is caught off guard. "Is that what you wanted?"

"That's not the point. You abandoned me, Jules."

"What do you mean? I'm here. I flew to Atlanta to be with you."

"You're here physically, which does count for something, but you're ... just going through the motions. I don't know that I can trust you anymore."

"Trust me? Eileen, I've never been unfaithful to you."

"That's not what I mean. I'm afraid I can't rely on you, that I can't be sure in my heart you'll be there when I need you most."

Jules examines the dishes, smeared with egg yolk remains and breadcrumbs. He has always thought of himself as trustworthy, a guy people could count on. Without looking up, he says, "I'm not a flake. I'm a responsible person." A shudder passes through his chest. "Aren't I?"

"Jules, I'm trying to explain what's going on with *me*. I'm suddenly growing up, I can feel it. Now the question is whether you're ready to grow up too. We're not kids anymore, we're adults. I'm ready for us to act like adults, to get married and start a family. If you're not ready, then —"

"Then what? Are you giving me an ultimatum?"

"I'm giving you a choice, Jules. A choice between committing to a future for us together or more floating around trying to..." She rolls her eyes while her fingers mimic air quotes. "...find yourself."

Anger wells up in Jules; she is mocking him. "Okay, I choose floating!"

"What?"

He stands up, his heart racing. "You heard me. Floating. Not marriage. Not accounting. Not ... this path. Something else."

Eileen flinches, as if a gust of icy wind blew hard across her face. "Meaning, something without me?"

Jules averts his eyes.

"How can you say that?" She stands to face him, turning red. "You're breaking up with me? Now? After what I just went through?"

"You gave me an ultimatum, a choice you said. I'm choosing."

Her mouth quivers and tears start to flow. She sniffles. Jules examines his hands, unclenches his jaw, takes a breath. He softens his voice. "Eileen, I'm sorry, I really am. The truth is I'm not ready to start a family, and I know that you are. I'm ... meant to do something else in life."

"Fine. Go do whatever that is. I don't care. Just don't come crawling back to me when you find there's nothing else out there. Don't come back begging to my father either. He's going to be so mad, after everything he's done for you."

Jules' stomach tightens. "Wait, don't say anything to him yet..." Jules takes another breath, and the knot loosens. "Never mind. It doesn't matter." He watches her crying, ashamed for causing her pain. "Eileen, you're a wonderful woman. This isn't about you. I need to find myself, like you said."

"Just go," she says between sobs. "Go. Get out!"

———

Three days later, Jules is back in Miami driving the big Chrysler, with Izzy in the passenger seat, and Max and Clare in the back. They are moving Max to the nursing home. Everyone is silent.

Since returning from Atlanta, Jules has been replaying scenes of togetherness with Eileen: their first dance, their first kiss, their disagreements, their final argument. She was so angry, so hurt. Would it help to call her now? What would he say?

Yesterday Jules told Richard the whole story. His friend offered counsel. "You did the right thing, Jules. I know it's hard and you feel terrible about hurting Eileen, but it would have happened eventually and then it would have been worse. In the meantime, you're going through a period of grief."

"Grief?"

"I've seen it in other friends after a breakup. You and Eileen were together a long time, and now that relationship is over. You cared about her, you relied on her, and you've lost her. So yes, grief. Your romance with her has died."

"Okay, so what do I do?"

"Be gentle with yourself. Don't beat yourself up with blame and regret."

Behind the wheel, Jules ponders Richard's advice. It's easier to be gentle with others than with himself.

Max breaks the quiet. "Where are we going?"

Clare responds. "We're going to visit some nice people. You'll see."

"Okay."

Jules sighs. Endings – first Jack, then Eileen, now Max. Is this the grief Richard described?

His dark mood is scrambled by the cheerful lobby of the nursing home. The place is well lit with white walls and framed landscapes. Staff members smile as they walk by. The chief administrator greets them and directs two aides to take Max's suitcases to his room. He escorts them to the "memory ward," where they are welcomed by a middle-aged nurse with a comforting smile. The administrator introduces her to Max and his family. She immediately turns her attention to Max, takes his hand in hers. "Hello."

Max responds by searching her face. His eyes widen. "Ida?"

"Yes." Before Izzy can speak up, Clare grabs his arm. She puts a finger to her lips.

"Ida …" Max quivers. "I didn't know. I would have…Can you ever forgive me?"

The nurse speaks softly. "Of course, Max. I understand. I forgive you. Don't worry, everything is okay."

Max begins to sob. Clare embraces him in a one-arm hug. "Did you hear that Uncle Max? She said everything is okay. You don't need to worry about anything."

The nurse continues. "That's right Max. I don't want you to worry about what is past. We are here now."

He wipes his eyes. "Will you stay with me, Ida?"

"Yes, I will be here. With you."

An aide joins them. "This is our friend Martin. Let's the three of us go to your room, so you can get settled. It's time to say goodbye to the others for now. You will see them soon."

"Okay." Max stares at Izzy, searches his face. "Who are you?"

Izzy sniffles. "I ... I'm your brother. I'm Izzy."

"Oh, Izzy. Don't cry brother, everything is okay. I'll be with Ida."

Izzy nods his head. Without acknowledging Jules or Clare, Max offers his arm to the nurse. "Such a gentleman. Thank you, Max." She wraps both hands around his elbow, and they shuffle away down the corridor.

Izzy sits at the rolltop desk, opening mail. It's been three weeks since Jack's funeral, and one week since they moved Max to the Jewish Home. Davey's on the back patio, daydreaming as usual. All these years they were four brothers living together. Now they are two. He was supposed to take care of everyone, but now they're dead: Ma, Bessie, Lilly, Jack, Lewis, and Joey. Max's mind is gone. Only Davey is left.

Has he done right by his family? Izzy was a good provider, keeping everyone fed and housed and clothed. He did what he was supposed to do. It's not his fault that people get sick and die, but it was his fault that Max lost his chance to have a wife and a child. Izzy had been so sure that Max had fallen for the wrong girl and that he had to intervene. Now he contemplates what might have been.

Marcia had turned out to be a good daughter to Max, though they only had two years together. She died from breast cancer, same as her mother. If it hadn't been for Izzy's meddling, Max would have known his daughter for her entire life of 39 years. Izzy paid for his mistake – after Marcia's appearance, his brothers ousted him as head of the household. They started making their own decisions: how they chose to spend time, what to buy, what to eat. Though their rebellious fervor faded over time, they never stopped reminding him of the sin he had committed, stealing a precious love from his own brother. Guilt hounds him like a headache that won't go away.

He scans the desk, spies the *Miami Herald* newspaper. A front-page story pops out. Meyer Lansky, "a former kingpin in organized crime," has died here in Miami. The article says Lansky was once a multi-millionaire who commanded huge organizations – he was rumored to have said 'We're bigger than US Steel' – but eventually lost his entire fortune and his loyal followers. In recent years, he was a powerless relic struggling with ill health and limited resources. He was buried yesterday at the Mount Nebo cemetery. The same place where Jack and Ma are buried. The same place where there's a grave waiting for him.

A crushing pain suddenly grips his chest. He can barely draw a shallow breath. Panicked, he tries to call out but is unable to vocalize a sound. He gasps for air, starts to stand, then collapses onto the floor, knocking over the chair that crashes down alongside him. Davey rushes in, kneels next to his brother.

"Izzy ... *ulp* Izzy, what's wrong?"

"I can't breathe," Izzy whispers. Davey has to bend down close to hear. "It's heavy on my chest. Get it off."

"There's nothing there."

"It's ... the Diebold safe. The big one from the lumberyard. It's full of money. Get it off."

"I can't. I'm going ... *ulp* to Clare's house, to ... *ulp* get help."

Izzy grabs Davey's arm and won't let go. "You need the combination. It's ... it's ... I forget. Ask the boy. He'll know."

"What boy? Jules?"

"Yes, Jules. He'll know how to open it." The safe is pressing Izzy into the dusty rug. It weighs a ton. "Davey, I tried to take care of you. The whole family. I tried."

Davey cradles Izzy's head. "You did take care ... *ulp* of us. We would not have survived without ... *ulp* you Izzy. You're my big brother, and ... *ulp* I thank God for you."

Izzy lets his eyes close. The weight on his heart has lifted. He floats above the floor, sees Jules bending over him. He exhales a final breath, the one he has held onto for so long.

Jules and his mom are led by Davey to the rolltop desk. She returned to Miami immediately upon the news of Izzy's death and helped Davey with yet another funeral as well as find him a small apartment near his synagogue. The apartment is clean and modern, with an easy walk to the synagogue and the grocery store. Several families and widowers from the synagogue live in the complex.

Now comes the work of clearing the house. "Let's ... *ulp* start with the money," Davey rasps. He produces a shoebox, removes the twine holding it together, and pulls out wads of cash in frayed rubber bands. He hands them to Jules. They are bound stacks of hundreds. One stack is all thousands, displaying the portrait of Grover Cleveland. Jules has never seen so much cash nor held a thousand-dollar bill. He does a quick count. "There must be twenty-five thousand dollars here."

"And ... *ulp* there are bank ... *ulp* accounts. Izzy took ... *ulp* care of all this. ... *ulp* I don't know how much. Here Jules, you're an ... *ulp* accountant, you will understand." Davey rifles through larger drawers and hands ledger books and bank account statements to Jules. "You ... *ulp* look it over."

Jules sits at the desk and starts poring over the accounts. Mom and Davey sit on the sofa. "Uncle Davey, where did all this money come from?"

"You know, we were ... *ulp* in the lumber business and painting ... *ulp* business in Brooklyn. Then when we ... *ulp* moved here my brothers worked at ... *ulp* the Floridian hotel, then investments, I don't know. Izzy ... *ulp* took care of all that. Jack helped him a little."

Jules is flabbergasted. There is so much money here. How could this be? Why didn't they use their wealth? Instead of asking Uncle Dave to explain, he focuses on practicalities. "So far, I've found certificates of deposits at several banks in Miami. All four brothers are authorized signatories. That means we don't have to go through probate for you to have access, Uncle Dave. You can simply walk in and get the money."

"I don't need much." He is quiet for a minute. "Can I ... *ulp* put Esther on the accounts?" He turns to his niece. "That way ... *ulp* you can get to the money when ... *ulp* I'm gone. We signed wills. Esther, it ... *ulp* all goes to you, Clare, and Max's granddaughter, ... *ulp* one-third each, but ... *ulp* you don't have to wait, you can ... *ulp* use it now. Buy yourself a ... *ulp* nice car."

"Thank you, Uncle Dave, that's very generous, but this is your money. I don't feel right spending it."

He shrugs, smiling at her.

Jules says, "To give her power of attorney on the accounts, you will both need to go to each bank together. I'll go with you to help."

"You're a ... *ulp* good boy, Jules. I have something for you." Davey pulls folded paper from his pants pocket and hands it to Jules. "Read it ... *ulp*, aloud."

Jules unfolds the two sheets of paper. It's a letter, handwritten in steady, flowing cursive. He reads so that his mother and great uncle can hear. "*Dear Jules, I am writing this down because what I have to say is too long and laborious for me to speak. After we buried Jack a few weeks ago, you asked me whether God has helped me make decisions in life and whether he can help you. I was feeling sorry for myself, as I have for 45 years, so I could not give you a proper answer.*

Now Izzy is gone, my second brother laid into the ground. As I said the Kaddish prayer for him, I remembered that he died thinking about you. Though he could barely get the words out, Izzy wanted me to tell you something strange. He said you know how to open a special locked safe. I didn't understand, but he could not explain further before his heart gave out.

In that moment at the graveside, I knew God was hearing my prayer for Izzy. God was so close to me that there was no distance at all.

I have not felt His presence like that since I sang in the choir as a young man.

After all this time, I finally understand. I don't need to sing with my voice to be close to God. I sing from the heart. That's all I need to do for God to hear me, know me, care for me. So, 'yes' is the answer to your question about me. God helped me decide to stop lamenting the past, to embrace this next phase of my life – a life with no brothers – as a chance to be with God again. That's why it is easy for me to leave this old house with its old belongings and stale memories, and move into a shiny new apartment, where I'll be surrounded by neighbors who attend my synagogue and who share my love for Judaism.

I also have a better answer to your second question: I don't know. I can't say whether God can help you make choices in your life. We all must answer that for ourselves. My prayer for you is that it does not take years for you to find the answer, as it has taken me. Love, Uncle David.

Davey undoes the top two buttons of his shirt, pulls out a gold necklace and works it over his head. He hands it to Jules. The pendant is a *Chai* – 'life'. It resembles Miriam's necklace, only larger, more masculine. "I want ... *ulp* you to have this. My ... *ulp* cantor gave it to me in 1935, after ... *ulp* my surgery." He points to his throat.

"Uncle Dave, I can't take this. It's too precious." Jules turns to his mother. Her hand covers her mouth.

"Yes, it is precious. That's ... *ulp* why you must have it." Davey takes the necklace and works it over Jules' ears and onto his neck. He clasps his thick hands on the sides of Jules' head, mutters a few words in Hebrew, gives a small squeeze, and lets go. Jules touches the *Chai* resting on his sternum. Davey nods.

After Jules helps Mom and Clare move Davey to his new apartment, he returns to the empty house to gather financial papers into moving boxes. He is still bewildered at the wealth that his great uncles were sitting on: over six hundred thousand dollars, mostly in CD's spread across eight banks. Yet all the while their house was falling apart, they wore dirty old clothes, and they lived on saltine crackers and TV dinners.

Jules wanders the house. He runs his fingers over things they used for 45 years: the table where they ate, its surface chipped; the beds where they slept, with mattresses indented from the weight of their bodies; the old-fashioned shaving brush they shared, its bristles unexpectedly soft; the high-backed chair where the chicken-leg lady resided. The utter stillness whispers that his great uncles are gone, yet these artifacts say that they remain. Soon everything will be donated or sold, including the house itself.

Jules pats Davey's *Chai* necklace, hanging around his own neck. He returns to the bathroom, claims the shaving brush. He will use this instead of the usual squirt from a pressurized can. Every morning their brush will nuzzle his face with shaving soap, a warm reminder. What other items are here for him to keep?

In a bedroom closet he finds a white linen suit stored inside a clothier's bag. The jacket – too big for him – sports a powder blue silk handkerchief in the breast pocket. Jules caresses the handkerchief, carefully folds it into his pants pocket.

Rummaging through dresser drawers he discovers a child's crayon drawing, inside a small glass frame. Though yellowed and faded, he makes out stick figures of a woman, a girl, and a man holding hands, with the girl in the center. The figures are labelled in a child's scrawl: Mommy, me, Grandpa Max.

On a bedside table, he finds an old photo. His four great uncles are standing tall in front of the Miami house, all wearing flowered shirts, their arms around each other. Thick handwriting on the back declares: "MY BROTHERS, 1935." Jules studies their faces. Despite the losses each of them had suffered at this point in their lives – Lewis and Joey were dead and Izzy's businesses had failed, Jack would never be with Howard nor enjoy a career in clothing, Ida had betrayed Max in the worst way, and God had abandoned Davey after taking away his voice – the four brothers were embarking on a new life in a new city, emboldened by their complicated love for each other. Jules stashes the photo, as well as the shaving brush, handkerchief, and child's drawing, into a moving box.

After filling the other boxes with financial documents and loading everything into his car, he surveys the living room one last time, draws a deep breath, exhales, and locks the front door shut.

Chapter 18
August 1981

JULES PULLS UP to the entry kiosk at the south terminus of the Florida Turnpike. He smiles at the attendant who hands him a ticket. He will be driving his beloved Mustang 350 miles north up the Florida peninsula, then west 2,500 miles across the continent to the Pacific Ocean.

The phone call two weeks ago with the academic counselor at the University of California in Santa Cruz sealed his decision to pursue a graduate degree in marine biology. After they reviewed his undergraduate transcript, she identified a suite of additional courses he would need before applying. The courses are offered fall semester, starting in three weeks.

Once he had made the decision, wrapping things up to leave Miami was surprisingly easy. Arnie Zender was baffled to hear his young accountant was resigning, and simply wished Jules good luck. His parents were befuddled but vaguely supportive. Richard said he was proud of Jules and promised to come visit him in Santa Cruz. Sydney Epstein told Jules he was a fool to be walking away from a wealthy future and his own beautiful daughter, just so Jules could play with fish.

In his car, Jules takes a deep breath to settle himself. Breathe in, breathe out. Now it's happening, he is changing his life. All the things that were previously so well-defined – love, work, home – are now in flux. Jules has never been so certain of uncertainty.

He presses the gas pedal and moves into the cruising lane. The air ahead is crystal clear, with no obstructions to the view of the distant horizon that Jules is speeding towards.

Glossary of Yiddish Terms

Boychik
    Term of endearment for a young boy or young man
Bubbeleh
    Affectionate reference to another person
Farshluggineh
    Crazy; mixed up
Farcockteh
    All messed up
Frum
    Religiously observant
Kvetch
    To complain
Mamma loshen
    Mother tongue; the Yiddish language
Megillah
    A long-winded story
Mensch
    A good person
Nebbish
    A nobody
Oy gutinue
    An exclamation, similar to "Good heavens!"
Pish
    Urine
Putz
    A worthless person (vulgar)
Shabbat
    Sabbath

Shivah
    Seven-day period of mourning following a funeral
Shlemiel
    A pathetic, inept fool
Shlimazel
    A consistently unlucky person
Shlump
    An unkempt person
Shmaltz
    Gross sentimentality; literally, chicken fat
Shmeckel
    Penis
Shmuck
    An obnoxious, detestable person (vulgar)
Shtickel
    A little something
Shtetyl
    Small village, usually in historical eastern Europe
Shul
    Synagogue
Tallis
    Prayer shawl
Treyf
    Non-kosher food
Tsooris
    Grief; pain of loss

Tokhes
    Buttocks
Yarmulke
    Skullcap worn by observant Jews
Yenta
    A matchmaker; also, a busybody

Acknowledgements

Creating this book gave me the opportunity to partner with a team of outstanding professional editors: Ceileigh Mangalam, Jennifer Silva Redmond, Ronit Wagman, and Nikki Boccelli-Saltsman. I am grateful for their patience and their insights into earlier, much rougher drafts. Heartfelt thanks go to friends who provided thoughtful reviews and hours of brainstorming with me: Mary Ann Gholson, Eli Simon, Sabrina LaRocca, Sheila Smith-McCoy, Jo Crescent, and Enrique Lavernia. Comments from numerous beta readers were also a great help. Gene Newman provided historical research about life in early 20th century Brownsville.

About the Author

After being raised in Atlanta, Jeff Lefkoff moved to Miami in 1980 to start his first professional job. There he encountered his great uncles – four elderly bachelors living together. One year later he moved to California, where he resides today with his wife of 35 years.

More at: www.jefflefkoff.com

Made in the USA
Middletown, DE
07 March 2025

72283259R00174